'A wildly original and alarmingly readable historical novel whose dark, blood-soaked narrative takes us by surprise at every turn. Lucy Ribchester brings to life the musical culture, both high and low, of eighteenth-century Edinburgh through the lives of a handful of women. Brilliantly written, the story is punctuated with violent deaths and abrupt, neatly-plotted reversals. Its protagonist, Isobel Duguid, is frankly unforgettable.'
– **Andrew Taylor, author of *Fallen Angel* and winner of the Crime Writers' Association Diamond Dagger Award**

'I couldn't put it down . . . Ambition, power, greed, desire – all seen through the lens of women's bodies and voices.'
– **Devika Ponnambalam, author of *I Am Not Your Eve***

'Written with passion and musicality it is both hugely enjoyable and stuffed to the gunnels with the appetites of life. Highly recommended.'
– **Mary Paulson-Ellis, author of *The Other Mrs Walker* and *Emily Noble's Disgrace***

'Lucy Ribchester has the power to take her readers to the heart of 18th-century Auld Reekie where she regales them with tales of opera singers and murderers, of cobbled streets and Old Town tenements, of audacious women and what can befall them. The writing is sublime, I loved every word.'
– **Elissa Soave, author of *Graffiti Girls*, winner of the Primadonna Prize, and *Ginger and Me***

'A gripping and grisly tale of opera, art and ownership set in 18th century Edinburgh.'
– **Lynsey May, author of *Weak Teeth***

MURDER
BALLAD

To Alison

MURDER
BALLAD

with best wishes

LUCY RIBCHESTER

Lucy Ribchester

Black&White

Black&White

First published in the UK in 2024 by
Black & White Publishing Ltd
Nautical House, 104 Commercial Street, Edinburgh, EH6 6NF

A division of Bonnier Books UK
4th Floor, Victoria House, Bloomsbury Square, London, WC1B 4DA
Owned by Bonnier Books
Sveavägen 56, Stockholm, Sweden

The right of Lucy Ribchester to be identified as Author of this
work has been asserted by her in accordance with the
Copyright, Designs and Patents Act, 1988.

Credit to author Joan Baez and publisher Chandos Music for lyrics to
"Diamonds and Rust"

Textured paper background © Shutterstock.com

This is a work of fiction. Names, places, events and incidents are either the
products of the author's imagination or used fictitiously. Any resemblance
to actual persons, living or dead, or actual events is purely coincidental.

A CIP catalogue record for this book is available from the British Library.

ISBN (HBK): 978 1 78530 537 5
ISBN (TPBK): 978 1 78530 621 1

1 3 5 7 9 10 8 6 4 2

Typeset by Data Connection
Printed and bound in Great Britain by Clays Ltd, Elcograf S.p.A.

www.blackandwhitepublishing.com

To Liz Ribchester,
thank you for teaching me how to read.

Well, I'll be damned
Here comes your ghost again
But that's not unusual
It's just that the moon is full
And you happened to call

Joan Baez, *Diamonds and Rust*

Such is thy power, O music! Such thy fame
That it has fabled been

Robert Fergusson, *The Canongate Playhouse in Ruins*

OVERTURE

The Fiddler's Wrath

Come all false-hearted women and your jealous husbands near,
For in my song about a foul murder you shall hear.

There was a wedded couple on the Netherbow did bide,
Maria and her Wenzeslaus were ever side by side.

A fiddler and a maestro was the husband's bonnie trade,
His bride composéd merry songs, and handsome melodies play'd.

But unto that sweet harmony in Canongate did come,
Fae the ships o' Leith, a fiery eunuch set her heart a-thrum.

His voice it did beguile the wife, her heart was put to test,
One night in Comely Gardens came she to the eunuch's breast.

Then Wenzeslaus abroad one day did spy the couple plain,
The sight did fairly stop his heart and drove him sair insane.

To fair Marie, he cursed and spat, to she he raged and riled,
But he could not forsake her, for she was big with his child.

The fiddler left Maria bleeding in her childbed throes,
And with his fiddle in his hand, strode to Carrubber's Close.

In cauld black shadows by the turnpike did he lie in wait,
Until the fine castrato did pass by before the gate.

The fiddler pushed the singer til he buck'd and fell down low,
And beat him cruel and bloodily, with fiddle and his bow.

On bended knee the capon cried, he begged sair for his life,
'O please believe me fiddler Sir, I never could steal your wife.'

The fiddler was a-flame with rage, the deil had seized his mind,
'I'll brak yer bones to splinters, for to touch the body of my quine.'

The corbies bore the skreiches lowde unto the castle rock,
His bluid did course a roaring river down to the Nor Loch.

The fiddler to the Playhouse fled, a-howling with death's sound,
'I'll tak my wrath here now' he cried, 'I'll burn it to the ground.'

For his wife had penned an opera that opened on that night,
But Wenzeslaus in violent rage did set the house alight.

Then Constables did capture him and chain him to his fate,
And dragged him to the Tolbooth through the penitential gate.

All Hallows Eve dawned grey; the fiddler stepped up to the noose,
His damned soul prepared to break and forever be let loose.

He trembled white and shivered cauld, he begged to tak the hood,
For there before the gallows grim, the bludied eunuch stood.

'You split my bones, you drew my bluid, you pulped my heart to gore,
But murderer, I'll haunt your soul to hell forevermore.'

The fiddler's final hour drew close, his crimes he did lament,
But swinging from the rope it was too late now to repent.

Traditional Edinburgh Ballad, eighteenth century

EDINBURGH

1791

ACT I
ST CECILIA'S

1

ISOBEL DUGUID STANDS facing her pier glass reflection, in the hallway of her apartment, on the sixth floor of the first turnpike, Fountain Close, Netherbow. Her eyes are closed. The cross-paned window in the parlour is open. She is listening. She can hear the sounds of the High Street below, echoing up the stone walls. Squabbling pigeons, howling bairns, drunk printers' devils cavorting at the end of their working days.

Isobel shakes her head back and forth and her ears pick out a higher chime, the gleaming rattle of her new emerald drop earrings. Her silk skirts graze the floorboards singing their own treble and Isobel has paid for copper embroidery on this gown too, which adds percussion to the melody, a scrape and a rasp that goes right through to her bones.

She is enjoying this, her music, when it is interrupted by a knock at the door.

Clessidro, from his velvet chair in the corner of the parlour, creaks to his feet. He grumbles as he crosses the parlour floor. 'I shall answer it then, shall I?'

'Aye, you're up,' Isobel replies, opening her eyes, squinting at herself. She begins to pat and flick clots of powder from her wig.

'I am now,' Clessidro mutters.

He wriggles past her, dragging his boots down the hall. He cranks the lock, swings the door ajar. From the cold of the stairwell comes the unmistakeable wheeze of a cadie who has just climbed six spirals of the turnpike.

Cadies move like crows through the closes here. Duckers and darters of Edinburgh, deliverers of good and evil, trunk bearers, letter carriers, gossip weavers, listeners, whisperers, knowers of everything. The way this man breathes with a whistle, even with his face half hidden behind the open door, Isobel can tell he has no front teeth, a black rot on his lungs. Six spirals, eighty feet up in the air they live, in their crumbling tenement tower, like rooks in a nest.

'Offer the man a glass of hock,' she yells down the spindly hallway. 'Give him a cup of water.'

Clessidro ignores her. 'What tidings?' he asks the cadie.

The cadie bears a note, for '—*wheeze*—Madam—*wheeze*—Duguid'. That word, *Madam*, grates on Isobel's ears.

She hears Clessidro pluck the letter from the cadie's hand and slam the door.

'Did you tip him a bodle?'

'No.' Clessidro holds out the letter.

'A groat?'

'No. For you, *Madam*.' Clessidro curtseys.

Isobel snatches it. 'So crabbit before a concert,' she murmurs. She contemplates the letter for a second, looking at her own name, their Old Town address, Fountain Close. She drags her nail down the thick, sensual fold of the expensive paper. She prises open the wax seal. She loves that sound.

The handwriting is a fussy cursive. She can hear in it the flourish of a tickling pen, the lick of wet ink, as she reads.

Dear Miss Duguid, —'Miss?' A screech to the ears.

I write as one aficionado of music to another. You may recall my letter of last month, when I wrote to enquire if you were that same Miss —dear God, screech— *Duguid to whom we are indebted for the ballad sometimes called The Fiddler's Wrath, about the murder of the handsome castrato Guido Guadagni, by the wicked violinist Wenzeslaus Herz.* —Well, that is she: 'Miss' Isobel Duguid. Go on then . . .

This ditty —Isobel puckers her lips. 'Ditty'? No.— *has, through time, travelled as far as London, where I am pleased to report it is providing a great many divertisse-ments on the streets.* —Well, no doubt. It's a fine work.— *I have heard it sung in the gardens at Vauxhall* — good— *and outside the Old Bailey* —marvellous!— *on trial days. I now write to acquaint you with my husband, a collector of folk songs and lyrical airs, who is in the process of amassing a collection of the finest ballads of Scotland to ensure the annals of history do not lose sight or sound of these precious relics of our time.*

Curious. Isobel has heard of these men, these ballad-scavengers, foraging the folklore of the countryside, hoarding their findings, scribbling them down in calfskin books.

We are both fortunate enough to have procured invita-tion to the concert at St Cecilia's this evening. —Most fortunate. Lucky yous.— *I understand you are on the bill as presenting 'Various Airs in the Scots Tradition'. It would truly be the pinnacle of our visit to your city if we were to hear the prima donna in person sing her own account of The Fiddler's Wrath, surely the city's most notorious and foul murder.*

This might be a little tricky. But Isobel does enjoy singing that ballad ...

Your servant always, —hmmmm— Mrs C. Abercorn.

P.S. It is my husband's intention to accompany each ballad he selects with a stave of the principal melody, and an etching of the founders or custodians of their respective compositions, when his book is published, so that their legacy be not lost.

Now that last line snags her eye.
She reads the whole letter again.

It is my husband's intention to accompany each ballad he selects with ...

Isobel knows the prudent thing to do would be to toss it — as she does most of the panegyrics that come from her admirers — out of the window, into the shit stream that trundles past Fountain Close, down to the Cowgate midden. But that line about etchings stays her hand. She hears it proffered in her head in a clipped English voice by a tall elegant lady, twiddling a sapphire necklace: *An etching of the founders or custodians of their respective compositions ... so that their legacy be not lost ... Precious relics of our time ...*

Though Isobel is a woman of music, there is something about the idea of her face scratched in indelible little gouges onto a copper etching board that is very tantalising.

But anyway, *Miss* Duguid? She goes by Maestra these days, everybody of consequence knows. Isobel hasn't been Miss for twenty years.

'Who's it from?' Clessidro asks. He is standing in the doorway to the parlour. He has picked up his brown bottle of punch and is swigging from it.

Isobel eyes him. 'Someone from the New Town,' she says. 'The Wretched Laird of Blahdeblahdeblahblahblah. More praise. *Again.*'

She tears the letter up. Isobel's ballads are not for collection. The word makes them sound like refuse. Her eyelid twitches.

Fine paper when it is ripped creates a shivering bass that she will never tire of. She drops the torn paper in a little pile on the stool beside the pier glass, where her array of powders and rouges and patches are gathered, clattering together. Clessidro is eyeing her now. Isobel beckons him with a crooked finger.

She clacks around in the pile of pots until she finds the bottle of rouge. Clessidro is standing too close. She can hear his laboured, alcohol-wet breaths. He observes her as she struggles with the cork, squeaking it in strangled half circles inside the glass rim. The concoction, a homemade mix of oil, beeswax and carmine, has congealed the bottle shut and she just can't get it to—

'You do know what you're singing tonight, don't you?' he asks her suddenly.

'*Various Airs in the Scots Tradition* is what the programme says,' Isobel replies.

'Because,' Clessidro's tone is warning, 'the committee made it very clear what they do and do not tolerate you singing. That ballad, for one …'

The cork of the rouge pops. Isobel gestures to Clessidro to stretch his mouth. His lips are thin and soft these days. Pulled taut like that, the stretch ekes the blood from them, renders them papery and fragile. She dribbles a glob of scarlet grease onto her fingertip and begins to pat it along the surface of his lower lip.

'I don't know which ballad you're talking about,' she says. 'I sing several ballads.'

'You know well—'

Isobel cuts him off. 'Shhhhh. Uhhhh.' She gestures for him to stretch his lips again and applies a second rubbing. She scowls as she works, but her touch is tender, pressing the sticky wine-coloured paste into the cracks and dry spots, following carefully the seashell curves of the lines.

'You know well,' he says, his voice straining with the unnatural pose, 'which one I'm talking about.'

Isobel lets him close his mouth and begins to rouge his cheeks. She is liberal and generous. She smears apple-shaped blurs that melt into the chalk lead base.

'"Vulgar" was how Dr Blair described it,' Clessidro says. '"Unneccessary" was the word Lord Moncrief used. George Thomson calls it "Doggerel".'

'Keep still.' Isobel thinks of the Old Bailey and Vauxhall Gardens. 'Divertissements' is what that letter said. She says the word divertissements in her head, extending the French consonants. Where does the stress on that word lie, tisse? Or ments?

'You won't sing it.'

14

'No.' Isobel shakes her head. She turns and dabbles in the pile again, wipes her fingers on a rag, finds the two or three frayed velvet patches she is looking for. She licks the resin on the back of them with the point of her tongue. Bitter as weeds. 'Turn your face.'

'You promise.'

She plants one patch, a heart, above his lip, to the right of his nose. The other, a crescent moon, she dabs below his eye like a tear. Clessidro has no scars — he is far too uptight to ever have lain with pox-carriers — but he likes to wear these mouches when he is in public. It makes him feel complete. Sometimes he wears the ace of spades on the opposite cheek. Tonight she can't find that one. She stands back, takes him in. 'Beautiful. Sort of,' she says.

'And you'll keep your promise?' Free of her fussing, Clessidro picks up his punch and goes to the window. He swigs as he looks out.

Isobel follows him, brushing wig powder from his raw silk-covered shoulders with her palms. 'Have I ever not?'

Clessidro chokes on his punch. It sprays.

'Your insinuation is unkind,' Isobel says, ducking to avoid the spray. 'I won't sing it.' She hesitates. 'I will sing *Stabat Mater*.'

Clessidro closes his eyes. 'Do not sing *Stabat Mater*.'

'Very well, I will sing *Erbame Dich*.'

'You will absolutely not sing *Erbame Dich*.'

'I will, and what is more I will—'

Clessidro cuts her off. 'Your chair's here.' He lifts the parlour sash high enough to lean out and calls to the chairmen, 'She'll be down as soon as she can get her arse round the turnpike.'

He turns back to Isobel and pokes her in the whalebone frame of her wide, flat skirt that spans the width of their tenement doorways. 'You'll need to fold up those hoops to get down the stairs.' Tenements were not made for grandeur but Isobel cares not.

She hesitates; a crotchet beat. She crosses back to the hall, gathers up the shards of torn letter and returns to the window. She leans out and scatters free the shreds of note. Like snow they fall onto the sloped close, landing in the travelling river of effluent — Edina's stinking roses — that ferries down the centre. Pulled under with a soft suck. Shit, like silk — like costly paper — has its own particular sound too.

'Come on.' She snaps her fingers. 'I don't want to be late.'

'Don't snap your fingers at me, you old bitch.' Clessidro wedges himself to the wooden frame, to allow her enormous wide-hipped gown, her cake-like wig, fissling on her head, to barge past.

2

THOUGH IT IS ONLY a couple of hundred yards as the corbie flies, from Fountain Close to St Cecilia's Hall on Niddry's Wynd, Isobel will arrive by chair. Clessidro prefers to walk. He prefers to use the musicians' entrance at the back of the hall, prefers to scurry unseen up the dank, bare stone staircase. He likes to trot alongside the pasty, knock-kneed, debt-ridden first fiddlers and soldier trumpeters on loan from the castle with a cap-doffing affectation that sets Isobel's teeth on edge. Clessidro is the Musical Director of the Edinburgh Musical Society and he is paid good coin for his Italian training, his violin playing and his voice. Isobel is constantly telling him he should swagger more, that if he did they might double his retainer and then they could have veal on weekdays. But instead, he acts like a Luckenbooth peddler granted an audience with the king.

There is something comforting to Isobel about taking a chair at dusk, when the cobbles are silvery and the tall buildings are swaddled in shadows. Something about the heft of the shiny black painted box weighing down the two long poles; the poles gripped in the fists of the tall chairmen as they sway with its load. To be lifted by muscular men, Highlanders in kilts, their hairy knees on brazen display beneath the swinging tartan pleats, men whom she is paying to lift her through the street — it is marvellous. Each step clops box against pole, knocks Isobel gently to and fro. Each step is a ringing bell, sounding her coming, the *lyrical air* of her success. Isobel needs no etching. Like this, ensconced in copper and ebony, silk and powder, on her way to the Edinburgh Musical Society, she already feels *eternal*. The hard frame of her dress, the metallic embroidery on the silk, scraping the leather upholstery inside the chair. How wonderful to be transported like this, like a relic, like a soul in a coffin, how marvellous to be carried as if one is immortal, like a diamond necklace in a velvet box.

Though her hoops are squashed up against her ears, and the view is obscured by a greasy window, she can enjoy the sounds of Auld Reekie as it sighs into the evening. Isobel likes to arrive at St Cecilia's from the Cowgate end, where she used to croon outside on concert days in her pinnie with her hankie on the ground for bawbees. The chairmen know this; they are always told. She likes to go this way. She likes to remember.

At this hour, the Cowgate howls its own opera.

Snuff spices the wind. The old lawyers are grunting their way out of coffee houses, the ladies are chattering about the concert about to begin. In Robertson's Close, Lord G____ is tupping his maids, two at a time, the sash thrown wide open. When will he learn?

Oyster shells crack under pattens, students argue about which way is to heaven and whether an orange exists; thieves pick their pockets while they are distracted by these conundrums. The Cowgate hocks and spits, twiddles pocket watches, farts. It roars at stubborn oxen on ropes.

Under the new South Bridge a lassie is singing a ballad about her lover, lost at sea. There is something about the way her voice swells under the arch of the bridge that touches Isobel's heart. This new stone causeway rattles when carriages pass over it, but when you stand beneath it, it is a great upturned chalice. It purifies the girl's voice, spinning it into silk, transforming it into something more than a tale of a dead sailor and an empty handkerchief.

'Stop!' Isobel screeches. She kicks the wood. The chair bucks and halts. Isobel still has a certain brashness to her voice — '*voice of a witch's child*', '*harsh as a ewe*', '*sends prickles up your back, like you've been whipped with a thistle*', some of the descriptions bestowed on her by the Musical Society board members, Clessidro likes to remind her — that can pull chairmen up at a single word.

She pushes down the window. It sticks, and she thumps it down. She fumbles in her purse, tied with a leather cord to her waist. She finds a bawbee, wriggles her wig and head out of the chair and tosses it to the singing girl.

The lassie stops mid-note as the coin arcs; she raises her hand to catch it, and as it slips through her fingers she drops to her knees.

'Thank you, oh thank you,' she cries, fetching up the bawbee with filthy palms. She doesn't seem to care that her dress, her apron, is now soaked to the thighs in brown puddle water. She looks as if she has been touched by the Virgin.

Isobel blows her a gloved kiss, waves. She has not forgotten from whence she came.

St Cecilia's Hall lies at the unsavoury, business end of Niddry's Wynd. It's a lane that was once covered in the jagged silhouettes of mansions. Now the new South Bridge has sliced off its flank like a side of steak, replaced the fanciful houses with regimented tenements, and St Cecilia's sits like a bunion jutting out from its foot, its pavilion grandeur borrowed from Italy, though somewhat incongruous at the mouth of the Cowgate.

As is Clessidro's custom — gallant fellow — he has suffered himself to climb down from his Calvary cross and enter the arches of St Cecilia's Laigh Hall to receive Isobel from her chair. He holds out a hand to help her down.

The courtyard is already filling up, and stuffy.

Clessidro looks around with discomfort, as if he might be at risk of being spoken to by one of the gentry.

'You'd better be on your best behaviour tonight,' he says quietly. He can see the old patrons eyeing up her gargantuan frock, thinking *not again*. Hoops are not encouraged in St Cecilia's, along with swords and too-high wigs. There isn't enough space. But no matter how many pints of claret Clessidro is fined at the monthly Musical Society meetings for Isobel's clothing, for her behaviour, they all know he will never manage to get her under control.

'The Society Governor is in, playing viol de gamba. Don't mess him around with the tempo.' Clessidro casts his gaze around the room. One or two of the gentlemen fiddlers are arriving now, in chairs similar to Isobel's. You'd never take them for second fiddles, with their fine instruments and painted cases, entering via the gilded pillars. But this is the Edinburgh Musical Society. The orchestra is made up of a mixture of professional masters and gentlemen amateurs who sit on the society committee. The employed violinists caper up the back stairwell with scabby fingers, ribs like spinet keys, eager for their coin, while the gentlemen who pay for the gaiety of being allowed to perform, come in by the Laigh Hall; bellies full of meat, brains so full of Malaga sack they sometimes forget how to count.

'You mind which of these musicians pays your retainer,' Clessidro says. 'If you want to keep yourself in dresses ...' He tweaks a frayed thread on Isobel's gown.

She slaps his hand.

'You will keep your promise,' he says.

'On that note ...' Isobel casts her gaze around the room. 'I have had a change of heart. About singing the ballad.'

Clessidro clamps his false teeth together. He hisses, 'But you did promise.'

'You know yourself I do not always keep my promises.' She smiles sweetly. A man and a woman, decked in lace frills and tartan bows, glide past.

'Your ballad stirs unhappy memories,' Clessidro says, his jaw still clenched. The paint Isobel applied carefully to his face has softened in the heat and his patches are beginning to slip down his cheeks.

'That's what ballads do,' Isobel says.

'The committee would like you to sing something nice this evening.'

But nice is not Isobel's music. Besides, she cannot win with this committee. They don't like it when she tries her hand at an Italian aria and they like it even less when she sings her coarse ballads. There is no point trying to please them.

21

Clessidro grips Isobel's arm. 'You know this is why they want you out of here. Because you bring disrepute and blood and gore, and you sing about something they would rather forget.'

'They like the blood and gore. It's why they invite me back.'

'You are deluded, *Madam.*'

'Maestra,' Isobel corrects him.

'Why can't you sing of bonnie banks like the other ladies?'

'You show me an Old Town bonnie bank and I'll sing about it.'

The chairmen wedge Isobel's sedan back out of the Laigh Hall, making room for more chairs to arrive. Isobel is waving graciously to the incoming patrons. 'I could sing a different ballad,' she whispers to Clessidro through her smile. 'I could sing an Aberdeenshire one about the boy whose tongue is cut out? Or perhaps the one from Dumfries where the man's bowels boil with burning lead. Do you think that would be more to the committee's taste?'

'You do push your luck Izz Duguid,' Clessidro snarls.

Isobel holds her smile. 'I will sing the soprano line on *Stabat Mater* too,' she says, moving away to greet a man in a brocade coat.

Isobel's dress is so wide she has to inch through the Laigh Hall sideways. She has to waddle in the narrow St Cecilia's corridor, and scuttle up the musicians' staircase like a crab. She did not think of this when the mantua maker was round. All she could think of was having the heaviest, biggest, broadest dress of all. She told Madam Potard, the mantua maker, as she stood with her measuring tape around her neck and her rattling case of pins, that she wanted to feel as if she were perched upon a great horse, as if she had six legs, all clattering along on glass shoes. She wanted to hear the scratch of the rough silk hem, the grate of the metal thread needling the polished pine floors, she wanted to leave the scrape of her mark where she walked.

Her hair has been dressed with the height of the oval room ceiling in mind, but she needs to take care as she dips under doorways, for the elaborate feather and curl creation, doused in cornflower and violet powder, threatens to snag on each frame. She leaves a savoury fog of jasmine in her wake.

At the top of the musicians' staircase there is a trompe-l'œil door that disgorges the musicians magically onto the upper landing — *ta da!* But before Isobel passes through it she gargles salt water from a jug in the cramped corner of the stairwell. This is where the musicians congregate before a concert, to warm up their fingers and complain about their lot.

Clessidro holds out a cracked Delft chamber pot to her, and she spits.

He puts it back in the corner, mucus frothing on the surface of the whiffing contents from its last user, which have not been emptied.

Isobel begins her round of vocal warm ups, each scale higher and louder than the last.

Clessidro, Isobel has noticed, never warms up his voice these days. Sometimes she wishes he would make some effort to demonstrate a form of cheer. His music is revered in this city. Auld Reekie! Edina! Home of the *Lumières*, centre of the world. He should be happy here. He has commissions galore. Not a week goes past when the Assembly Rooms doesn't premiere a piece of his music, and each is received with adoration by the *Courant* and the *Edinburgh Review*. He teaches half the aristocracy and if he didn't have such stubborn morals he'd be enjoying the favours of their bedchambers too. What more does he want?

Scotland is not an extravagant place, but Isobel knows neither of them would survive in this profession of theirs in London. They would go down there hoping to take over the King's Theatre stage and end up being fucked in the bum by impresarios in some grubby bagnio, both of them. They would end up in the stocks or the clink, or the Bedlam. She has told Clessidro many times that this is where they might end up if he doesn't start behaving a bit more like a Maestro Musical Director. It is no good. All he can do is muster up just enough effort to get through these Friday concerts, so he can go to the oyster cellar afterwards and drink.

Never mind. Tonight it is not her concern.

Tonight on Isobel's mind, the more pertinent question is: what shall she sing?

The bill says *Various Airs in the Scots Tradition and Italian Arias*. They have been rehearsing *Stabat Mater* with the orchestra, and although it was not planned that they sing it tonight, no one can begrudge it as a last-minute change. Clessidro will no doubt sing one of his own compositions. Then there is the question of her own solo programme. Isobel's Scots Airs are all *a cappella* so she can decide as late as she pleases which of them to sing. She will start with something not too violent, perhaps *Andrew Lammie* or *True Love Murdered*. She will obviously sing *The Twa Sisters* because it is her favourite and there is never a dry eye in the house afterwards. And then, should she really venture to try them with *The Fiddler's Wrath*?

It would have a kind of symmetry with *The Twa Sisters*. But she has not performed that ballad at St Cecilia's for some years now. Clessidro has forbidden it, and his cruel words in the Laigh Hall about her bringing disrepute do make her pause. Do the patrons *really* not like it?

She can't help thinking about that letter.

The finest ballads of Scotland
Precious relics of our time
An etching . . .
Accompanied by a stave of the principal melody . . .

She will sing *The Fiddler's Wrath, merci,* because it is a *precious relic of our time,* and her *aficionados* in attendance tonight have requested it by post, and her dissenters — the committee, whoever — will have to lump it.

With a flourish, the harpsichord player strikes up the opening chords of *Stabat Mater.* The small orchestra — violin, viola, viol de gamba (*Lord McAllister, Society Governor,* Isobel remembers), serpent, oboe — join in. Isobel rustles the fabric of her skirts. She smooths her bodice. She nods to Clessidro, standing next to her.

She clears her throat, lifts her chin, breathes a full swelling of the chest, and she sings.

Some of the front row wince.

Isobel Duguid does not have the vocal cords for *Stabat Mater.* But Isobel cares not.

She belts and she puffs. She trills. Clessidro, standing alongside her, sings the alto line but his sweet counterpoint is no match for her volume. She shrieks. She gives full warbling vibrato and she defiles the hallowed Latin in front of the lawyers and clergymen, who pay their guinea-a-year membership for front row seats. She tips back her illicit wig and she fills the oval room with sound. It is impossible not to be swept away on the broomstick tails of her undulating voice. Isobel hits the high notes with full force. She crows the grace notes. She growls the treble. She did learn the arts of *melisma* and *rubato* once, but now she has — wilfully — forgotten them.

'Has she made a pact with Deil to get on this stage?' she once heard a front row man whisper to his friend.

The friend replied, 'Ah, if so, you'd ha thought he'd give her a better voice than *that*.'

Clessidro once told her that the Musical Society treasurer George Thomson had threatened to slice off his ears and nail them to the Mercat Cross if he was made to listen to Isobel sing *Stabat Mater* in the oval room of St Cecilia's ever again.

'If he does,' Isobel had said, 'how will he listen to the sound of his own voice, canting in the coffee house?' She had sung it again the following week, noting the treasurer's ears were still fixed to his head.

The name Isobel Duguid regularly features on the Musical Society committee minutes in connection with this or that gripe — sometimes in George Thomson's florid hand, sometimes in others.

Clessidro, when he arrives home from the weekly meetings in the upstairs room of the Fortune Tavern, likes to recount the conversations they have had about her.

'She mustn't be let loose on any Handel.'

'If she wears hoops and a high wig one more time …'

'Why can't she sing about bonnie banks instead of murders?'

Seated round the square table, over black cork and calves foot pies, claret and curd florentines, they discuss what to do with the problem of Isobel Duguid.

'If Isobel Duguid is to continue to perform at our Friday concerts,' one of the gentleman fiddlers is said to have asked, 'how exactly should we explain her to our visiting guests?'

George Thomson concurred. 'I have nothing against the common man's music. I once arranged an air I learned from a shepherd. But I'd no sooner let this Duguid beldam soil the stage with her rhymes loose and indelicate as cannot be sung in decent company, than I'd … nail my ears — and *I'll do it this time* — to the Mercat Cross.'

'It's not that we don't approve of women on our stage, you understand.' This particular committee member still, after fifteen years, had a habit of speaking slowly to Clessidro, as if his understanding of English was poor. 'But they need to keep their paps out of sight. Those bodices of hers—'

'And the wigs—'

'And the hoops. She'll never get into heaven with those hoops on. How she moves in them—'

And invariably, as the whisky was poured and the snuff was passed around, they would return to the subject of Isobel's dress. And that, said Clessidro, would keep them going for a good quarter of an hour while he finished the claret and brought the meeting to a close.

Isobel's dissenters are always thwarted in their plans to unseat her. Many have tried, all have failed. For reasons unknown to the committee, Clessidro, their beloved Maestro, the society's prized *castrato musico* from Naples, will never, ever hear of having her dismissed. Every time anyone is drunk enough to ask him directly if they can do away with her, Clessidro gives the same response.

He sighs. He looks down at his cravat. He takes another swig of the *gratis* claret as if to fortify himself for what he is to say. He meets no one's eye, and he says, 'No no, Maestra Duguid. She is a good singer of her own manner. She stays. She sings. She is me, and we are as one. Or both we go.' If they want Clessidro to stay, they must also have Isobel.

Some of them have offered to forfeit the rest of her retainer, to keep her in her Old Town tenement, if only she will keep shut her mouth.

But Clessidro will not have it. He is loyal.

And he is too valuable, too cherished a musician for the Edinburgh Musical Society to throw away. Listen to him singing now: that sweet, cultivated, melancholy voice, like a lark with its wings clipped and a vast, tragic view of the forest. He can make you weep with a single *do re mi*. He is only the second castrato to visit Edinburgh, and castrati are no longer ten a penny these days. Already the Musical Society is competing with the London stage for the last of the travelling *musicos*, and the barber surgeons of Naples have, to the dismay of music fans everywhere, developed morals. They will not find another Clessidro to sit on their board, to sing at their concerts, to parade to visitors, not for the salary they pay him. So, he comes with the woman they must suffer — of all indignities — to call '*Maestra* Duguid'. She is his baggage, his travel trunk, and she caws and cruins her *ditties*, and the committee of the Edinburgh Musical Society must tolerate it, as they would a corked bottle of porto on the table of a colleague.

Now Isobel swerves from a high to a low note and the viol de gamba player drops his bow.

These grousing, backstabbing board members, she has no time for their cant. Some of these songs Isobel learned before she could speak a sentence. She learned them from her stepmother. There is no truth in the notion that murder ballads are not part of the heritage of the country. They may not be pure nor hearty but they are as old as the heather, older than corbies and pig's blood and smoke.

Besides, Isobel knows deep down what the patrons with their bums on the benches think. The committee may be allergic to her ballads, even some of the patrons may complain out loud, but she sees the knee-trembling thrill that shivers through them when she sings her most savage tales. There is a rattling of jewellery, a shifting of silk on the oval room's curved benches, when she sings of murder. There is a feverish grip that takes hold of the air as the ballad's ghosts scurry up their rigid spines.

Come all false-hearted women and your jealous husbands near,
For in my song, about a foul murder you shall hear.

Now she is singing it; *The Fiddler's Wrath*. Now there is silence. They will never admit it, but some of them have paid their ticket price to see this.

Now come their indrawn breaths.

Isobel commands the stage. This is her home. This is her music.

She stamps her buckled foot to mark the beat.

His voice it did beguile the wife, her heart was put to test,
One night in Comely Gardens came she to the eunuch's breast.

She is taking them back twenty years, to a crime some of them still remember, a crime in the dark dungeons of their worst fears and most ghoulish fascinations. It is a crime some might claim is too close to their hearts to stomach hearing sung aloud.

There was another castrato, back then, who sang concerts for the Edinburgh Musical Society. He was a man whose grace bordered on mystical, whose skin, whose fragrance and tongue are woven into the lore of Old Town memories. The fact that he was later beaten to death in a close, his handsome face pulped and splintered by the blows of a *violin* is not something anyone in the oval room wants to think about now. To see the town's favourite fiddler hang for his murder, to hear of the vulgar affair with the fiddler's wife that started the whole thing, this is nothing any of them wishes to dwell on. It is done, buried. The sorry story is one they do not want to remember, thank you.

But Isobel knows, really, they do.

They would love to have lovers *fae the ships o' Leith*, these duchesses, these baronets and lawyers' wives, sitting here. They would love to try the *tender breast* of a castrato for their favours, to have husbands that beat the life from their lovers, then came to them with open arms coated in jealous blood.

Isobel knows she is selling both a terror and a fantasy, and they are purchasing it handsomely, they are gobbling it. She stamps and she roars.

The corbies bore the skreiches lowde unto the castle rock,
His bluid did course a roaring river down to the Nor Loch.

Afterwards they will pass by Carrubber's Close, where it all took place twenty years ago, and from the safety of their chairs they will shudder. They will crane their necks to look for the bloodstains on the surface of the turnpike walls.

But those stains were washed away long ago. Isobel knows fine well that the only *memento mori* of that murder is preserved in the words of her ballad.

3

FTER THE CONCERT, the stewards around the hall throw open the outer doors to the cool Scots night. They waft the scent of patron out with hard paddles. Spermaceti wax slides gracefully down the curled branches of candelabra that dangle from the oval room's glass dome — a cyclops's eye in the ceiling. The oval room walls are painted a serene sage, which holds the music in a verdant spell during the concert, but afterwards makes it an oddly sickly space for socialising. When people are on their feet the airy hall feels too small and crowded, the kind of space that compels one to hush one's voice, for fear the room itself is alive and listening.

Isobel is milling among the murmuring crowd, swishing her voluminous skirt this way and that. There is a din of fans clacking and swarming, the loutish laugh of the farm poet Burns — he's here tonight — with his waistcoat open and his shirtsleeves rolled up, casting his beady eye over the society daughters.

Isobel doesn't hear the woman approach until she is right behind her, almost on her heels.

The woman's footsteps are light, pottering, her jewellery tinkling. Isobel hears the squeak of an indrawn breath, and she turns.

The woman lets out a strangled gasp and trips backwards. She raises her hands to steady herself. Her jewellery is gaudy, her dress too slight, too frivolous for Edinburgh, though she wears no wig. She has thick, coarsely pomaded hair. She laughs and clears her throat. 'Excuse me.'

She seems tiny, like a wren. Isobel, by contrast, is huge in her wig and frock. If you include her hair she's as tall as Sam MacDonald, the giant Highlander who walks his stag up and down Parliament Close, menacing the locals.

'Madam Duguid.' The woman gathers herself. 'I hope you will forgive—' she has a frog in her throat, 'excuse me, the imposition. But did you receive the note I sent to your lodgings? I am Mrs Abercorn, the wife of Percy Abercorn, the ballad collector.'

Isobel stares at her with undisguised curiosity. Is this the *She* who penned that letter on expensive paper, so flattering of *The Fiddler's Wrath*? She doesn't look like the sort who would be into gore. She looks instead like the kind of woman whom Burns, wherever he is, might compare to a flower or butterfly. She is slender, with glassy dark blue eyes and a demure carriage that belies her haughtiness. Her blood-brown curls are fussily arranged in sausage ringlets on top of her head, and her skin is as translucent as rice paper. But then they do surprise you, these New Town ladies, who appear so fragile, but have such violent inner lives.

'I was most grateful, most charmed by your missive.' Isobel murmurs. Et cetera. She churns her hand. 'But . . .' she hesitates; she can't help herself, '*Maestra* Duguid, if you please. Not Madam. Never Madam.'

The woman's eyes widen. 'Of course. I'm so sorry.' She raises her glove to her lips, performing shock.

Isobel smiles warmly.

'It is a local tale, *The Fiddler's Wrath*, is it not?' Mrs Abercorn asks. Her teeth are as sharp as a piglet's. 'And ... and did the couple you sing of in the tale ever sing *here*, at the Edinburgh Musical Society?' Mrs Abercorn gazes around the room. 'What was his name, the fiddler, an unusual one — Wenzeslaus. And she was Maria?'

'They were the Herzes. She was called Marie Eliza, but that didn't fit the verse.'

'I see. And the lover's name? That isn't mentioned in the ballad.'

'He was Guido Guadagni—' Isobel lets her mouth hang for a moment. Isobel's teeth are all her own. She is proud of them. Only one has yellowed, and it is to the side, you can't really see it. 'He was a fine singer. So I hear.'

'I see, I see. And Wenzeslaus ... was a fine fiddler too?'

'The best. His fiddle was a Guarnerius.'

'No!' Mrs Abercorn puts her hand to her lips again. She has a very faint cast of smallpox scars across her cheeks, covered over with the slightest layer of pale paint. 'And it was smashed to pieces?'

'Over the head of Guido Guadagni.'

'A tragedy,' Mrs Abercorn murmurs, and Isobel is not certain whether she means the dead castrato or the smashed, grossly expensive violin. Her voice drops to a whisper. 'It's said he was handsome too, wasn't he? The eunuch? It is hard to envisage such beauty, cruelly ruined, left in an alleyway. It is a barbaric practice. Horrible.' She shakes her head. Her gaze slides sideways. 'And yet the way it tunes the voice. The voice of a *musico* contains this quality that you can't, you just absolutely can't ...' She trails

35

off. Isobel sees her looking around the room and knows she is looking for Clessidro. Isobel would rather not get onto the subject of Clessidro's voice and how marvellous it is. People — concertgoers — once on it, tend to get carried away. 'Long live the knife,' Mrs Abercorn says softly.

'I was there at the fiddler's hanging,' Isobel interrupts. 'It was a dreadful affair. Very gruesome.'

'My goodness,' Mrs Abercorn whispers. She leans close to Isobel. She smells faintly of sherry. 'Do you recall it? I've never been to a hanging.' There is something obscenely craven in her voice. And now Isobel definitely suspects her to be one of those with special interests in the grim. What else could please her about hearing the tale of a man who had bludgeoned his wife's lover?

'I don't recall it differing from any other hanging.'

Mrs Abercorn's eyes widen. 'You have been to many hangings?'

'My friend, this is Edinburgh. We live on top of one another in the Old Town, Laird and criminal. It's hard to avoid the goings-on of life — or death.' She clears her throat. 'He took to the noose with dignity, if that is what you mean.' Isobel senses she wants something more. 'Perhaps ... he shivered. I think it's only natural that such a murderer would be fearful of hell.'

'And was it as you say, in the ballad?' Mrs Abercorn asks. 'Did he really see the ghost of the dead castrato appear before him?'

'Ah now.' Isobel is delighted she has asked about this. 'That I must own was a fancy of mine. I thought it added a sense of ghostly closure to the end of the tale.'

'You fabricated the detail yourself?' Mrs Abercorn's lips hang parted. 'That is marvellously clever of you, Maestra.'

Isobel nods in agreement.

'Tell me, do they still play his music — the fiddler's, what did you say his name was?'

'Wenzeslaus Herz,' Isobel says.

'Yes. Wenzeslaus Herz. Do they still play his music here? At the society?'

'Heavens no,' Isobel says. She glances around at the society members, jostling and drinking their whisky nips. 'It brought great shame on the Musical Society. It was in all the broadsides at the time. They don't court that sort of attention. Some people don't even like to hear his name mentioned. Any of their names, in fact. We call them the castrato, the wife, the fiddler ...'

She persists though. 'The wife, Marie Eliza, yes? It is said in your verse that she composed an opera. Is the score then held by the Musical Society library?'

'I believe it is lost to history. You are very interested, Mrs Abercorn.'

'It would be a curio, would it not? An opera by a woman.' She draws conspiratorially close, narrowing the gap between them; two women, who must surely, surely want the same thing for one of their sex. 'It would be a shame if it were lost forever.'

But Isobel is not playing that game tonight. 'The Canongate Playhouse burned to the ground,' she says flatly. 'I say so in the ballad. You can buy a print depicting the charred ruins if you wish.'

'With every score of the opera inside?'

Isobel shrugs. 'I'd think that even if there were such a score left, the music of both Wenzeslaus and Marie Eliza is cursed. Disgraced, at the very least. It was scandalous.'

Mrs Abercorn colours and blinks meekly. 'I see. Are they all buried in the city? Or was he taken back to Italy?'

'The castrato went into a pauper's grave at Greyfriars. But Wenzeslaus the fiddler was given to the anatomy school.' For the first time Isobel notes Mrs Abercorn wince. It doesn't stop her. 'For dissection. His bones are probably long dissolved in acid or tossed in the midden like cow bones. I don't know what they get up to in there. As for Marie Eliza I presume she must be buried here somewhere. Anyway, I believe there is claret downstairs, or some of our country's very palatable whisky.' She is getting bored of these questions. Can she go now? She wants to go and collar Clessidro before he departs for the oyster cellar. He owes her money for tonight.

But no, Isobel is not quite excused yet. Mrs Abercorn has turned now to a man on her left in a velvet coat and cravat and is tugging on his sleeve. 'Percy,' she says. 'Percy.'

Percy is deep in conversation with the harpsichord player.

'You will recall my husband is collecting ballads,' Mrs Abercorn continues. 'He is eager to meet you. Aren't you, Mr Abercorn? Mr Abercorn's heritage is Scottish. Come, Mr Abercorn,' she snaps. 'Come and meet the ballad singer.'

Isobel bristles. Ballad singer. She sang *Stabat Mater* tonight. But what can she do? It is not untrue, is it? Why does that title still shame her?

Mr Abercorn turns now and Isobel extends her hand. He is not a tall man, though taller than his wife, but he has a solid presence. His balance leans slightly forward, coupled with a robustness of belly and chest, which sends him protruding into the space in front of him. He wears a plain, unfussy brown periwig, and his small eyes hold a vacant but pleasant stare. There is something Isobel does not like though about the rasp of his palm; it has the devil's dryness, the texture of death. She shivers and her earrings rattle, like chandeliers, like bones.

'Mr Abercorn is collecting ballads from among all Scotland, both pastoral and urban,' his wife continues. 'Yours is a singular tale. We have not come across many such *murder ballads*. Isn't that right Percy?'

Percy is gazing over Isobel's shoulder, eyeing up the wealthier patrons milling behind her. There is a crack as his wife squeezes his hand. 'Percy. She was *there* at the fiddler's hanging.'

'Dreadful,' Mr Abercorn says, shaking his head, clenching the pain out of his fingers. 'Such an unusual subject for a ballad.'

'Percy collects ballads,' Mrs Abercorn repeats. Her posture has stiffened. Her smile is inappropriately bright. Isobel can't quite put her finger on what it is she doesn't like about her.

'It's not so unusual,' Isobel says. 'Songs of murder are as ancient as the land. You can always find the last words of criminals being sold at the foot of gallows. Or in town squares. An opera might cost you a shilling, but a street ballad is free to all and can cheer you on a cold day.'

'Ah. I'm trying to steer clear of the cheap kind of broadsides,' Percy says. 'The ballads I'm after are of a purer significance.'

Oh here we go, Isobel thinks. Bonnie banks. But the thought of the etching mentioned in the letter pops into her head and she stays her tongue. She wonders how she might steer the conversation that way.

'As I am aware,' Percy says, 'the ballads traditionally sung in the lowlands of Scotland were of a more pastoral bent. Natural songs passed from nurse to bairn celebrating the wonders of Scotland, her lochs, her graceful maids, hearts broken in earnest, noble wooers, indeed her banks ...' Warming to his subject, Percy gestures, painting out the scenes.

There are many societies and salons in the city, all of which exist to lubricate discourse, and yet Isobel cannot help wondering what this discourse entails, for she has never heard a man but that likes to hold court at his own pace. She looks to Mrs Abercorn for solidarity, but Mrs Abercorn is gazing lovingly at her husband.

He is still reeling off a list of venerable subjects for Scots ballads. '... Rosslyn Castle, Culross Harbour, *Jennie o' the Glen*. And though I haven't heard it myself, I have heard tell of a tune called *The Braes of Ballenden*. Then we cannot overlook *The Lass o' Patie's Mill*, if we are speaking of bucolic tales—'

'Wasn't she murdered by her lover?' Isobel wonders aloud.

'—*Jamie Telfer of the Fair Dodhead* ...'

'That's the one where the captain is shot through his ba' stane!' Isobel cries. 'Can there be anything more gruesome than that?'

'*O Can Ye No Sew Cushions*,' continues Percy. 'That's fine and bright, good for a sturdy-voiced wife to sing as she reaps the harvest, and there was one, slightly more tragic than gruesome, I believe you sang it tonight. *Binnorie, O*. You gave it a different title.'

'*The Twa Sisters*,' Isobel says.

'I've heard it before. The tune sounded familiar.'

'There were echoes,' Mrs Abercorn says, 'of the same tune in *The Fiddler's Wrath* that I noticed, were there not?'

'Were there?' Isobel feels a prickle travel up her spine.

'And *The Twa Sisters* tells of a murdered woman,' Mrs Abercorn says, 'who also returns from the grave to confront her killer, just as yours does.'

The room smells suddenly sharp and dangerous. Isobel does not like the suggestion she feels is being made about the originality of her ballad. She flicks a speck of wax from her dress. 'Sometimes other tunes and words can accidentally drop into your compositions when the spirit of the muse is in you. Ask Mr Burns. He has collected many an auld wife's country verse, to which his name is now put.' Her grin is a barb. 'If the tune of *The Twa Sisters* is echoed, and some parts of the story, it is by accident. That ballad is entirely my own. Just as Signor Pergolesi was given due credit for *Stabat Mater*.'

Mrs Abercorn smiles lightly. 'Of course,' she says. 'Percy, I think *The Fiddler's Wrath* is an interesting ballad for your book, don't you?' She taps her husband's arm.

'You must call on us one afternoon for tea,' Percy says absently.

'Is Master Clessidro here?' Mrs Abercorn is looking around the room. 'I'd love to congratulate him on his performance. Did he compose that oratorio he sang with the organ? It was just astounding. Perhaps he is in the Laigh Hall.'

'He doesn't show his face much after a concert.'

'Whyever not? There is no such thing as a shy musician, surely.' Mrs Abercorn chuckles.

'He's not shy. He just knows what happened to the last castrato who plied his trade around here.' Isobel turns to leave but no — again — not yet. Mrs Abercorn stays her with a hand, and now she is reaching into her husband's breast pocket, dithering her fingers under the soft lace trim. Isobel waits impatiently, rasping her skirts back and forth against the floor grain. Mrs Abercorn wiggles out a calling card from Percy's pocket, and hands it to Isobel.

Isobel glances down at the elaborate scrawl. *Percy Abercorn Esq.* The address is Young's Street. New Town.

'Do come to us, *Maestra*, I beg. For my husband's book. It would be a pleasure to have you come to us in person. Because he intends to produce, of each ballad custodian or composer, an *etching*, for posterity.'

Isobel smiles warmly and tucks the card down between her paps.

4

CLESSIDRO IS STANDING at the top of the musicians' staircase, holding an open bottle of punch. He lurches. 'You said you would never sing that fucking ballad here again.'

The punch is strong. The fumes from his breath are stifling.

Isobel wedges sideways through the door and goes to rescue her cloak from where it has been tossed on the stone floor.

'I'm talking to you, Izz Duguid.'

'*Maestra* Duguid—' She wags her finger.

'Maestra up my arse,' Clessidro slurs.

Isobel pretends not to hear. 'I think I sang well tonight.'

He sprays punch with his laughter.

Clessidro is a turkey cock when he's drunk. He's a ranting, raging cunt. Isobel can feel her skin heating to boiling. Twenty years she has been waiting to scrape a compliment from his mean little lips, even a small one. It will never come. Why does she bother still trying? Why does she care? She has everything she wants. 'If they really despised it, they wouldn't clap at the end. Would they?' she says.

Clessidro is silent.

'Would they, *Maestro Clessidro*?'

He curses and spits green bile on the floor. 'It's not even your fucking tune. You stole that too. No, you copied it. That's worse.'

'It's not yours either, is it?'

He squeaks the gob of spittle into the flagstone with his foot. 'You mustn't call him a *fiery eunuch*. It's insulting.'

'It fits the verse.'

Clessidro grinds his false teeth. He swigs from his bottle, sucking the clay rim like it is a cold stone teat. He is always like this, tired and grumpy, after a concert. Isobel shan't remind him of the luxury of being allowed to sing on a stage, in a room, an oval room designed to reflect sound in the most flattering manner. She shan't remind him of the comforting drip of the candelabras, the perfumes of bergamot and jasmine hazing off the cotton handkerchiefs of the concertgoers. Her nails clench into her palms as she thinks; she shan't offer him the chance to sing for his supper under a bridge, in a stinking market square at dusk, in Parliament Close, instead of at the Edinburgh Musical Society Friday Concert.

They leave St Cecilia's and traverse Blair Street. At the old poultry market they enter the new South Bridge through a small door. The bridge has been built like a rotten tooth, brittle on the outside, empty on the inside. At night you can climb into it and slither all the way down the turnpike staircase to the oyster cellar at its root.

These vaults have only been open a couple of years but already they echo with drips of mouldy water, they flutter with bats and beetles and scuttering rats. The fat of the fish-oil lamps makes coughing shadows and a cloud of smoke so thick it gums your ears. The underground lairs were built to be work-shops, saving space above ground, a luminous idea birthed by an architect sat at a table who would never have to work in them. For a while the artisans enjoyed the novelty, and you could hear jewellers at their craft, cobblers banging wood and leather, watchmakers' boys running up and down the stairs spilling stars of metal. But it only took a couple of years for the rats to move in, and the jewellers moved aside. Now you're as like to hear the sounds of tupping and reeling, Scots Porter sloshing out of tankards and women tripping on oyster shells from midnight till dawn, as you are to hear wives and men at work during daylight hours.

'I don't want oysters,' Isobel says, going sideways down the dark, curved stairs. Her skirt grazes a sooty patch on the wall and she tuts. 'I want a pasty.'

Clessidro helps himself to half a dozen rattling fat oysters from the bucket on the table and pours them each a pint of black cork from the carafe. Isobel leaves him and waddles through the soot-stained arch to the next chamber, where the baker-butcher-piemaker-whatever, Meaty Pete, is measuring out his mock venison for the next day's batch.

Isobel doesn't ask Meaty Pete what's in his pie. It's rich and sloppy, starchy and earthy, and the pastry — double crusted — cracks like wet sand when she bites it.

When she returns to the oysterhouse chamber, Clessidro is sitting with a face like a skelped arse. She inches round onto the bench, using her pie-free hand to steady her wig.

'Are your oysters bad?' she asks. 'You look ill.'

He grimaces. 'It's not the oysters make me ill, you know it.' He tips and swallows another, then throws the shell on the ground. He smells of brine and vinegar. 'You have to stop singing that ballad. You're tempting the devil.'

'Deil be damned. The only thing I'm tempting is the curiosity of New Town pigs.'

He regards her. 'What do you mean?'

The card of Percy Abercorn Esq is stabbing her in the right tit. Something tells her not to mention it.

'What did that letter say, that the cadie brought?' he asks. 'I saw you rip it up. What did it say?'

'Are you determined to bicker?'

'I know you, Isobel Duguid. Sometimes I think you forget that. Who were those people you were speaking to, after the concert?'

'I can talk to the patrons afterwards, can't I? Why were you spying?'

He downs his black cork and pours another. The cellar is full now, noisy with soused advocates and disgraced gentry. Clessidro always goes through a passage of melancholy before he is drunk enough to find his cheer. On Isobel's life, he'll have his shoes off and be stripping the willow up and down this dungeon, up to his neck in Lairds' sons and not-so-fair not-so-maids, before two in the morning.

'They liked your Oratorio by the way. The woman I spoke to called it *astounding*.' She thinks this ought to placate him a little.

He nods and tips back more beer. Isobel finishes her pasty. Satisfying. She lets the silence between them do its work, washing them into better moods.

They sit for a while, wordless in the companionable din, and it becomes half-pleasant again. Friday evenings like this make Isobel content. *Ventum est aequilibrium,* as a scholar she once knew might say — she has everything she needs. She doesn't remember the last time she slept without a roof over her head. And she has music. Music, music everywhere. Even now, a fiddler is striking up. Clessidro's sour milk temper is a small price to pay for what they both have these days. Anyway, he is calming down a bit, now the concert is over, it seems.

He takes his jacket off, rubs his hands.

'I don't want to dance,' Isobel says.

'I didn't ask you,' he replies, climbing over the bench, snagging his groin where an embroidered fleur-de-lys is coming loose. He yanks the thread away, and stumbles over to where a set of dancers is assembling.

Clessidro never knows which side of the dance to place himself on. Gentlemen would like to see him play the role of the lady, ladies would like to see him play the gent. Tonight, a dandy in ruffles slaps him on the arse and whoops, 'Come capon, give me a birl.'

Clessidro is genial now, his bad mood put aside. He knows his bread and butter is to let these fools call him 'capon', to ridicule loudly and publicly his mutilation, while at the same time sighing in ecstasy at the *divine* quality of his voice, an inhuman voice, a gift only God could bestow. He lies on the hair that divides angel and monster. They want him in their beds, even as they insult him, they want to pry his legs apart with their curiosity. Edinburgh is a learned town. Everyone here wants knowledge, but it's not always a good thing to be on the receiving end of the thirst for it.

He lines up opposite the dandy, clapping his hands, stamping his feet, ignoring the greasepaint and mouches sliding from his face. Isobel sees him then, very suddenly, in another age, another person entirely, at a masquerade in Comely Gardens, many, many years ago, rushing through the pear orchard, flushed, laughing, drunk. The shock turns the hairs on her neck to ice. She drops her head, turns back to her porter glass.

Fuck knows how long Clessidro will be at his cavortings. He is birling like he has deils on his tail. If Isobel looks too closely she can see them. And she knows then that she must leave the oyster cellar before she gets drunk enough for anyone to see the deils on her own tail.

She picks her way through the stompers until she reaches Clessidro, panting. He wheezes and takes out his handkerchief, wipes his face, smudging the rouge.

'Key?' She holds out her hand.

'Knock on the door,' he says. 'Just wake Mary.'

'Don't be a prick. She has to be up at six to make your fire. Key.'

'How will *I* get back in?' he whines. But he tosses her the key to 7 Fountain Close. It slips from his palm and falls, chiming beneath the feet of a puffing lady in silk shoes. Isobel has to lower herself down slowly in her hoops, as if she is curtseying to this New Town wifey, to snatch up the key before it is kicked away in the dance set.

When she rises again, Clessidro is holding something too. He twirls it in his hands, peers at it in the crackling gloom.

'Give me that.'

He has Abercorn's card.

'Fell out of your tits. You should be more careful when you bend over. Christ knows what else might fall out of there.'

'Give it back.'

He screws his eyes at the lettering, then makes a sudden, startling noise like a cat, a threatening screech. 'You watch your tongue around people, Izz Duguid.'

Isobel snatches the card. Clutching the key, she turns and hustles up the stairs.

In the sudden cold open space above ground, her ears begin to ring. She snaps her fingers at two chairmen, leaning against the bridge wall, whistling in mournful harmony some old ballad.

5

EDINBURGH HAS CHANGED MUCH, during Isobel's lifetime. Stand still for too long in this city and you'll grow dizzy. Someone will have thrown a building up where last you looked. They will have hammered whole streets over the top of other streets, walled in the ghosts of the old tenements with chiselled new chambers and exchange halls. They will have conjured a bridge out of thin air, hollowed it out and created a labyrinth inside it.

When Isobel first arrived, they had just begun draining the Nor Loch, to make way for the North Bridge, the first of the new bridges. Amidst the effluent and swamp water they found the bones of all the criminals that had been drowned there over the years, of which her mother was one. That was Isobel's first lesson; bones never stay out of sight in Auld Reekie. Drown them, wall them in. They will find a way to float back up. They will bang on the doors and scratch on the ceilings of the sealed off streets.

No one throws their piss out of the windows anymore, but they find other ways to get rid of their excreta and some of it can still land on you. Isobel will never let her guard down. She is a canny woman, and she knows what it is to live on both sides.

Today Isobel is turning over a new leaf. Instead of taking a chair, she will walk to the New Town. She has a new *robe à la polonaise* she wishes to show off in the streets, a frothing, shimmering, sea-green silk gown with skirts looped up, *retroussé*, bubbling over a pale pink bodice. Confident Clessidro is still abed, though it is early afternoon, she sneaks down the turnpike, placing each of her clopping pattens carefully to still the echo of wood on stone.

The day is fine, a spring day, a very Edinburgh day, bright and crisp with a temperate edge, as if the sun has been warned by the Calvinists not to be too lurid in its display.

The hem of Isobel's skirt grazes her ankles as she walks and her heavy tread (helped by the pattens) draws attention to the creaking silver buckles on her aquamarine shoes. She is a fine sight, and she makes an even finer sound. She dominates the air around her as she walks.

Mrs Abercorn's residence is on the brand new, aptly named, Young's Street. Not the fanciest of the New Town houses, but none of the houses that side of the swamp are anything approaching mean. She walks past the new Theatre Royal that is buzzing with crowds, a tumbler outside performing flips while a boy hands out playbills for *Macbeth*.

Ever since Isobel was a wean, she has had sound in her heart. From an early age she could hear things other people could not. Small sounds. Birdies breathing. Leaves falling. Horses clopping a mile away. People whispering behind yellow gorse bushes.

These ordinary noises came together as music in her head. Rattling carts over dirt paths formed the beat. Birds added melody. Dead leaves shifting made harmonies. Toss in the regular dirge of market sellers, chapmen, criers of broadsides, corbies, muck inching down a shallow hill, shrill laughter, and you have yourself a chamber piece of nine instruments. Isobel hears music wherever she goes; it's not something that can be shut out.

When she was a little girl, in her village some way south of Edinburgh, she would walk the hedgerows singing the songs she had learned from her stepmother. Almost all of her favourite ones involved gruesome, grisly deeds. As the wind in the hawthorns made the orchestra, and the bullfinches and great tits trilled the descant, she would sing about the vengeful hands of Lamkin the murderous stonemason, who slaughtered his Lordship's wife and baby, or about the slain Earl of Moray, or the jealous stepmother who baked her husband's daughter into a pie. And if it was autumn she would gather blackberries from the bramble bushes, pinching the bubbles of their fruits to burst, and she would pretend to herself that the deep juice staining her fingers and ringing her mouth was blood.

If that you would your daughter see Good Sir cut up the pie
Wherein her flesh is minced small and parched with the fire.

As Isobel emerges into the New Town, the air clears and thins. Sound carries in its velvet, in the spaces between the clouds. In the Old Town the sounds ricochet and zigzag from sludge to pigeon-infested steeple, getting lost in the washing lines that hang between closes, changing direction, smirring into cries and clangs.

In the New Town you can hear birds.

Beautiful songbirds, blackbirds, sparrows. The carrion crows are ravens here and even they sound noble. No wonder everyone around here believes they can think so clearly. Anyone could carry a basket of thoughts on top of their head in such peace.

Into this adagio of calm Isobel comes stomping, her pattens thwacking the sharp-laid new setts, cutting a clean rasp on the wood pavements. She brings the ribald hustle of the city's gouty heart into this sparkling new space, where goods are sold not by grating voices from red-raw throats, but by the soothing chime of bells on shop doors.

There is a perfume shop on Princes Street.

There is a shop that sells pianos and sheet music.

Paper, crisp as silk, tickling the piano's wood as the pages are turned. That rasp, that open-throated gasp: *gorgeous*.

There are no poultry markets or fleshmarkets in the New Town, but there is a single flower seller wandering down George Street, like a lonely dog-violet that has blown off course. She can only be about ten and she has ginger hair and a sweet, peat-smoked voice. 'Fresh daffodils, Dutch tulips, Marigolds.'

The chairmen here don't bang into each other and swear. The horses don't shy or screech because the roads are plenty wide enough.

Isobel gives Mrs Abercorn's Young's Street door a Cowgate knock and waits to see what the maid makes of her.

6

MRS ABERCORN HAS BEEN on edge ever since Friday evening, ever since the cadie collected the letter from her hand, its ink still fresh and bitter smelling, to deliver to Fountain Close. Then came the waiting game: preparation for the concert, the usual ablutions, wondering what dress would not single her out as an incomer. Clutching Percy's arm, picking their feet through the sticky Cowgate, finally finding the concert hall buried up one of Edinburgh's terrifying black-mouthed closes, and then hearing *her* voice in the flesh; hearing the infamous Isobel Duguid — Mrs Abercorn hesitates to use the verb — *sing*.

All through the concert Mrs Abercorn had twiddled and twisted the printed copy of *The Fiddler's Wrath*, which she had purchased for ha'penny in Parliament Close. She couldn't stop herself, even when her gloves turned damp from the force of her grip. Twiddling and twisting, as she heard that carrion crow voice murder tune after tune. Isobel Duguid's *Stabat Mater* will never, ever, leave Mrs Abercorn now. At one point Percy had put his hand upon her knee to still the jigging of her leg.

Even after the concert, that ballad had continued singing a racket inside her purse, until she burned it.

Now it is ash in the parlour. The words are no more deadly than the fluttering of a robin's wing. They rustle in the grate — toothless ghosts — and soon the maid will come and tip them far away into the compost pile at the bottom of the garden.

Mrs Abercorn is still getting used to her new house. Percy had wanted somewhere more rural. 'What is the point,' he had said, 'of moving away from London, if it is to another city?' He had wanted Perthshire or Kirkcudbright. He had talked at one stage about moving to one of the islands, Skye or Rum.

'Don't be ridiculous,' she had told him. 'They would throw you off a cliff.' She could picture him in his velvet frock coats and silver-buckled shoes, wrestling with skuas, scraping his heels on seaweed-slimed rocks. Feasting on boiled eggs that stink of fish, trying to pick off the delicate shells with his soft puffy hands. The thing about Percy is, he never considers the reality of his fancies. He has a fantasist's sensibility and he refuses to see a vision through to its logical conclusion. It remains always a romance to him. He does not think of Scotland for instance, but of *Caledonia*. When he imagines the islands, he imagines an etching he has seen, of the basalt columns on Staffa; he hears the roar of the waves inside Fingal's Cave, but he does not feel the wind suffocating him, or the violence of the sea as it flicks salt into his eyes. Sometimes Mrs Abercorn does not know what her husband thinks about himself.

He had said to her of this move, 'I'm thinking only of my book of ballads.'

Already one of his Oxford compatriots had gone to the Lake District in search of ballads. He is currently scrabbling up dells, scuttling through fields of sheep dung and hemlock and — by his letters — collaring any shepherd he can find to let him sit by his hearth and donate his words. Another friend is collecting in Gloucestershire, and a third in Shropshire. Percy had thought Scotland would be the exotic choice.

'Edinburgh is not a city,' she had told him. 'It is a village. You'll see.' She had not told him it was the place where she was born. Percy believes his wife is a Londoner through and through. Why would he not? She speaks like a Londoner. She has the gall and the grace of a woman brought up in Clerkenwell. She knows how to paint over her smallpox scars and when to refuse the wine bottle.

The hammering on the door goes straight through her.

She grips the handles of the chair and prises herself up. She is still a young woman, but she has been wearing an uncomfortably formal dress every day since passing her husband's card to that singer. She has been waiting for the knock. If one is lady of a household, one must make an impression.

She will answer the door herself.

Percy is not home; Elspeth is busy at the linen.

She wants to speak to this ballad singer alone. She wants to ask her about her tale; where it comes from, where she heard it, how she came to sing it on the St Cecilia's stage, what it means to her.

Wives can collect ballads too.

7

S ELL ISOBEL DUGUID'S SOUL for coal if it isn't the woman herself, Mrs Abercorn, that answers the door. Isobel tries to stave off her shock. She doesn't want to seem rude, but this is curious: where is the maid?

'*Maestra* Duguid. How good of you to come.'

'Thank you, Mrs Abercorn.' Isobel doesn't wait to be invited over the threshold. Mrs Abercorn pins herself to the lintel to make way for the *habit polonaise*.

Mrs Abercorn's Young's Street hallway is short, her dwelling meek, a demonstration of modesty. The first thing Isobel notices is its quiet. The lamps here burn smoothly. They do not hiss and spit with impurities. They burn with a sigh, that is more like a whisper. Beeswax slides down the candlesticks. It is all very tasteful. None of it advertises its expense.

Who are the people in the hall paintings, Isobel wonders, as she casts her eyes across them. Old men in puritan hats. Women in brown wigs. The gloom mutes any clues. They could be Mrs Abercorn's ancestors, or they could be some tat she picked up in a curio stall at the Luckenbooths.

Isobel removes her pattens and leaves them by the front door. The hall echoes softly with the sound of her buckled shoes.

The hostess's feet, by contrast, in their leather slippers, scurry smoothly across the lacquered floor as she moves past Isobel, into the parlour, across to her chair by the window. Isobel halts just inside the parlour threshold. She glances past her hostess's shoulder, through the window. It's a narrow street outside, a dark street almost like the Old Town, with mews barns being constructed on the other side for the owners of the grander houses nearby to keep their horses in. But instead of the Old Town sounds Isobel is used to, there is nothing. Everything is muffled, smothered. The mews builders today are nowhere to be seen. Isobel and Mrs Abercorn could be the only people in the world in here. The floor seems suddenly like an ice rink, treacherous, noisy, thin in hidden places, designed to snare intruders. Her heels ring out far too loudly as she steps into the room. They announce every shift of weight. They give away her state of mind.

'Tea?' Mrs Abercorn asks, in her sparrow voice. She is not a Londoner, but she is a foreigner here.

Where is Percy, Isobel wonders. *Where is the maid?*

A noise upstairs startles Isobel, a scrabbling like beetles across the floorboards. She glances up. The chandelier trembles in a draught.

'Yes, thank you,' she says, and sits without waiting for an invitation.

Mrs Abercorn squeaks a trolley towards her and pours two long, splashing streams of hot tea into a pair of toile-patterned bowls. She hands one to Isobel, rattling against its saucer. Isobel lifts both saucer and bowl, leaning her lips over the hot liquid surface, and slurps.

Mrs Abercorn perches on the edge of a sage velvet chair by the window.

'How long have you sung at St Cecilia's, Maestra Duguid?'

'Too many moons to remember.'

'And the patrons don't mind you singing such violent songs?'

'People wish to hear about violent deeds. It is what we see when we look around us.'

Mrs Abercorn laughs.

Isobel prickles at that. She thinks of the rats mauling seagulls, of cows shrieking in the slaughterhouse, of the dead fish thumped onto slabs on the market stalls, of the screams of women at dusk, the closes so tight you can never tell which land or which floor they are coming from. She thinks of the ballads she learned as a child, blood soaking every verse. This tea-sipping sow may have cultivated manners, but she knows nothing of the world. 'If you live in a place for long enough,' Isobel says, 'then you'll see it everywhere.'

Mrs Abercorn sets her teacup neatly down and sits in the chair. The upholstery breathes out as she leans back. 'You know that my husband is a collector of ballads,' she says. 'But I believe I too can spot a piece of work that is of great interest. Of special merit. Is that the only ballad you have composed?' She picks up a small leatherbound notebook and dips a quill into a dainty blue-black inkwell.

'It is the one for which I am known. Well ...' Isobel has an urge to scratch her head, but she is wearing a wig and wouldn't be able to get her fingers underneath it discreetly enough. 'It depends what you mean by composed. Most of the works I sing are of common ownership. They were taught to me and I have passed them on, perhaps making them my own with fancies. But *The Fiddler's Wrath* is different. I did write that one down. The tune I wrote, as well.'

'I see,' Mrs Abercorn says, scribbling a note in her book. 'And what was it about that particular murder that moved you to write it down?'

All of a sudden Isobel is afraid — of what? She does not know. She knows there are people in this town who can see through her wigs and her paint, her copper threads and her horsehair hips. There are people who can see through silk and skin the way architects see through walls, to see what raw materials were there before the stone was moulded, to see what they could build instead: because what has been moulded can always be remoulded, from stones or blood.

This woman, who is so very interested in her ballad. What else has she got her eye on?

'I suppose,' says Isobel slowly, her wig still itching. 'I suppose I had for some time been moved by the muse to put my name to something. There has been so much music in my soul from an early age. But when you fraternise in these enlightened circles, as I do now, it becomes only natural to want to emulate their modes of creation and preservation. My people may have passed songs mouth to mouth for hundreds of years, but that has no currency in this city anymore. If ever it did.'

Mrs Abercorn thinks on that for a moment. Against her will, Isobel begins to fidget. She can't help herself. Mrs Abercorn is stirring something in her that she hasn't felt for some time, some challenge to her right to be sitting here, talking about a work of music she has written down. There is something in Mrs Abercorn's voice that is reminiscent of someone else Isobel knows, that crawls under her skin and pricks at her insides.

'I understand,' Mrs Abercorn says. 'Your country heritage is not given the respect you feel it deserves. It is why my

husband wishes to record your folklore.' She pauses. 'But ...
you say you saw the man hanged? Was that when you first
heard this tale?'

'I might have read of it in a broadside, to know the names
of the victims.'

'The *victims*?' Mrs Abercorn stops scribbling and looks up.
'You mean there was more than one? I had thought only of
the castrato.' She scribbles another note. She has a pressing,
scratching way of writing that is unsavoury to the ears.

'There were two victims. Marie Eliza, the wife, was as much
a victim as her lover, wasn't she? Although she did not die by
her husband's hand. The pain of the murder led her to lose her
life, and that of the child she was birthing.'

Mrs Abercorn stares at Isobel. Her quill slips. She puts it
down carefully and picks up her teacup. 'Then there were three
victims, were there not?'

'Yes. Yes, I suppose there were. The child died also.'

'Heavenly soul.' Mrs Abercorn looks down at her notes. She
takes a sip of tea then picks her quill back up.

Isobel thins her eyes. 'And so, now to talk about how this
rendering of my composition in your husband's book will
progress, Mrs Abercorn? Will there be renumeration?'

Mrs Abercorn's face gleams, opal bright. 'I had thought
posterity was renumeration.'

Clessidro, that is who it is. There is some note in her voice
that reminds Isobel of Clessidro. A part of her suddenly shrinks.
She hates the power Clessidro still has to make her feel green
and brash. This woman has the same hardened gaze as
Clessidro's. Who has given her that mineral core, that bright,
hard stare, Isobel wonders.

'We all have to eat,' says Isobel, though in her head she is counting not bread and milk, but the cream Italian pastry horns that fill Mr Morello's window.

'My husband shall give you three pounds for the ballad. Sterling.'

Isobel snorts. 'Three pounds sterling. That's sixty shillings. One hundred and twenty bawbees. I could make that in two weeks if I sang that ballad under the arches of South Bridge. The patrons pay more at the Edinburgh Musical Society.'

'Very well, make it five pounds, and when the book is published you shall have five more for it.'

Despite her prosperity now, her regular engagements with the Musical Society, Isobel will never tire of money. Old habits die hard. She loves the sounds of coins. Delicate farthings, tinkling bawbees, the bell chime of a good guinea. But . . .

'It's not enough, Madam.'

Mrs Abercorn lets Isobel brew her avarice for a second or two before speaking again. 'My husband will etch a very poetic picture of you in his book. Now, I know you are famous in Edinburgh, but this book could make you famous forever. Edinburgh's Murder Ballad Maestra, Isobel Duguid. Immortal. And the melody too. He will print a stave of the principal melody. Your — composition.' She smiles. Her teeth snap together.

Are those teeth real? Or pulled from a young country girl in the street, and sold to her by a barber? Isobel can't tell. Why does she want this ballad so badly?

Mrs Abercorn reaches into the pocket of her dress and takes out a pair of very tarnished guineas. 'A deposit. It is an extremely interesting story. I think you know that.'

Isobel does.

'It would be a shame if it were lost to time. If you — *prima donna* that you are — were lost to time.'

This is true, Isobel thinks. Edinburgh has various ways of commemorating its citizens. There are death masks, which are reserved for the extremely noble or the extremely venal. Then there is the anatomy school, where your flesh could end up in a bucket of acid, your bones rattling as they are hung on display for the scholars to study. And then there are etchings.

There is a man called Mr Kay, a printmaker, who owns a shop on Parliament Close and sketches locals of curiosity he sees passing by. He displays these etchings in his windows to reflect who is important to the city, either by the gravitas of their role in civic life or by the irresistible eccentricity of their personality. Isobel has often wandered slowly past his shop, where he sits outside with his sketchpad and his stool. Up and down and up again she walks, certain that he must be seizing the opportunity of furtively drawing her. She has a recurring fantasy that one day she will be passing by, arm in arm with Clessidro, and she will stumble upon her own likeness in his window, huge and lively, elegant, pensive and a little mysterious. She cannot wait for this moment. She cannot wait to see Clessidro's face, his mouth slowly open with . . . what? Surprise? Disgust? Rage?

It is yet to happen. Of course, Mr Kay has already sketched Clessidro, throat open, mid-song, accompanied by two fat little putti with their fingers tangled in the strings of harps.

'Who have you commissioned to create the etchings?' Isobel asks.

'Oh I don't recall.' Mrs Abercorn shrugs. 'A local artist. His name escapes me now.'

Isobel hears a noise above. It's not the chandelier this time. It's a low murmuring. She cannot help but glance up at the ceiling. 'What is that noise?' she asks. The tune of the murmur begins to form in Isobel's head, helped by the ticking of Mrs Abercorn's clock, which Isobel can also hear now, in the hall.

'Ah take no heed of the scratching,' Mrs Abercorn laughs lightly. 'I keep a caged bird in my bedroom. A canary. Beautiful thing. Mr Abercorn bought him for me from the docks.'

And that is when Isobel knows her hostess is a liar. Because caged birds may scratch at their bars with their beaks, they may even sing, but they can't murmur psalms, softly under their breath.

Still, Isobel pockets the guineas.

Already she has begun dreaming of how high her hair will appear in the etching.

8

B Y THE TIME ISOBEL leaves the Abercorns, the city
is beginning to breathe out for the evening, to let her
stays hang loose.

It is a beautiful night, the calmest, palest of spring nights.
It is a night where Isobel can see, just by tilting her head
upwards, the cool crags of Calton Hill, where the gibbet used
to stand. Now builders, working through the evening, are
clearing a path for a pleasure walk. It is to be the finest of its
kind in Europe. Mr Hume's idea, an idea turned into stone,
carved and cut into the world by tradesmen.

Isobel loves the sounds of an early spring evening: doos and
swifts circling, fulmars lost from Leith. There is an evening
vapour that hangs in twilit Edinburgh, and seems to trap sound
in its oily residue, softening it. Chickens are being carted back
home from the poultry market, pecking against the bars of
their cages on the wagons. Merchants from Dean spill grain
as they traipse back to their mills, and the flower sellers are,
like their own buds, slowly closing for the night.

On another night Isobel might have had mind to stop and
watch the actresses pull up outside the Theatre Royal and hustle
in by the side door. She loves to poke her nose, from time to

time, in the snack sellers' baskets to see what they have, for she once used to peddle China oranges at the Canongate Playhouse, in another lifetime, in a previous incarnation of herself. Isobel has in her heart a calcite love of theatre. She adores the irrational urgency of it all. Who cares about a play? Who cares about a concert? No one in a play is real. And yet it is the most vital thing in the world, and you must be on time, early in fact, to chatter, to be seen, and if Mrs Siddons is hoarse, or if the thunder machine collapses through the rigging onto the stage, if two drunk old Jacobites start a duel, or if the *prima donna* happens to miscarry in the dressing room, if, if — God forbid — Isobel Duguid *loses her voice*, then the whole thing comes falling down, flimsy as a house of cards. And yet no one dies, the world goes on as normal. Usually.

Everyone is excited to see a play, or to hear a concert, to fly through another person's dreams for a while.

The courts are closed now. There are the men, hurrying home in black, from the buried chambers they make their living in, back across the North Bridge to the New Town. Who knows what turned their noses puce, what makes their brows frown? They are men of thought. But as the evening comes, their thoughts go to slumber and they fill their bodies with alcohol and flesh.

Sticks and straw strewn on the market floor.

Muck in the gutters. The shite cleaners don't come until well after the taverns have closed. Dusk is peak slime time for Auld Reekie.

And yet Isobel could skip with joy. Tonight, she could skip through this mulch because it is spring and she has money in her purse and a fine new dress, and the summer season is almost upon her, and soon she is to appear in a book. It is high time for standing in the drizzle at pleasure garden masques, *ridottos* at the Theatre Royal. It is time for Edina's long foggy evenings and they always remind Isobel of the first summer she came here. She can feel the ghost of her past self in the air, with all the promise she thought she once had.

She could skip up past the Luckenbooths to the castle, slip her hand inside a soldier's uniform. She could sidle down to Meaty Pete's, clamber down the staircase that winds behind his ovens and in the bowels of the bridge place a bet on one of Jem Barbary's fighting cocks. She could dance a ceilidh with street children, underneath the windows of the New Assembly Rooms.

She is thinking of all this, while inching her way up Advocates Close — a shortcut to the High Street, but a smelly one — in a practised waddle, straddling the waterfall of slurry burbling down the close's central gutter. She is waist deep in her memories when Clessidro steps out into her path, blocking the light at the High Street end. His figure is unmistakeable, his lolling stature, his haughty bearing, the bottle of grog in his hand. He is like a bad penny, a grim stink sent by a witch, an omen.

'Were you following me?' she calls out.

'If I was following you, would it not be logical to see me behind you rather than in front?'

Isobel catches up to him. 'Who knows with you? You might shapeshift into something else next. A bat? A toad?'

He grabs her arm. She almost slips in the muck, but she steadies her feet in time.

'Shut up,' Clessidro says. 'Be quiet.' He eyes the slime. 'You don't want to pull us both into the river of shite, do you?'

'Are you drunk?'

He must have been following her. He must have hot-footed it up one of the other closes, past Goose-Pie house, to catch her and stand in her way.

Clessidro clutches Isobel tighter. She can hear his nails beginning to shred the fabric of her sleeve. 'You're going to tear my new dress.'

'Your dress, Isobel Duguid, is not what you should be worrying about. It is your tongue. Do you want to be hanged, like your mother? What were you doing in that house? On Young's Street?'

'You did follow me!'

'I was in the New Town anyway and I saw you. I'm teaching Lady Douglas to sing. And she's commissioned a piece for her masquerade.'

Isobel removes Clessidro's claws, one by one, from her arm. The embroidery has come loose on his own coat. She remembers when that coat was fine. Now it hangs off him. He is shivering. His eyes are welling, his nose running. 'It is only that I worry about you Izz. Your tongue, your tongue—'

'My tongue has served us well, as well you know. Anyway.' Isobel jingles her purse. 'I have guineas. Shall we eat some mussels and drink some wine?'

Clessidro sighs and shakes his head. But he allows Isobel to take him by the arm and together they begin to walk up the High Street towards John's Coffee House. They cut a curious figure, his old clothes, her flamboyant gown. He brings her continental chic. She brings him ... what? The local touch?

'What piece will you pen for this masquerade?' she asks.

'I don't know, probably a sonata. She wants something she can play herself.'

'That's exciting,' Isobel says.

But Clessidro is still distracted. 'That woman,' he says. 'I saw her at the concert. There is something about her. Something ...' He waves his hand vaguely, in the affected, Italian way he has cultivated.

'Her husband wants to put my ballad in a book.'

'A book?' Now Clessidro stops. He looks feverish. 'Are you mad Izz?'

'No. I'm as clear eyed as the day. A book is fixed, final. In a book, nothing is hearsay. A book holds no rumours, no gossip. A book is fact and fact alone. A book makes history truer than ever it was. Paper can be torn and scattered but books that lie between boards are closer to stone.' She will not tell him about the etching, about the stave of melody. He will laugh — he will see straight through her motives — and she cannot bear his scorn tonight.

'A trial is fact,' Clessidro whispers. 'The printed courant makes history true. What more do you want?'

'You underestimate what these New Townies are capable of.'

Her hair, as high as the new bridge. Her shoulders strong, her dress, white as a dove. They will ink the lines of her lips. They will blacken her eyes. They will draw her in full-throated song. Maestra Duguid. A composer. They will print her words and print her tune. It will be her song, for as long as the ink is soaked through the paper.

A poet once wrote a villanelle about Clessidro's voice and published the poem in the *Edinburgh Review*, and seldom does he let her forget it.

He shakes his head. 'No, no. I think you do, Izz. You push things to see how far they will go. That ballad brings nothing but trouble. It's a hell-hag's curse.'

'Tssss.' Isobel is angry now. 'Come. Let's talk of it no more. I want a drink,' she says.

9

PERCY IS STILL ACCLIMATISING to the Edinburgh diet.

Elspeth, the housekeeper who doubles as cook on weekends, has, to his mind, a very peculiar palate. Percy is a sensitive soul, and he can tell if a cow has been fed on grass or grain. He finds the meat up here of a very sour flavour, and frequently wonders aloud if it is off. Elspeth has the local tongue and she wonders aloud if the London meat he has eaten hitherto in his life has instead been off.

He finds the wine too cold, the seafood too pungent. He finds the berries tart and the abundance of kale and turnips to be incompatible with his digestion. Percy delivers forlorn monologues about English mustard over the dinner table, and since the Abercorns have no friends yet in Edinburgh it is Mrs Abercorn who has to endure these alone.

'I spoke to that woman today,' she offers, to take Percy's mind off the food.

Percy spits a shard of leek onto the side of his plate. He looks confused.

'The singer, from St Cecilia's.'

'Singer?' Percy sips his wine and grimaces.

'The ballad singer.'

'The crone in the pink wig?'

'It was cornflower blue and peony, Percy. And I found her evocative. She has a very Edinburgh disposition, don't you think? A woman of great pluck. The kind of ballad singer you are looking for.' She takes a nonchalant sip of hock.

Percy chews this over, with another mouthful of cock-a-leekie. They call it a soup, but it seems to him more like a stew. His teeth are on their way out already and he is making a meal of its toughness. 'What do you mean? When I think of Edinburgh what springs to mind is fresh air and progress.'

'She has something of the Old Town about her. I don't know just — something. I think she'd be perfect for your book. A perfect subject of the city. Quintessential.'

'I was fancying someone a little more innocent.'

Mrs Abercorn pretends not to know what he means by this. 'But if you wanted pastoral we should have gone to Perthshire.'

'*I* said we should go to Perthshire.' Percy puts down his fork.

'Oh Percy.' Mrs Abercorn tops up her wineglass from the bottle. She has drunk more since coming here than in her entire Clerkenwell lifetime.

'Don't you think we should go to Musselburgh and speak to the fishwives?' he says.

'Now fish is somehow a more wholesome thing. And they must have ballads at Musselburgh.'

'I really think you won't find a more singular ballad. It has everything. Murder! An affair! Musicians! I think there is metaphor to be mined there.' Mrs Abercorn knows the word 'metaphor' is usually certain to pique her husband's interest. He likes to believe he thinks on two levels, always. Mrs Abercorn, on the other hand, knows that sometimes the simplest explanation is the truest; a thing is sometimes no more than itself. 'As I said, Percy, I spoke to her today.'

'You spoke to her?' Percy picks up his spoon and clears his throat. 'I get so blocked up without mustard to clear my nose. I must speak to whatshername and failing that I'll have some shipped. You must be able to get mustard here. You *must*. Ha. You spoke to her? That woman? Where?'

'She came to the house.'

'Here? She was in here?'

Mrs Abercorn knows her husband is thinking of the rented upholstery. 'She didn't sit down Percy,' she lies.

'But even so. You didn't let her see any of the valuables, did you?' He casts a glance at the crockery cabinet.

'No Percy. But I have agreed that you'll pay her ten pounds for the ballad.'

'Ten ... what? Why would you do that?'

Sometimes Mrs Abercorn wonders about her husband's faculties. She has never set foot inside a dreaming spire and yet she has more common sense drunk than he has sober.

'Percy.' She puts down her glass. 'If you want this to be your coup, your big poem, the magnum opus inside your first collection, you may have to part with coin for it.'

'I don't believe Wordsworth and Coleridge have ever parted with coin for a country ballad. Or that chap Burns. Or George Thomson or Thomas Percy.'

'I know, dear. But you are an Oxford man. You have a keener eye and sometimes that means you have, when necessary, to pay for what you find. Gold is worth more than ... than common clay. Or fish. You know you don't even need to stick to her words. Instead of being a collector, you could produce your own work, put your name to it. *Inspired* by the ballads of Scotland. That would be a fine idea.' Mrs Abercorn has to be careful now, because if she pushes Percy too hard she will scare him off, or worse, she will incite his belligerence. No poet wants to admit their wife does half their work.

Percy chews his lips for a long time, in that way Mrs Abercorn loved, once upon a time, to witness. They met at a concert in Dean Street. She was singing Handel. He had sat in the front row and chewed on every note she sang, peculiarly distracted yet focused on her at the same time. She had found it charming. Now some of Percy's charms have gone off a little with age.

'I did not think of an urban ballad, that is the only thing.'

'She does not have to be an urban figure. She could be, for instance ...' Mrs Abercorn casts her eye around the table. She doesn't want Percy to know how carefully she has been thinking this over, how acridly the sulphur of her rage has been burning inside her. 'She could be a saltwife. Salt is extremely elemental. The most primal of all of the foods. She could be of the sea. The sea that lies at the mouth of a great city.'

Percy seems to have lost her. His mouth is hanging open. Mrs Abercorn fears she has let herself go too far. 'Well, perhaps she need only be a street ballad singer. That too is a symbol of the times. Let us think on it, Percy dear. We should also consider putting out some invitations.'

He bristles and swallows a piece of chicken. 'I do not like this craven social activity. We should let our calendar evolve naturally, like the season.'

'Very well,' Mrs Abercorn sighs. 'We shall let our calendar evolve naturally. Like the season.'

10

'SIT DOWN, MAESTRA DUGUID,' Mrs Abercorn says. Isobel looks around the Abercorns' parlour at the assembled company. Percy is here and he has brought a friend, a Dr Campbell, come to gawp at the specimen Duguid in her full feathers.

Isobel eyes the sofa. Mrs Abercorn, or her maid — *someone anyway* — has covered the soft devore upholstery with an old and itchy-looking blanket of tartan. After a moment Isobel sits.

'The most excellent news,' Mrs Abercorn announces, 'is that my husband has found a printer for his book. You are to become one of the most famous and notorious characters in all of Edinburgh.' Mrs Abercorn claps her hands. She applauds herself. She has, rather vulgarly, set three guineas out on the table, like a test. To see how coarse Isobel is. To see if Isobel will peep.

Isobel will not peep.

Percy sits at the writing table in the corner of the room. The charcoal pencil he holds in his right hand has left a black dust on his white cuffs. His wife takes her usual chair. Dr Campbell perches on a tufted ottoman before the hearth — ever the gent, he insisted Isobel take the sofa. She fidgets on the prickly tartan in her thin muslin skirt. She wore it to be humble and discreet, but now she rues the decision.

'Well, it is delightful we could all come together this afternoon,' Mrs Abercorn pronounces. She has her notebook on her lap, her swan feather quill and ink on the side table. Her tea is a foul-smelling brew of lapsang souchong — ham hock and piddle fumes. Isobel has never cared for it since the days she used to smuggle it ashore for money, up her skirts. 'I think we rather hoped you might be able to tell Percy and Dr Campbell as much as possible about the ballad for Percy's book — everything we spoke of the other day — and then perhaps,' she simpers, 'if it would not trouble you, we should be honoured if you would give us a little private concert, so that Percy can take down the words. Does that sound agreeable?'

Isobel casts her gaze over at the two men. Percy is swatting charcoal dust off his cuff. Dr Campbell returns her stare, then roams his gaze from her wig — pristine, dainty, fragranced with jasmine and tuberose today — down to her shoe buckles, plain pewter, but polished.

'Yes, I should think that sounds agreeable,' Isobel says. Her words come out stiffly. Isobel does not like these small gatherings. They offer the worst kind of social intercourse. They have not the relaxed intimacy of a tête-à-tête, but they make her feel more exposed than if she were at an assembly or concert.

'Very well,' says Mrs Abercorn brightly. 'As far as you know, when did the affair between the castrato Guido Guadagni' — she checks her notes — 'and Marie Eliza begin?'

78

'It's hard to say. They were part of the same musical set. Canongate Playhouse, Musical Society concerts.'

'And you knew them through the Musical Society?'

Isobel hesitates. She glances at Dr Campbell. She knows him from somewhere but can't place him. 'I wasn't performing with the Musical Society then. My introduction to that circle came later. But you'd see them, up and down the High Street. Hear little rumours. Edinburgh is very small.'

'That I am beginning to appreciate.' Mrs Abercorn chuckles to the room. Her husband and Dr Campbell oblige by joining in. 'You did not know Marie Eliza then?' Mrs Abercorn goes on.

'I knew *of* her. She was known. In Edinburgh. She was a singer. A composer. Everyone knew her to look at. She performed with the Edinburgh Musical Society, and on stage.'

'And was she beautiful?' Mrs Abercorn asks.

Isobel falters. Her thoughts split all of a sudden and she can't get them back into their correct pattern. 'Depends. Perhaps.'

There is a noise upstairs, the grating of wood on wood, grain against grain.

'Your bird has woken up,' Isobel says.

'Bird?' Percy frowns.

'It is Elspeth, Percy,' Mrs Abercorn says firmly to her husband. 'I asked her to air the beds.'

Dr Campbell leans towards Isobel, 'You have lived in Edinburgh exactly how many years?'

'I couldn't say. Lots, that's all.'

'I only ask because you mentioned the Canongate Playhouse just now,' he says. 'It must have been over twenty years ago that it burned down.'

'Twenty-two,' Isobel says.

'It's in the ballad,' Percy explains.

Dr Campbell turns to Percy. 'She is most sharp in her memory, for the education she must have had,' he says. 'Did you say she was *from* Edinburgh?'

'I was raised in a village,' Isobel says.

Dr Campbell stares back at her now. 'And there was a school, in the village?'

'There was.' Not that Isobel learned much, other than to avoid locking gaze with the sexton who ran the place, when he walked the rows of desks, quoting John Knox and peering down the lassies' sarks.

'Interesting,' he says slowly. He turns his head to Percy. 'I'd say she is around forty-five. But you can never be sure with women of her class. There is the chance she is younger.'

Isobel is certain now she does know this Dr Campbell. She is sure she has heard his voice before. At the Pig and Wig Society? In fact, this whole caboodle is conjuring up faint memories for Isobel of a time when she 'performed' for the Pig and Wig Society, standing naked on a long table while the learned men surrounding her passed round a gouged-out cattle horn that they took turns to pleasure themselves into. You get to Isobel's ripe age — forty-three, thank you Dr Campbell — and find you've crossed paths with all the learned men of the town, in all the wrong places.

'The vices of the Cowgate and Lawnmarket cannot be under-estimated for the mark they imprint on the body,' he says.

'You would know,' she snaps.

Dr Campbell's only reaction is a cool, light smirk. And now she knows exactly where she has seen him. It was a long time ago. But he was friends with Jas le Corbie — a poet, of sorts — at the university, with whom Isobel once shared lodgings and a bed.

'You must know a great deal of ballads,' Dr Campbell says. 'I think I recognise you, from singing them around Parliament Close.'

'That was a very long time ago,' Isobel replies. 'I've swapped the cobbles of the Luckenbooths for the St Cecilia's stage for many years now.'

Mrs Abercorn, who has good instincts for sniffing a squabble — developed through dining with Percy and his Oxford men — leans forward. Her voice is pacifying. 'We all believe,' she says, 'in the lifeblood of the music of women like you. You are the keepers of our country's very tradition. And for that you do us a great service with the load you carry.'

Isobel is not sure how to respond to this — with gratitude? She will not look at the guineas. She will not look at the guineas. *Women like me . . .* What happened to *precious relics of our time?*

'But back to the crime.' Mrs Abercorn hastily scans her notes. 'What made this murder speak so deeply to you that you felt compelled to pen a ballad about it?'

'It was a very vicious murder, the worst the city had seen. Murder is a popular subject and one I have always sung of.'

'Then, it wasn't any personal connection with the victims?' Mrs Abercorn waits.

And then, against her will, without warning, Isobel looks at the guineas. She knows Mrs Abercorn sees her do it.

The noise upstairs again, a brusque drumming this time. Isobel can't help but glance up. When she looks back, Mrs Abercorn is still staring at her.

'This business about the Canongate Playhouse being burnt to the ground,' Campbell says. 'I recall it was the violinist Wenzeslaus Herz who was accused of setting fire to it. But is it true it was because his wife had an opera there? That he set fire to it, to *punish* his wife, for her affair? Is that not just a confection for your ballad, and the real reason was something to do with the kirk?'

'We may never know his motive for setting fire to the Playhouse,' Isobel says. 'But like any ballad, the questions we do not have answers for are what keep us returning to the story, are they not? To try out our own answers on them, until we find one which makes sense.'

Dr Campbell snorts, as if he has suddenly heard a cat speak sentences. He takes out a cotton handkerchief and wipes his nose, then inhales a peck of snuff. 'I think you have found a very good subject for your book, Mr Abercorn,' he says, looking over his own eyeglasses into Percy's eyeglasses. 'From the little I know about Edward Bartley, about Stanhope and Goodwin, they are all focused very much on collecting anthologies of the pastoral ditties for their records. I think you, Percy Abercorn, may have found your niche. No one is collecting ballads of the urban kind or writing about their singers. No one at all.'

Dr Campbell pauses a beat — a quaver rest — while he thinks on his pronouncements. Then he guffaws; a sound like an oboe with a blockage. 'What a delightful woman you are, Madam Isobel Duguid. The very best. Your mother was from Midlothian?'

'She was from the Borders.' Isobel adds, 'She was hanged as a witch.'

There is a pause while Campbell frowns at her. Is she telling the truth? Isobel can see him calculating the years. Then, 'Even better,' he says, shifting his gaze to the two English visitors. He corrects his glee. 'Though we have, gladly, moved on from such dark ages.' He shifts on the ottoman. 'It would be extremely authentic of course, for a ballad singer, if she had a child in her arms.'

'A howling babe,' Percy muses. 'In a bundle. They do in London I know. There is a Hogarth sketch. I wasn't sure about up here.'

'I'm not a ballad singer, in the common sense of the word,' Isobel says. 'Not any longer. I am a composer. A singer.'

Mrs Abercorn says gently, 'Percy dearest, *Maestra* Duguid is a singer—'

'The Prima fucking Donna,' Isobel snaps.

'The Prima — Donna,' Mrs Abercorn says, 'of the Edinburgh Musical Society.'

'But you are not ashamed of your past, as a street ballad singer, surely?' Dr Campbell smirks again. 'And it is true that you still sing ballads, is it not. Even if they are — forgive me — *compositions*, written on broadsides and sold for a penny, instead of handed down from nursemaids. You do not deny that, do you? Else why would we be here?' He laughs again, quietly, to himself it seems; not to her anyway.

The ceiling creaks. Isobel feels an unbearable rage. An unbreakable cage around her.

'Well,' Dr Campbell snaps to attention. 'There is time enough to fill your book Percy, with more than one tale. I daresay you will find a ballad singer with a child in her arms somewhere around the Luckenbooths. Now Isobel, I think it's high time we heard this infamous song of yours.'

Isobel sulks for a moment, rearranging her skirts. She swills saliva around her mouth, using the silence to nurse the slights to her pride. But she has never been able to resist an audience, never able to shun the chance to share a tune. So she stands.

She clears her throat and stamps her foot with a sturdy beat. She sings loudly, heartily.

Percy isn't used to such sounds in his own house, she can tell.

Mrs Abercorn taps her toes in time. At the end, they all clap, and it's an eerie sound, clipped and polite against the long, gory residue of the final note.

Percy says, 'Yes. Yes indeed.'

Campbell is staring at Isobel the way the front row patrons do. She knows he too is thinking: *What pact did she cut with the deil to end up on that St Cecilia's stage, with her mare's tongue and her high hair?*

But Isobel needs to mind that there is only one more of these *sessions* to endure. And then she will be immortal. She will be Isobel Duguid, *Prima Donna* of the Edinburgh Musical Society, who Entertained the Town with Salty Tales of Gruesome Deeds. The woman who composed her own ballads — words and song — such as this very melody, printed here ... Ballad singers are not recorded in this way. You never know their names. Their names are Traditional Ballad and Auld Scots Air. They are never Bessie May the Fishwife or Singing Sally of St Giles with the Oyster Pearls Glued to Her Teeth. Surely this is more than Isobel could ever have hoped for, far better than singing at St Cecilia's, far better than a burnt opera and a hanging.

Her witch-daughter voice. *Her* mare's tongue. Her murder ballad.

Mrs Abercorn sees her to the door. As Isobel steps across the threshold, Mrs Abercorn gently clasps her elbow. 'Maestra Duguid. This child,' she says quietly. 'The baby that died the night of the murder. It's troubling me. Did they christen it, with a name? Your ballad doesn't say much about the child, and it worries me,' she says. 'To think of an innocent that died without taking a breath, in an unconsecrated grave, unbaptised, somewhere in the city.'

Isobel almost laughs at this notion. To think so solemnly of one unbaptised babe among the thousands of tiny bodies in their caskets, tucked into the caskets of their mothers or just wrapped in their shrouds, scattered shadows on which the city walks. There are more unbaptised babies buried beneath the turf of Edinburgh than there are rooks in the eaves.

But then she sees the crease in Mrs Abercorn's brow, and it softens her; she can't help but think of her own unbaptised soul, her mother standing on the gallows before she could see her — Isobel — painted with the holy water. She says, 'I believe Wenzeslaus gave her the name Cecilia. Patron—'

'Saint of Music,' Mrs Abercorn finishes. 'Very pretty.'

Isobel says, 'You are fond of music Madam. Do you sing or play, or compose yourself?'

Mrs Abercorn smiles, but she can't disguise the sound of her teeth grinding together. 'I am from a musical family. But I myself have scant talent for performing. Still, I am proud of them. Very proud.' She proffers her hand, the guineas jangling in her palm.

Isobel takes the guineas and puts them in her purse. 'Thank you.'

11

CLESSIDRO IS GONE from the tenement when Isobel returns.

His trunk is gone. His clothes are no longer strewn over the washstand in their shared bedroom and spilling out of the chest of drawers. His unwashed peony and oyster scent is cleansed from the air, and his cackle's last echo has faded. His teeth are gone from the nightstand.

There is none of his sheet music skating around the floor with the draught.

The bedroom absorbs her tread. For a moment she feels suspended. She is a beat of silence, a minim rest. She is indrawn breath, and Clessidro — her ague, her bile, her rot, the stain on both their souls — is really gone.

Did she dream the last twenty-two years?

Dr Campbell's question about the Canongate Playhouse is still chiming in her head, making her doubt her own understanding of what is true and what is false. She did see Wenzeslaus Herz set fire to his wife's opera. He did it with a tallow candle that he ripped from the pit wall. She can see it now, in her mind. And she can see the rest of the ballad playing out before her too.

Is Isobel well? Can one history truly erase another? Is the only world that matters our perception, and can it be bent as such, or is there such a thing as pure truth, watched over by a single God, unbreakable? And when such questions are debated by Dr Campbell, or by students like that rat-rogue Jas le Corbie in salons, in taverns, in cellars and supper rooms, do they understand the torment of a mind afflicted with that question in the real world, beyond the salon windows? Or are they only pleased to have been able to dream up such ideas? And if they are only pleased with their ideas, is that pride any worse than Isobel's was when she took ink to paper and decided she would write her ballad?

Flimsy on a broadsheet; firm in a bound calfskin book.

Isobel slips her purse, with the guineas in it, from round her waist and puts it on the side of the washstand. The room is hot. The baker who lives below them has fired up his oven and there must be a local feast he is baking for, for she can smell cakes from down the chimney breast.

Clessidro is gone. If she runs, could she catch him? Carbuncle that he was, would she want to catch him and yank him back into this midden? He belongs with her.

Her betrayal is only just beginning to sink in.

Perhaps that tremor on Isobel's breast, that twitch in her eyelid, is not hurt, but guilt. Clessidro is gone because she sold her ballad. She sold her ballad and when she sold it, she sold what bound them.

She slides into the cool bed and waits for the oven below to warm her aching feet, sore from traipsing across the North Bridge over the Styx of the Nor Loch's dregs, so many times, from Old Town to New Town, back and forth, back and forth, and back again.

12

PERCY SNORES SOFTLY. Once upon a time his body was as comforting as a whale. He was a great leviathan to which Mrs Abercorn clung, to stop herself from being swayed around by the winds of the world, to stop her being pulled into the spiralling deep. His snores were as regular and reliable as the earth's heartbeat. If the apocalypse were to come, if the horsemen bearing their torches were to descend on them, and the house burn to the ground — as it does frequently in Mrs Abercorn's dreams — Percy's snoring would still go on, and on, and on, carrying her above the rivers of smoke and sulphur.

But since coming to Edinburgh, she is no longer comforted.

Now the rhythms of his snoring change at will, they slow down and they speed up; they stop suddenly. In her dreams, she is no longer carried. Instead she steps on a burnt floorboard and descends, not into the sea, but into a pit of fire.

Or perhaps it is not a pit of fire, but the snapping of a trapdoor on a gallows, and she is being hanged for an unknown crime, for one she did not commit. She screams. She wakes.

Percy's body is sprawled flat on his back, snoring.

She curls tightly next to him, her white shift drenched in sweat.

13

THERE ARE FIFTEEN SUBSCRIBERS to Mr Abercorn's *New Book of Traditional Edinburgh Ballads*, seated around the dining table when Isobel's grand entrance is made.

Mrs Abercorn had tried to stuff her in the butler's pantry, to make her emerge — surprise! — at the right moment. But Isobel was having none of it.

Isobel has had her fill of being stuffed inside confined spaces for the entertainment of the learned. She has cut herself free from giant pies; she has worn a wig made of Charles II's mistress' nether hair. She has stood on tables and crawled under them, and sang when she was told to, and stopped singing when she was told to, and tonight she will appear through the double doors like a lady, thank you Mrs Abercorn.

She is wearing her two-yard-wide mantua, and nothing could have persuaded her not to.

From behind the hall door, she can hear their voices. She can hear meat being sliced, jelly softly falling apart, gravy being slopped onto plates. Wine hitting crystal. Two women laugh and a fork scrapes porcelain. A tinkling jig. Someone can't be bothered making his way to the commode so he calls for the table chamber pot. His pissing makes a noise that recalls, strangely, the sound of money tumbling onto stone setts.

Isobel cannot hear sentences but the beginnings of phrases.

'She is . . .'

'She *was* . . .'

'She *sounds* . . .'

Then silence.

Now Percy Abercorn is clearing his throat. The sounds shrink. Percy's fingers fiddle with the loose screw on the side of his eyeglasses, a small scraping. He is drunk, he is staving off burps with every sentence.

'My good people,' he says. 'I want to thank you for welcoming myself and my wife to your beautiful New Town.'

There is some applause. These people love to congratulate themselves. As if they personally were down on their hands and knees, scraping away the bones of the dead to make space for all this crisp new stonework. All they had to do was hand some money to a banker.

'I cannot fathom a finer city from which to begin chronicling the lives of those guardians of our folk tradition and heritage, than here in Edinburgh. They are not pretty stories, and nor should they be. But they must be told, because their darkness speaks of our humanity as much as any tale of bucolic beauty.'

Bravo Percy, Isobel thinks. *Maybe his wife wrote his speech.*

'And what is more, we have with us tonight the very singer who inspired the magnum opus of this volume, the woman whose melancholy tale resonated so much with my wife, that she could not forget it. It took over her mind. For days, she begged me to seek out this singer. And when I did, I was just as struck as she.'

Bit of a fib Percy, Isobel thinks, recalling his list of more suitable ballad topics, that he reeled off on the night of the St Cecilia's concert, *but never mind. We're here now, aren't we?* She has been promised her extra five pounds after this performance; all in all, for this ballad she's been pledged as much as she earns in half a year at the Musical Society.

Mrs Abercorn startles her by opening the double doors suddenly, and the burst of sound and light makes Isobel realise what a strange position she is in, standing there, mute in the doorframe, all eyes on her. The ladies, interspersed between the men, are poised with amusement, heads cocked to the side, laughter half in and half out of their mouths, hair frizzing in the warm, food-steamed air. The men are in various states of curiosity, leaning across their soup plates, or back against their chairs. They all still have their jackets on, despite the heat from the hissing fire. Moisture is beading down the creamy wainscotting — Isobel can almost hear it.

Mrs Abercorn takes her hand. There is a devilish hot dryness in her palm that for some reason makes Isobel want to run. Instead Mrs Abercorn pulls her, shuffling, forward.

The room feels muggy and quiet now, fabric and breath blanketing whispers and stifled coughs. Their eyes, their blinks, are like small percussive chimes. Their wigs whistle, and the friction of necks turning and craning and turning back again sets something off kilter in Isobel's spine.

'Isobel Duguid. Some of you may know her from the Edinburgh Musical Society. But to us, she will always be a ballad singer of the streets of Auld Reekie — isn't that what you call it here?' Mrs Abercorn laughs lightly.

'What?' Isobel snaps. 'I don't sing on the street anymore.'

'Hush,' Mrs Abercorn whispers.

'No. I'm a musical Maestra these days.' She raises her voice, eyes the patrons. 'I did sing at Parliament Close, and I was an orange seller — for a while. But that's different.'

'It is part of the poetry of the work, to conjure up the profession of the singer as humble,' Mrs Abercorn counters. 'That is all.' There is a small silence. They are all looking at Isobel, and it is not Isobel's preference to be silent and looked at. She would always rather be listened to and in the dark if the choice were there.

'Shall I sing now?' she blurts, for she cannot bear the silence; there must be sound, now, in the room or she will perish.

'No, no. Percy will read.'

Percy creaks open his pristine leather copy of his new book. Tanned to the softness of a tongue, and crimson too. No expense spared.

He puts on his eyeglasses. He clears his throat. He reads. 'This is my version of the tale,' he prefaces.

'"Come, all false-hearted maidens", the Ballad singer sighed,
As she lay down her babe at the filthy road's side,
"Come hear how my mistress I did betray,
In Old Edinburgh's Canongate one day
Jealous of her beauty, her voice and her hair,
I beat to death her lover, a castrated singer fair,
And now their spirits haunt my soul, they are my load to bear.

Though I was never hanged for it, my fate I cannot halt,
For I must carry round their tale, as heavy as salt."'

He reads.

And he reads and he reads.

Isobel's horror grows. What is this? It is not her. That is not her in his poem, and that is not her ballad and that is not what she sings and why is she standing here, in front of these people, to listen to this? What is happening and what has she done to deserve it?

He reads, and as he reads on, the poem grows ghastlier. Isobel, he says, would sing with her babe in a basket, bent-backed outside Marie Eliza's gilded door, and the flaxen-haired opera singer would but throw coins, though never gave her notice. Isobel, he pronounces, the crone who hawked her songs on hanging days, was jealous of the lovers, she saw them to-ing and fro-ing on the Royal Mile, watched their furtive liaisons, and soon began to covet the grotesque-bodied castrato for herself. And she would wait, and she would wait, watching them, an axe in her hand until one night, until one night ...

Isobel cannot bear it.

He cannot go on.

For a second her dizzying thoughts stop, and she thinks: *Is this a better story than mine?* But then rage takes her.

'Stop!' she cries.

Percy will not stop. He is in full flow:

'The ballad singer's soul eroded so, hate rinsed it clean away,
In her throes of spite she barely knew night from day,
The eunuch lover crept into Maria's flower bed
And lo the hag did beat him in the temple of his head,'

'It is not what happened!' Isobel screams.

Is she mad? Is she hearing this? Is this a joke? Do they all believe him, or is she part of a pageant? How many copies of this book have been printed? And where is her fucking murder ballad? Where has it gone? Has it vanished? Has it been mutilated, obliterated by the force of a literary man's will, never to return? Where is the tune? He isn't even singing. The sounds are all blazing one big bonfire in her head. She can't tear apart her thoughts; they are like fighting cocks, surrounded by laughter, by indrawn gasps. Why would the Abercorns do this to her? What did Isobel Duguid ever do to them?

Isobel becomes grimly aware that Mrs Abercorn's fingers are gripping her arm. She has the strength of a coiled eel and she is not letting go.

'You're hurting me. I want to leave. Give me my five pounds and let me leave.' Isobel wants nothing more than to run from this lewd burlesque and drink herself blind, back in the Old Town where she belongs.

'Stay,' Mrs Abercorn says. 'For you have run, Isobel Duguid, and you have hidden, and you have lied, and you have sung and printed your lies. But on the grave of my father you shall answer for your lies. You shall answer for your crimes.'

Isobel's heart stops.

'On the grave of . . .?'

She is from a musical family.

She keeps with her a woman who sings quiet psalms.

Clessidro is gone, a ghost evaporated, and it is Isobel, she sees now, all along, who has been the fool.

She sees now in Mrs Abercorn's face the ghost; two ghosts, in fact. Very faint, behind the paint and the smallpox scars. Just a hint really, the nose of one, the other's eyes.

'Cecilia Herz?' she asks.

Mrs Abercorn nods. 'Yes,' she says quietly, 'I am not dead. I did not die when my mother birthed me, as well you know. I am the daughter of the man you saw hanged, daughter of the woman who died with a broken heart. And as you lied about me, I want to know how many more lies you have told. When you sing ballads about dead people, you should always tell the truth, for their children will return as living ghosts to hold you to account.'

Isobel is shaking now, she is trembling, and there are two men beside the double doors, standing in front of the double doors in fact, and they were not there before. The sash window is locked. Mrs Abercorn sees her looking at it.

Isobel says, 'Wenzeslaus was taken by the constables. They caught him. Bloodied. Setting fire to the Playhouse. It was him. The whole town knew it was him.'

'He might have been hanged for it, but he was no more guilty than his unborn babe.'

'How do you know? You were only born that night.'

'But I know.'

Isobel has no reply to this. She tries to think of something to say, but her thoughts are crumbling.

'Can you, Isobel Duguid, on the bones of your mother,' Mrs Abercorn says, 'say truthfully that Wenzeslaus Herz did kill Guido Guadagni? That he did beat him to death with his violin, in Carrubber's Close, as you sing in your ballad?'

The silence smothers. Sound cannot survive without air and there is no air left in the room.

Just as Isobel thinks she's about to suffocate, she surfaces from the rotten mire, gasping, and when she has caught her breath, she says in the same quiet voice as Mrs Abercorn's, 'No. No he did not.'

Mrs Abercorn is still as a gallows tree. Slowly she asks, 'What you did that night killed my mother. Is that not so?'

But Isobel will not answer this. How can she? What, is she supposed to pull up an answer from her soul that has lain knotted and dormant for so long? She could say, 'It is not so simple.' She could say, 'You do not understand.' But she doesn't. She says nothing. It is her time. The ghosts have risen, and the rattling skeletons of the dead have come a-guising, clicking and clacking their jig.

Mrs Abercorn gestures to the two men standing by the double doors. She says, 'Take her to the Tolbooth.'

ACT II
TOLBOOTH

1

M RS ABERCORN,
       Cecilia Abercorn,
       How should I address you? '*One aficionado of music to another?*' One liar to another?

I wonder if your breakfast has been as luxurious as mine — slop of oats in a tin bowl? (I didn't eat it, I'm waiting until one of my other *aficionados* can bring me some mutton or partons, or at least some bread and cheese.) Or is the view from your Young's Street home half as pleasant as mine (the arse of a drunk Redcoat)?

Cecilia Abercorn, indeed.

I'm not the only one peddling falsehoods, am I? How simple a disguise marriage is for a name. How much you think you have the measure of me.

You believe — I *know* you do — that one with a brain as coarse as mine must be too simple to know when she is being spoken down to, or over, or about; to know when someone's tongue has slipped, and to watch them bend down and pick the slithery thing back up, so they can stick it back in their mouth and carry on as normal. You think I am not quick enough to catch yours or your husband's careless remarks, your dropped words.

And you believed — I'm certain you did — that once my voice had been stopped, that once you'd had me bundled off to the Tolbooth, that would be the end of it all. Shut up, out of the way, I could rant my songs to my heart's content, while your husband peddles his own mangled version of a murder he knows nothing about. You believe that I can bawl and cruin and sing to the rats and the corbies, the cooing-doos and the madmen, and the gaolers will only have to bang on the door to brank my mouth.

But do you know what I can do as well as sing? I can write! With quill and ink! Just like you! There you go. I'm quite the performing hen.

When it came to using the last bawbees I had for bread or for paper, I chose paper. Your husband knows the power of the written word, and so do I.

How lucky he is. Are those whose stories he takes for his book so lucky? We don't get to choose how our words are sent out into the world, or how they are changed. That is the risk you take when you put your heart into a story and tell it mouth to mouth.

I knew the power of the printed word. And you are right, Cecilia. I used it wrong. But now I will put right my tale. I do not care to save my own life from the noose, but I will not have lies about me printed in your husband's book.

So you're going to have to shut up for a wee while. Because it's true, that what happened that summer is more complicated than will fit into a ballad.

Go ahead and burn this at your peril.

Read it if you dare.

2

DEAR CECILIA,
I will own that I was angry last time I set my quill to paper.

I had not slept. This room smells of vitriol and mould. The window is grated and though it lets in little light, it lets in all the sounds of the night in their ghastly beauty. And I still bore you a grudge for the trick you played. I felt taken by shock when your Town Guardsmen unveiled themselves at dinner, for I had believed them to be guests — which was, I think, your intention. I have never before had my hands put in irons in all my life, not as an orange seller, ballad singer or even as a smuggler. It hurt, Cecilia. And the spectacle bit my pride. You cannot countenance the path I have trodden to take me to the level of comfort in which I live.

However, I am grateful for the guineas you deposited at the gate. The warden has brought me some barley broth and a small bottle of porter, and I do admit this has given me some cheer.

The drunk soldier who shared my bed when I arrived has gone now, and I have only a small sad lassie in her place, accused of concealing her pregnancy and disposing of the baby, and she sleeps for most of the day. This gives me good time to think and to write.

I have taken your act of generosity as a sign that you would like to continue reading my treatise. I am sorry our paths had to cross in this way, and I am sorry I have told some untruths. It was not my intention to deceive, only to report the events no more or less than as the public and the broadsheets had them at the time. If anything, my crime has been to accept the story others conjured, and not to disclose my familiarity with the events, of which, you guess correctly, I am a part.

I shall start at the beginning, and every day I shall write to exhaustion, and when I am done then you shall know the truth. For does not every child deserve to know from whence they came?

3

I WAS NOT BORN IN EDINBURGH, and my mother did not hang for witchcraft, as I tell people. This practice was abandoned before I was born. But as you can imagine, I do not let that come in the way of a good story. It pleases me to think of my mother cavorting with the deil, rather than, as she was, Alice Duguid, a frightened, panicked scullery maid, like the one in the bed next to me, who was hanged for trying to do to me what that sorry lassie is said to have done to her own babe.

As for my father, he may have been the Earl of D_____ (for my mother was in his service at the time I was born). Or he may have been the Earl's coachman, for I am told there is a local ballad sung in these parts of a maid seduced by a coachman, who later concealed and tried to drown her babe. Or he could have been the Earl's trumpeter, a man brought from the Earl's West Indian plantation, who brought the people of the village a great deal of joy with his music, though many of them did not deserve it for the life they had stolen from him. Let us go with him. Let us assume that music is in my blood, as it is in yours.

I was brought up by a midwife, Mrs Rixon, and the first time I heard a ballad it was sung by her. Mrs Rixon used to travel on a small pony great distances to tend to the women who could afford to pay her, and I was left alone from a very young age, with nothing but some milk and bannocks and my own company to keep me cheerful, sometimes for a whole day. If she knew she would be away for several days she would bundle me into a sheepskin and strap me to the front of the pony's saddle with two sturdy belts, the way she did her bag of midwifery tools. I would travel with her, soaked and freezing through the winter nights, parched and clammy through the summer days, and we would ride to villages and houses that could be ten miles afield.

Through the delirium of pitch dark, or the glaring sun of the day, she would keep me from grumbling or howling by singing to me. The pony's walk was her beat, the slap of its shod feet in the dirt, and the way it threw me lightly from side to side became a rhythm that rocked me into a peaceful trance. She would sing about all kinds of things, forget-me-nots that grew in clots, bluebell woods and bickering birds, boys that stole ponies from the stable block and rode abroad to steal a glimpse of their sweethearts. She sang about women who dressed as men and went to sea to seek their fortune, about dogs who smoked pipes and rode goats, girls who walked the streets in cat-skin robes, mermaids with silver combs in their hair. Her own father had been a sailor and he had taught her many shanties, and his mother was a dairymaid who knew milking songs, and so on back the tales went through time, gathering some and losing others along the way.

But my favourites — and I think they were her favourites too — were the darkest tales, the bleakest, cruellest and most murderous. A child can understand when an adult to whom they are close nurses a passion for one thing over another. They can hear the shift in tone, the clarity and fever in the voice.

I remember the songs so vividly. I remember *The Strange Banquet*, where the guildsmen of the village were cooked by the devil. Tailors pickled, sheriffs roasted, yeomen brained into sauce, a mayor stuffed *with jelly in his belly*. Then there was Lamkin, the stonemason who took revenge on the Laird who did not pay him by slaughtering the Laird's wife and baby. She often sang *The Twa Corbies*; I always remember the line, 'Ye'll *sit on his white hause-bane, And I'll pike out his bonny blue een,'* because it was so gruesome to me, the revelation of the body as bone and veins. Of course she sang *The Twa Sisters*, as well you know. But there were also songs about bogles and witches, Sawney Bean and his cannibal family, who were said to live in the caves not far from where we stayed.

I do not know why she sang such brutal tales. Often she sang them at dusk, as we were riding through the twilight. If I close my eyes and try to stir my memories of these times I can hear magpies chattering high in the trees, leaves crunching under the pony's hooves, startled hares scattering twigs and sometimes the call of one horse rider to another on a gloomy, lonely path. Perhaps there was something talismanic in the way she sang her most violent ballads at this time of change. When the light begins to be pulled down beneath the cloak of night, this is when the walls between the two worlds are at their thinnest. Maybe in her gruesome words she was somehow saying to the devilish sprites on the other side, *Mark me, for I see you. I know you are there, and I have darkness in me too with which to fight yours.* Sulphur. Plagues and fire. Blood and guts. That was Mrs Rixon's way. Or maybe she was signalling to any lurking highwayman that she was not to be reckoned with. Come not near the mad woman for she will sing to you of murder and butchery.

It was my favourite time of day. Still is.

When you are a child, you take what you are told, and you do not think only of the words to such songs, but also the joyous music, the delight of the rhyme. But the words, they seep in somehow, don't they, in the end. And if they are cruel and bleak and savage, they can lodge in your soul, and like the food you eat, stick to your bones, bloom inside you to become part of who you are. What did your nurse sing to you, Cecilia? Let me guess. *Stabat Mater? Caro Mio Ben? Ring a Ring a Roses?*

If I had a child, I would sing them *The Stepmother's Cruelty*, which is about a girl who ends up baked in a pie.

We were used to blood and guts. Sometimes Mrs Rixon sang to the women in labour to soothe them as they sat on the birthing stool, screaming and crying. I was seldom present in the room, for most of the houses we visited were large enough to have a kitchen, and I would be sent there more often than not, to watch over a pot of hot water on the stove. But I could hear the sounds of her songs as they travelled through the walls or down through the floorboards, the heavy clap of her feet to mark the beat, the stubborn calmness of her voice. Sometimes I would catch the tune of what she sang. Often it was merry, but if it was dusk she would sometimes sing murder ballads to the birthing women too.

Then the wait. The silence, the breath of relief as the baby's petrified shriek came birling through the house, a demonic sound; terror, a child's first feeling in our world. And the cheers, the whoops, the opening and slamming of doors, the rich plunk of corks being wrenched from bottles, glasses clumsy, clinking. It all trickled down into the kitchen where I sat with my eyes on the millpond of the cauldron, still waiting for the first hot bubbles to rise.

Or the silence that didn't end. No song. No shriek. Soft crying. Whispered words. Mrs Rixon ushering me back out onto the pony, wrapping me in the pungent sheepskin. Singing her sorrowful, bloodied ballads through the trees, all the way home.

I was happy as a child, and I thought for a while that eventually the time would come when I would take over the trade of midwifery and ride a pony to great houses like Mrs Rixon did. But at some time during my late childhood, I began to feel the stifling force of the village around me. I wanted money. I had seen it in those houses I'd visited. And silk dresses. And Japanned wood. And a fireplace as big as a chicken coop. I wanted to know where those people went when they were not lounging in their houses. Where did the miller sell his grain? Where did the farmer drive his cows, once a month? Where did the milk go? Where did their spinets and fiddles and books come from? Where were people tried and gaoled and hanged as they were at the end of songs? I knew it wasn't in our village.

I also suspected that were I to stay there was a strong possibility I should end up with child myself, and I could not guarantee that I would not try to do what my own mother had.

Have you listened to me much, beyond that concert you came to, some Fridays ago? If you had, you would have noticed

109

that for all my grim tales, I have sung not once about mothers who dispose of their babies. Though that is the most common kind of dark ballad you will hear in these parts — for it is the most common kind of murder — it is not one that I can bring myself to take a coin for. It is a haunting of my mother I cannot bear to conjure. And I have scruples, Cecilia. More scruples than your mother or father gave me credit for. You will learn of them. You will learn how music bartered me a life that could have been filled with misery, violence and death, for a life where I only sing about those things.

After leaving the village, with my schooling no more than a few numbers I could scrape on slate with a pencil, a catechism, some phrases from Shakespeare, and a nous for how to keep still and silent when men in cloaks peered over my shoulder, I took the road along the coast to Edinburgh with another girl who also wanted more for herself, called Beth.

After trekking along the coast far enough to catch sight of Bass Rock, we were given passage on a fishing vessel and ended up in Newhaven, a harbour on the edge of Edinburgh. Most people when they arrive in a strange land gravitate towards the kirk for sanctuary. But the kirk has always put a bit of the fear into me. Perhaps I know myself too well, that I am possessed with a little of the devil, and it is that which repels me from the holy water and the sacred stone. I was drawn instead towards the sea, where sailors wait to leave and women wait to see them come home alive again.

We were taken in first by a pair of saltwives, who were kind to us and gave us a bed in their cottage in return for our helping them cook and sweep the hearth. I have said they were kind but their appearance terrified me more than the bogles in Mrs Rixon's ballads. Their feet were worn to pegs, toes like tree roots, and they sucked the cockles out of shells one by one for they had no teeth. They also had ballads that they sang as they loaded their salt baskets, and in the evening over the stove, but theirs were waterier and more despondent. Ghost ships. Drownings. Storms and monsters. Men who left the house one day and never returned. Bodies never washed up, appearing only as spectres in mist. Their ballads were full of absences, empty spaces, lives interrupted and never resolved. There was something sadder and more upsetting about a disappearance, about an empty rocking chair, than there was about blood.

Although I am glad they took us in, they were also an omen for where I thought I might end up if I let the days fall past without trying to find myself richer lodgings.

Beth found a fisherman, I found a smuggler. She ended up with a fine townhouse in Granton Square, for her fisherman turned merchant and sold oysters to cellars as far south as Birmingham. I ended up a smuggler's dolly, hoiking loot back and forth between ship and shore. And look where I am now.

The smuggler was a flash man and he had a fine, clean house, stuffed to the rafters with trinkets and feathers and china ladies and glass baubles and all kinds of gewgaws. But though he was rich by the standards I knew, he was mean as wolves with his pennies, and he lived with his old mother who kept the contents of the house under her sharp gaze. I wasn't allowed to touch anything, not a silver plate, not a looking glass, not a brandied fig, without her permission. He kept his wine chest locked and ledgered and his coffee beans weighed to the grain, and his house stank of the mackerel he kept smoking in his chimney to disguise the scent of tea. She called me 'The Lassie' and she walked abroad with a fan dangling from her wrist and a Chinese silk bonnet even in the bleakest rain, and yet she didn't know rotten meat from good and couldn't hold a tune.

I sent a winkle shell once, back to Mrs Rixon in the village, wrapped in paper with the address scrawled in the smuggler's quill in my shaky, unpractised hand. But I never knew if she received it and because I moved lodgings after that she had no way to write back to me.

I carried all the treasures of the world up my smuggling skirts. I used to hide all kinds of things in my hoops, to evade the customs man. Bottles of sherry, saffron. Tea was always popular. Did you ever consider why I barely touched those lovely black brews you put before me when we were in your parlour, in the delicate porcelain cups? It is because I cannot consider tea without also thinking of it bundled in bandages, swinging beneath the nethers of a young smuggler girl as she clings to the side of a boat to take her to shore, so she can have a shilling, and make the tea merchants rich.

I drew the line at pineapples. But I did smuggle China oranges from time to time, and it was this that led me to the next verse of my life, which is to say, perhaps the most fatal one.

I would share boats with the hoors who went out to the tea clippers when they anchored. Can you imagine, Cecilia, what it is like to travel aboard a doxies' bumboat? You might like to think they are full of cheer, very jolly places, as they are drawn in the postcards you have probably seen for sale in the tat stalls down Leith. You would very much like to believe those postcards you have seen I'm sure. You know the ones — buxom wenches in their frills, paps pushed to their collars, cheeks rosy, eyes wide with surprise as a sailor sticks his whatsitcalled up her neveryoumind.

But the sad truth is that most of the women on them have to be blind drunk to do their job, and the banquet of poxes gifted on them by the sailors makes them itchy and bad-tempered. They did their best, and I liked some of them — Scratching Lucy and Violent Jenny — but they were an omen too. For a while, I endeavoured never to let a man near my privates for as long as I lived. I aspired to become a nun of sorts, wedded to myself. I'm sure even you know by now that in a city like Edinburgh, that's an opium dream that doesn't last.

I am tired now, and running out of ink, but you shall hear more from me soon.

4

I F BY THE TIME YOU READ THIS I still have the misfortune to be in the Tolbooth, please do me the favour of finding out where Billy, the old turnkey, has gone. I cannot bear this new curmudgeon who tells me I am not to request meat in here for it is not his wont to make feasts for murderesses. He has taken away my shoe buckles, lest I use them as missiles through the grated window onto the Luckenbooths (which I hope you know I would never do), and I have not even had my trial, but this is of no consequence to him. He denies me porter and tells me I am to have nothing but water from the cistern, brought daily in a bucket, and I am not to clean my underlinen on a Sunday. I have tried to pay him, but he does not want my coin, nor my rings, nor cloth. I wish for Billy back, for Billy sings and what is more he has promised me one day he will bring a piglet of his own for me to pet, which would cheer me greatly in here. Perhaps you could make enquiries Cecilia, it really is the least you can do.

Anyway, back to China oranges up my skirts.

Several times a week the ships would bring fruits into the harbour. We — me and the smuggler's men — fashioned a cage with which to carry them, from jute rope and sheep's bones and oak staves from old coopers' barrels. It had to be invisible beneath the heft of my skirts and only constructed behind the front portion, for I also had to be able to sit down as we were rowed ashore. On an ordinary day I could take around twenty of the fruits. They would swing as I walked, bouncing off my calves and thighs and if they were good, their skins would be sharp with juice and release their fragrance in little spits of oil and I would smell lovely, like a rich woman. For my troubles I was allowed to keep four per journey, each of which sold for tuppence on the shore at Newhaven.

Then one day I marked as a gentleman stepped off one of the boats. I had learned to spot a rich man in a crowd of sailors, but this man was different. He had something about him. He was what you might call a 'Macaroni', Cecilia — you with your society words — because he had sparkles at his throat, a silk ruffle and a coat that was dyed in bright, costly colours. And though he had been on a ship and looked as tired and as sick as any, his periwig was pristine and powdered and he wore gemstones on his buckles. I liked the look of his buttons. They were a different colour to the rest of the coat. I thought they'd look good on my own frock. And I liked that he was humming a tune. He had a strange-shaped box which looked like a coffin but which he carried as if it was a baby. He wanted one of my oranges.

'How much?'

'Where ye fae?' Wasn't I blunt in those days?

'Venice,' he said. And immediately I saw in my mind's eye a picture of canals and masked hoors, for Venice was all some of the sailors on the ships would talk about.

I sold him an orange for tuppence and asked what was in his wooden case. He opened it to show me. Would you countenance it my friend, but it was a fiddle; a gleaming, well-oiled, nut-brown fiddle, with the head of a lion carved at the end of its scroll.

'You're going to sell it?' I asked.

He shook his head.

'Give us a tune then.'

'Ah friend,' he said, and he laughed. 'If you wish to see me play you must purchase a ticket for the Edinburgh Musical Society or the Canongate Playhouse.' Haughty fellow. How on earth would I know what those were? Down here with the doxies. It had never occurred to me that musicians could be brought, like lavender, or fruit, from over the seas, for a society of people to sit in a room and hear them play.

He was a fine, groomed fellow and he spoke English well, and said he was here to make music in concerts and plays. While I was helping him find a coach to take him into Edinburgh, I told him I liked music too and knew many songs and should probably like to sing in a concert, for it sounded like a fine thing, and he laughed and told me that the only way I would ever get into the Canongate Playhouse or the Edinburgh Musical Society would be to sell my oranges, where fruits were offered for sale at the intervals.

My pride was hurt, which he saw. I found him a coach, and while the coachman was loading his trunk onto the roof he turned to me, still clutching his fiddle case. 'I'll tell you though,' he said, before we parted ways. 'If you were to take those oranges into town and sell them at the Canongate Playhouse, you should get not tuppence but sixpence per orange.'

Well, Cecilia, you can imagine how my ears pricked at that. His carriage rattled away over the setts and I never saw him again. But I thought on what he said, and the way he looked

and smelled (Expensive. Eau de Cologne doesn't come cheap).
I resolved that very afternoon that I would save the rest of that
day's oranges, and find out where this Playhouse was and make
the journey there myself.

At that time I was still lodged in the smuggler's house, a tall
thin tower on the harbourfront, and I was sharing the smuggler's
bed nightly where he smuggled his — modest — goods up me
when the fancy took him. So you can imagine the opportunity
to make money for myself in this way, so I might one day have
a chance of saving towards having my own lodgings, wasn't
something I could let pass me by.

It was a trek, the journey away from the water, uphill, all the
way to the strange country of Edinburgh. The city was being
built, as it always is, columns raised, stone hammered, roads
flattened.

But the clamour of the Old Town that greeted me! I might
have known by then that I loved sound and song, but I did
not know the full range of noise the world had ready to cram
in my ears, to stuff me with.

Oh God, I can live without sight, I can live in the dark, I
can live in the mire of this Tolbooth cage, I can live without
my wigs and my skirts and my hoops, but don't ever take away
the sounds of Edinburgh's Old Town.

Those tenements, packed tight as thieves' dens, open windows
echoing every crow call, every drip, every sigh; the knock of
the soup spoon against the side of the pot, the smash when
the wife flings a bottle at her husband and misses, the whip of
sheets, shaken to be strung between closes, the cries of poultry
sellers and their caged birds' calls. All this, all catcalls, greetings,
whistling, cajoling in Parliament Close, fishwives, saltwives,

Irish tin flutes, the laugh of girls with no fears, only fancies, pipes, ballads, drums from the castle barracks. Marching soldiers. On hanging days, the scream of fainters in the crowd, the noose's choke. All this, and don't ever try to tell me that music is only what you hear in concert halls, written by men like Handel, or your father.

I was stunned by it. I was drunk on it.

You are too late, Cecilia, to see the Canongate Playhouse. Two decades too late, for your father razed it to the ground in a rage. That much is true. Now there is a fancy new Theatre Royal in which I have never set foot, but where I don't doubt there are orange girls who scurry from box to box, ferrying lovers' notes for tuppence and offering extras while the play is going on.

Finding myself on the fishbone spine of the Royal Mile, with all its crumbling closes leading off it, I had to find someone to ask where the Canongate Theatre lay. And the person I clapped eyes on happened to be Jas le Corbie.

Jas is a small player in this tale, Cecilia — though he'd like to think he was a bigger one — but remember him. Because, like the hand on a compass, he was to bend my fate, and his will was strong. Free will? Sometimes yes, unless you hitch your cart to someone whose will is freer than yours. Jas was a scholar at the university. He knew these games. He knew how to talk his way into or out of anything. But it was he who taught me the currency of words, the exchange of ideas, and I suppose I must be grateful for that.

Of course Jas le Corbie wasn't his real name. He was James Crowe. But he had aspirations of becoming a poet — don't they all, at that age? — and so when he was around town, trying to make his mark in the taverns and salons and coffee houses, Jas he was.

I found him — or rather, he found me — peering down Sugarhouse Close that night. He was leaning against the wall, smoking a long, thin clay pipe. The bowl on the end had been fashioned into a naked woman with engorged breasts, facing him, and he was holding it to his lips by cupping her grainy buttocks.

He called over to me, 'A threepenny bit says I can guess where you came fae.'

I had been catcalled earlier in the evening, but not in such a pompous way. He was wearing black and brown, when the rest of the Mile down this end was dressed in green and copper, red and blue. He was viciously plain. Later he told me the absence of colour helped him to think.

I said, 'I'm looking for the Canongate Playhouse.'

'Why? Are you a spy, an assassin from the kirk's men come to shut down the play?' He turned his pipe towards me, made it into a musket and aimed it at my head; blew my imaginary skull to pieces.

'I've got oranges to sell.'

He looked up down my body, making a show of peering about my person. He looked in my hair, behind my back, could see none. 'Where are they?' He sniffed. 'I can smell them.'

I still had them in the cage, up my skirt. 'Never you mind. Are you going to tell me where the Playhouse is?'

'You're too late for the play. Started at half-past six. The only two things that are punctual in this city: the kirk and the theatre. Why don't you try the kirk instead for your oranges? There's not much difference. There's a man on a stage, gloating to the sound of his own tongue, and if you pick the right kirk they have wine too.' He led me back out of the close and pointed with his pipe down the hill, where a pair of red doors were flung open. Men dressed in black, like him, were filing in. Then he pointed up the hill to another close, a discreet entrance to a modest stone building, women and children slipping through the door.

'It's not Sunday,' I muttered. 'What are they doing?'

'Why hush your mouth!' He feigned offence. His eyes grinned. 'Evening prayers. For the souls of the chosen. And even for the chosen there's more choice in the kirk than the theatres, if you can't decide what kind of God yours is. Of theatres, there's only one here, and even that, only sometimes, when the kirk men can't be arsed shutting it down. And there's nothing there that passes close for a God in its morals.'

'I'll try my luck in Parliament Close,' I said, turning away. I'd heard tell that was the place to go to, for buying and selling anything — fruits, books, trinkets, women.

'A fellow heathen, then?' he called, as I made to leave. 'I reject the kirk too.' He took a puff on his pipe. Smoke rose from between the woman's legs. 'I'll show you Parliament Close,' he said, and took off at a clip ahead of me.

I felt like a squat moth, fluttering alongside his gangling legs that strode the Mile. He told me as we walked, 'There isn't a play at the Playhouse tonight in fact, but an opera.'

'A what?'

'An opera,' he said again.

I had never heard the word. I parroted, 'Anopera.'

'An,' he said. 'Opera.' He turned his head to me as he walked and smirked.

It was such a sensual word; it sang itself. 'An opera,' I said.

'A Beggar's Opera.' He looked at me and laughed. He laughed heartily. I couldn't fathom why.

You see now, Cecilia, the tricks that are played? The veils that deceive? That it tickled the man who wrote that title, *Beggar's Opera*, to mix those words, 'beggar' and 'opera'. But you had to know what each was to know that they were words that belong far apart, to different worlds. I was not party to that joke then. It was not a joke made for me.

Jas le Corbie regaled me as we walked with tales of the university. He was a scholar, studying philosophy. He believed he knew every word in the world that was worth knowing. He tipped his three-pointed hat and cried, 'Hulooo' to men we passed, who greeted him back. He had a maddening power of twisting and playing with his words, to take something I had said and turn it into something that amused him, or to pluck a word just out of my knowledge to confound me, as I hustled to keep pace with him.

'Go back to the Playhouse tomorrow night, you'll be in good company, and I'm sure you'll sell your oranges. Come on, Parliament Close doesn't wait either.'

We turned a sharp corner and entered another close. It was a gloomy alleyway underneath an arch of windows which joined together two buildings on either side. Through one of the open windows I could see a woman above me, plunging her hands in and out of a bucket of water while steam rose.

There was a low square door cut into the wall. Jas turned into it and I followed him through. Immediately I smelled the familiar scent of kirk wood and cloth, heard the hushed echo of our feet on the flagstones. The sounds of the street were dampened.

Was this a trick? Was he trying to deceive me into saving my own soul? 'What are we—'

He cut me off. 'It's a short cut,' he said. From behind one of the pillars he led me to, I could catch glimpses of the robes of a minister, flickering shadows as he moved.

Jas jabbed me in the side of my stays and pushed me into a pew. 'I thought I said—'

'Hush.' He pointed to the preacher and directed his gaze that way.

The kirk was mostly empty. No one had prayed in the evening in my village either, at least never in the kirk. Some lawyers sat in the front pews, still in their robes, some apprentices, and a few couples from the tenements, shopkeepers and merchants still in their day clothes.

I have no love of kirks. Our village minister preached brimstone on Sundays and found God in the underwear of the local village girls the rest of the week. Watching the way people clung to his words, like they were climbing into lifeboats, unsettled me — still does. I understand the power of an echoing hall, of listening to a person singled out at its head. I just don't find that kind of rapture and comfort in the kirk.

Jas had crossed his long legs, one over the other, he had knitted his hands closed on top of them, and he was listening with his head cocked to the side and a smirk on his face.

He was blocking the end of the pew. I had no escape.

The minister's voice, echoing round the dark stones, felt like the thrum of a dirge. As his voice began to rise and the words blended into one hammer of sound I felt a warmth at my waist, looked down and saw Jas le Corbie's bony fingers probing beneath the laces of my stays. I flinched out of his reach. I slid my bum along the smooth pew. The minister's voice rang out and Jas slid closer to me, pressed his hip in its wool breeches up against my brown linen skirt, wriggled the finger further now underneath the thick corsetry fabric. It felt like a worm, probing, burrowing. The startling warmth, the thinness of it, seeking, searching, its determination to wriggle into me. I feared he would tear my sark.

I thought I understood now what we were doing in the kirk and I shifted to move away. But he caught my waist with both his hands.

'Is not this spiritual?' he whispered. His voice was tight with mirth. He ran his hand up the stiff stomacher of my bodice until I felt the dry tickle of his fingertip creeping over the top and onto my bosom.

I have said I had no love of the kirk but I did not want to be part of this spectacle of his, whatever rebellion he was enacting and had co-opted me to play a role in.

'I just want to sell my oranges,' I murmured.

I watched him look around the dark stone arches, his face calculating the danger, weighing up if he thought I was the kind of girl who would scream. It would echo in here. It would be loud. I held his wrist at bay.

'Very well,' he whispered.

We shuffled back out into the evening light of the High Street.

'I'll take you to Parliament Close.'

I made to walk away into the evening crowd.

'I promise,' he called. I turned and he looked me in the eye.

I did not believe him. But I went with him.

Jas took me down closes, over sludge piles, past wooden slabs with fish heads stuck to them. He took me past old blind men with ballads pinned to boards, beside broken green glass in the gutter, spread handkerchiefs, past the man they call Gingerbread Jock, doing his jig, while girls in pinnies with flour and soot on their cheeks clapped and laughed.

That fucker, Jas — James Crowe — that night, did not lead me anywhere near Parliament Close in the end, but instead to the Cowgate. He led me down the bleakest of alleyways, and to the tune of two cocks fighting in some basement den, pressed my back against the wall.

'I will discover where your oranges are kept,' he said.

I sized up his sinewy face, his fine stubbled jaw. I contemplated hitting him in the teeth or crying out or running. But instead, I stayed where I was and I observed him as he helped himself. I did not flinch. I did not close my eyes. I watched closely the shapes his face contorted into as he performed the act. I observed my defilement in his eyes — this beast of refinement who helped himself to me the way he helped himself to words. And I began then to brew my own ideas about this city. As he bustled in and out of me in a strained rhythm, I began wondering what he had in his muck-strewn garden of knowledge, that I could pluck from him. In short, while I did not enjoy the act the way he did, I smelled in the midden crook where his neck met his shoulder something I wanted to possess: an opportunity.

That night was my debutante's ball into Old Town society, my introduction to the *Lumières*, and the place among them they had carved for girls like me. But I knew right then, that at some point I would fashion my own knife, I would carve a better place.

5

P AY ATTENTION NOW CECILIA, for behold, here
comes the entry of the *Prima Donna* of my tale, which
is to say: your mother. And lo, she is not descending
from the heavens on a crescent moon, no, nor wandering
winsomely through the forest with sylph-like gossamer billowing
around her feet, singing about Orpheus.

She is, however, at the Canongate Playhouse. Though as
you'll learn I did not meet her upon its stage.

You are dying to know what the Canongate Playhouse looked
like, aren't you? For certain you have been inside theatres in
London and Bath, and I daresay even Scotland, but you have
not been inside the theatre that your father burned down, the
theatre where your mother's opera was rehearsed. That place
will always be a cave inside your head, a dark box in your heart,
a locked room that you want to step inside, but can't, no matter
how much blood you can smell through the lock, no matter
how many other theatres you visit.

The Canongate Playhouse was a fox's den, built on a whim
on top of an old straggly garden, and smaller than you'd think,
far smaller. The stage could not have been more than ten yards
across at its widest. The whole place was lit by cheap tallow,

and it hissed and smelled — all the time. Beef and crackling. All was dimness inside, all wood; it was nothing like St Cecilia's. It was like being in the belly of a ship, and it was run by sailors from Leith, who hauled the scenery and flew the trapdoors and rolled the thunder machine with their gargantuan, tattooed arms.

Every step you took inside that place was amplified — not echoing, just loud. It was pure loudness, pure raw sound, sound incarnate. The building was encased in stone, keeping the devils inside and the kirk outside. But the timbre, the acoustic, came from the wood with which it was floored and panelled. Plain wood in its simplicity is the most beautiful instrument of them all. Strike it, slap it, kiss it, shout against it, set fire to it and hear it cackle.

Your mother always said there was a kirk-like silence in that building when it was empty. But I never heard it empty. From the second I stepped through the turnpike, it was always a place filled with actors calling up and down stairs, crying along the garret corridors for more paint or more rouge or more water, or testing out their voices on the stage. I remember the set men scraping wooden beams along the floor, the wardrobe mistresses with their arms full of whispering silk dresses, hoops, petticoats, stockings, so many stockings, a basket of silk snakes. They were kept, like snakes, under lock and key, in a trunk in the attic that smelled of nutmeg. The attic was where the actors dressed, and to get to it you had to step outside the building, go down the close a little way, and walk up a separate turnpike. There, at the top of the building, overlooking old Holyrood Abbey, behind two dormer windows, the actors and the singers would undergo their transformations.

The musicians were housed at the opposite end — down in hell, if you will, in the basement. Down there the trapdoor to the stage creaked, and the orchestra pit was so tiny the bugle must have stuck into the kettle drum player's armpit.

When I arrived that second night, the audience was just beginning to filter in. They were lined up along the close, leaning against the wall, swords and buckles rattling, lurid cheeks, the stink of thick wig pomade on them. These early birds, these young rakes were after the best spots in the pit to watch the ladies enter. The ladies arrived later, I learned, taking up the best spots in the boxes in which to be seen. Some of the better quality hoors wandered between the boxes and some of the orange seller girls were going up and down the line, offering their baskets too.

I followed this queue, drawing quiet stares, picking up on strange, dropped words from the conversations; 'court of session'; 'terrible luck'; 'best price'; 'odious man'.

A cadie in a torn tartan coat was leaning against the curved wall of the narrow turnpike. He looked out of place in his grubby breeches, with his brown wig askew, and that drew me to him.

'I have oranges to sell,' I said. 'Can I sell them here?'

He pointed me in the direction of a man collecting tickets from the patrons as they filed in the door, who said he would make space at the front of the stage, but he would take a penny an orange for the continuance of his protection.

'Protection?'

He ignored me. He needed a penny, which I gave him. Without looking at me, he continued to take tickets as he ushered me inside.

I followed the trickle of patrons through the open door and into the theatre.

The sound. The sound roared. It raged. It was like the thick of a marketplace, but as if each calling vendor was belting their cries into your very ear. It was dizzying. Men in the pit greeting one another. Ladies whipping their fans with riotous force. High glee. Low laughter. Footsteps cavalry on the painted pale green boards. A trumpeter warming up. The tuning of the kettle drums. The sound rose and arced into the high boxes, the gilded bannisters, the plain-panelled Gods. It was a storm, a war charge.

And above it all, a sing-song line was coming from in front of the benches, right before the stage. 'China oranges, sixpence. Sixpence a China orange.' Two girls with sausage curls were swaying their baskets back and forth, roving their eyes, pushing their bosoms towards the men whose palms hovered over their fruit.

I followed the crowd down the side aisle, feeling the nerves of the imposter with each thump of my feet on the floorboards. I wondered if the other girls would push me aside, if they would jealously guard their pitch. But the girl standing before the orchestra pit, with the crimson bodice and the black hair, smiled as I crouched and hitched up my skirts. I began to pull oranges from the cradle inside.

She laughed as I stood up. 'That's a magic trick,' she said.

I felt foolish for they all had baskets, and I had to balance my oranges on the lip of the orchestra pit, where they rolled about, falling off the edges and knocking into the candles. Then a boy in an apron who was busy lighting the candles went to fetch me a basket from the black void at the side of the stage.

I peered into the gloom, into where he had disappeared. I could see nothing in there. It was as dark as the grave. There were sounds, muffled and hushed — musical sounds, sounds of dragging and rustling — but I couldn't really make any of them out. Those wings, as they were called, they were the crossing place, the place where people who existed only for the duration of the play were born and where they disappeared afterwards.

I learned the names of the orange seller girls — Meg and Jeanie, and there was Eleanor roving the boxes — but there were half a dozen other girls that came on different evenings.

'Don't offer them to anyone with a white cockade on their breast, or in their hat,' Meg said.

'Why not?'

'Jacobites. You don't offer a Jacobite an orange if you don't want to get your face slapped.'

'Watch out for them trying to pinch your tits,' said Jeanie. 'They'll pretend they just want a feel of the oranges but then they'll make a mistake, oopsie daisies, my hand went too far up, that's not an orange is it? If they do that ...' She pulsed her fist closed. 'Juice to the eye. You'll be an orange down, but it's worth it to see how much it smarts them.'

I wondered if this was their way of trying to frighten me away. But then I grew distracted by two men in long cream flared coats, as they approached and stood waiting to purchase our fruit. They were talking unguardedly about one of the sopranos in the opera.

'She will be on tonight, it says so on the bill.'

'I'll want my ticket price back if not,' the other said. 'It's hard to believe she can sing as well as she looks.'

'She's a daughter of the Corris, you know the violinmaker. Not a rose, but a bit of a thistle.' The first one raised his hand and made a lewd gesture. 'And it's rumoured she fiddles too.'

The second one laughed. They reached the front of the queue. 'Not in public surely? I mean it wouldn't do — for a woman to play violin that is.' They both cackled.

'What's he, then, her husband? Apart from a cuckold?' The first man rummaged in Meg's basket, found the orange he liked, handed her sixpence from the purse at his waist, hanging by his sword.

'Wenzeslaus Herz. A Prussian. Cut his teeth in the Venice season. He plays well, composes too. But he gambles, so they've had to whisk her onto the stage for their supper.'

There were more whispers. The girls were very interested in the gossip about the Herzes, particularly about Wenzeslaus. They said *she* — the soprano — had disgraced her family by running away to Venice with Wenzeslaus Herz, that Wenzeslaus was the catch of Europe, that he had sold his soul to the devil to play fiddle the way he did, but that he had a bold temper, and that the Herzes had been forced through his debts to return to Edinburgh with their tails between their legs, on a contract for the Edinburgh Musical Society. No one could deny though that together they made a handsome couple. I wanted to see this Wenzeslaus. I was curious about him. I took a wander up and down the aisle before the pit, swaying my basket, glancing over the lip of the barrier.

I had marked a man striding into the orchestra pit just a few moments ago, in a waistcoat, shirt and breeches, with his fiddle under his arm, his walk wide, almost bow-legged, as if what lay between his legs was encumbering him. He had the air of a man who bluffed at cards and expected to be looked at. Now he was seated in the centre, in — what I later learned was — the principal fiddler's chair. This was he, then. Wenzeslaus the demonic. Wenzeslaus the Prussian. Wenzeslaus the virtuoso. Wenzeslaus the cuckold. He looked tolerable. Handsome. Absorbed in the task of tuning his violin. Maybe this is hindsight but he did also have that air some men possess, that twitchy air that warns you not to come too close, not to poke or tease them. But maybe that is hindsight. I don't know if he made that much of an impression on me in fact.

I was more curious to see her.

In *The Beggar's Opera* that night, she was to take the role of Lucy Lockit, a fiend who poisons the girl that steals her fiancé. What did I imagine she might look like then, after all the chatter and the whisperings I'd caught? Six heads? Snakes for hair? Thorns for lips? Eyes that burned jade and ate everything they saw? It is hard to think back on a picture that existed only in the mind, which has since been erased by reality. And of course, no one's soul is revealed entirely in their face. But I think I expected her to have a quality about her that went beyond the rest of us — not the grace of blossom, but the hard edges of a gem. And in that, I was not wrong.

It was so strange to see a story like *The Beggar's Opera* unfold that night. Do you know it? About the villain Macheath and his adventures with rogues and thieves? All set around Newgate Prison in London. Actors were playing villains, beggars. Polished voices were singing the songs of the street, loud, robust, clear. In the closes, the noise of insults is muffled, but in the chapel acoustic of the Playhouse you could hear every crisp 'Jade', every amplified 'Slut' and 'Hussy'. *Is this what the rich pay for?* I thought. To see respectable people take on the roles of the folk they could look at for nothing in the Cowgate? Is this how they make sense of us, by making stories of us?

Your mother's entrance arrived. You could tell there was a great moment brewing, for the audience seemed to hush at the same time as swell in their fidgeting and whispering. They were no longer chatting or catcalling the singers onstage, but there was a restlessness in their attention.

The actress playing Mrs Peacham was still onstage, finishing her song. She shuffled in and out of the wings a few times. The orchestra struck up the last verse of her song again. And then the crowd began to boo.

They were vicious, all these ladies and men in their fine clothes. The line between diversion and menace began to splinter and I wondered why it was they hated her so, when Meg told me Mrs Peacham was singing the Lucy Lockit aria and the *prima donna* had not appeared. I glanced at Wenzeslaus. His eyes were on the soprano onstage, but he was sawing away at his violin like he would break it. The whole orchestra were out of time with each other now, the bugles hesitant, the kettle drums ploughing on.

Mrs Peacham tried her best with the aria but she struggled with the pitch and kept skipping words. A curl of orange peel flew past my ear as it was flung at the stage, and it was then that one of the stagehands in his apron came on, cleared his throat and announced that Mrs Marie Eliza Herz had missed her cue.

A fight broke out. Tired of waiting for the *prima donna*, some of the pit were already singing in slurring tongues, and a rendition of *Culloden* was competing with *Bonnie Prince*

Charlie from the boxes, though the play had nothing to do with that battle. Three drunk students in their gowns stood up and ripped a wooden bench from its fastenings and held it up as a battering ram. I was shocked. I had seen ceilidhs in my village grow feral in the wee hours, but I never imagined when I saw the rakes lining up in their silk and wigs and powder, that this lawlessness could take place in the theatres. The man at the Newhaven dock had painted them to be genteel; he had laughed at my coarseness, my naivety.

Stagehands now rushed the stage, and Meg, the orange seller, caught my eye and tweaked her thumb at the side aisle that led to the turnpike and back outside into the close.

I was stuffing my last three oranges into the pockets of my skirts to follow her, when I heard a cry from the wings: 'A physician! Is there a physician in the audience?'

The fight was now drifting like fire into the aisles. As more bodies were jostled, more tempers were pricked. I could smell the stink of sweat, wine and soured eau de cologne, that whiff of untethered rage that spreads like a disease. Jeanie grabbed my hand and yanked me. I tripped behind her a few paces.

And then I broke from her grasp.

I don't really know what compelled me to do that, Cecilia. Sometimes you never know when fate is leading your hand, or whether your own conscience is shaping your path. I am not, as well you know, a physician. But what I did know was this: there was a woman missing from the stage, and I had been brought up with hushed knocks on our cottage door in the middle of the night; Mrs Rixon packing her leather bag, saddling her pony and swaddling me in the sheepskin if she thought it was to be a long trek. There were many reasons a woman with the reputation your mother had might fall ill. But I knew the most common one.

I ran back into the theatre and asked two of the stagehands to hoik me up onto the stage. I told them to go to the Maut Ha tavern next door and ask for a bucket of hot water and a glass of cold white wine. They looked uncertain about taking my orders but they disappeared. Then I took my first steps across the threshold into the black maw of the wings.

Wooden pulleys, cloth curtains, panicking sailors stripped to the shirtsleeves. Everyone was trying to snuff out the candles before they caught cloths or were tipped over.

'Show me where the actors' room is,' I asked a man who reeked of leather. He pointed me outside the theatre to the north turnpike. I was halfway up the chilly spiral staircase when your father barged past, winding my kidneys in his haste, with the scroll of his violin.

I followed him up and along the narrow galley. The room he turned into was painted pale green like the theatre, lit by fish-oil lamps that had left black streaks up the walls.

There she was, lying on the rug. Her skirts were soaked with blood. No Medusa hair. No cunning lips. She was doubled over, curled into a ball and hugging her stomach.

It was a stuffy late spring day, and though the dormer had been opened, the tiny room was packed to the ceiling with costumes, hoops, swords, all of which seemed to hoard the heat in them. The wardrobe girls were tripping over their petticoats in panic, and there was a rancid smell of frightened sweat and copper blood. Next to her there rolled a glass carafe with a dribble of water left in it. The singer who had played Polly

Peacham was bent over with a wet cloth, making cooing noises. Your mother was making a sound like a nanny goat. I knew that sound, the most punishing of labour pains, which knocked the woman into strange animal places in her soul.

Wenzeslaus shoved me out of the way. He dropped his violin — the Guarnerius — on the bare floor and knelt next to her. 'Eliza, Eliza, my love, is it the baby?'

Marie Eliza couldn't speak. She made the feral noise again.

I grabbed the arm of the closest girl. 'Go down to the stage and see if the boy has returned with hot water and wine. I sent for it from the Maut Ha. And see if someone can fetch some clean cotton cloths and—' I dropped my voice. 'Perhaps some tansy or rue. I don't know if there's a garden nearby you can take it from, but the Physick Garden east of the loch isn't far. Go on.'

Wenzeslaus had marked me now and was staring up. 'Who is she?'

'I'm an orange seller,' I stammered. 'But my stepmother was a midwife. I thought I could help.'

'What's going to happen?' he demanded.

Marie Eliza was panting now. That sharp scent of blood and terror in the room was coming from her. Now the woman who played Mrs Peacham appeared. As she stepped through the door, she began instructing Wenzeslaus to unbutton his breeches. 'She needs raw leeks, and her husband's water, fast. Quick to it.' She was out of breath from running up the stairs, her voice hoarse from singing.

Your father reached for his crotch.

'Stay,' I told him. 'That doesn't work. I've sent for water and she's fetching wine.' I pointed to the girl.

'Who is she?' Mrs Peacham asked Wenzeslaus.

137

'The orange seller,' the wardrobe girl replied. 'Am I tae go fir the wine?' Her jaw hung open. The room was stifling. Nobody seemed to want to leave. Marie Eliza groaned and rolled onto her back.

'Go and fetch the wine,' I shouted.

'Piss in that carafe,' Mrs Peacham, at the same time, bellowed to Wenzeslaus.

'Don't do that, she'll only sick it up again.' I knew the old wives' method and it had never worked, and frequently made the woman sicker. It was in the middling and finer houses, of merchants and millers, bookbinders and stonemasons, and sometimes Lairds, that you had to do battle with someone who'd had enough education to read a pamphlet on medicine, but not enough to read a current one. Wenzeslaus looked between the actress and me. His eyes were helpless.

He panicked. He made his choice. He picked up the carafe from the floor, unbuttoned himself and pissed out a small golden dribble. Mrs Peacham held the carafe to Marie Eliza's lips.

'Did anyone find a physician?' Wenzeslaus was asking, to no one, to the room.

I didn't know what to do. Seething, blushing with rage and humiliation, I knelt at Marie Eliza's head and whispered, 'Spit it out. There's medicine on its way.'

The piss came pouring right back out of her mouth, along with everything else in her stomach, all over the ankles of Wenzeslaus's silken blue stockings, a huge spray, mixed with her vitriol. He dropped her hand and hopped from leg to leg, mopping himself.

The door was slammed back then, and through the crush of bodies someone bustled in a physician. In his black calf-length coat, with his tricorn hat still on his head, he looked a vision of death. The cluster of people fell silent and shrank back like devils before a cross.

I did not let go of Marie Eliza's hand. I was mesmerised by the force of her pain. I couldn't let go. She clutched me every time a squeeze of the womb twisted her insides. We were bound by that unspoken thing all women are bound by, that curse that unites the village midwife to the fainting lady, that thing knotted in our bellies that torments us all whether it fruits or not.

The doctor removed from his coat pocket a small shining knife. He clicked his fingers and a boy loitering near the door passed him a rag from beside the dressing room mirror. He gave the knife a wipe.

Marie Eliza saw it then, the glint, her fate. She began to scream. 'No, I don't want the knife. Not the knife.'

'What are you going to do?' Wenzeslaus whispered.

'There's wine coming,' I said again, but my voice was a thin worm among the clamour. And the doctor was already bending down, his knife tip poised against the vein in the crook of Marie Eliza's elbow.

'Hold her down,' he cried as she writhed. She screamed, and a large ruby bead formed against the blue vein, then slithered down to her alabaster palm. She shrieked. She rolled herself over and vomited more of her husband's piss over the doctor's shoe buckles.

He didn't seem to care or was too absorbed in the task of bleeding her to notice. He knelt in the stinking puddle and began pumping the blood from her arm with his fist. Each time his fingers gripped, they drew a cry from her, and every few minutes she would lean sideways again and retch, though she had nothing left in her stomach to bring out. It looked excruciating. But what did I know of anatomy to tell him he was wrong? I hadn't been to the university. I hadn't even fucked an anatomy student at that point.

What I did know though, was that bleeding a miscarrying woman was something Mrs Rixon would never have done. She would have soothed the woman with warm water and wine, and with her words and songs, and then she would have reached her practised arm inside, until she touched the neck of the womb, and if she felt the sac there, unbroken, she would have applied astringents, vinegars, toilette waters, witch-hazel, all gently, all lovingly, inside the woman to stem the flow of blood and try to save the baby.

But if she had felt a foot, a head, a tuft of hair, burst from its sac, she would have gravely braced the woman for what was to come, and pulled the dead child free with her bare hands.

All I could do was hold this screaming woman, while she puked the piss Mrs Peacham had given her, and bled from the arm the doctor had slit, and wriggled, and screamed, and I was useless. I was the orange seller.

And all I could think to do was sing. And all I could think to sing were murder ballads.

So, I started to sing her *The Twa Sisters*.

'There were twa sisters lived in a bowr,
Binnorie O Binnorie,
There came a squire to be their wooer,
By the bonnie mill-dams of Binnorie.

He courted the eldest wi' broach and knife,
Binnorie O Binnorie,

140

But he lo'ed the youngest aboon his life,
By the bonnie mill-dams of Binnorie.

The eldest said to the youngest ane,
Binnorie O Binnorie,
"Will you go and see our father's ships come in",
By the bonnie mill-dams of Binnorie.

She's ta'en her by the lily hand,
Binnorie O Binnorie,
And led her down to the river strand,
By the bonnie mill-dams of Binnorie.

The youngest stude upon a stane,
Binnorie O Binnorie,
The eldest cam' and pushed her in,
By the bonnie mill-dams of Binnorie.

O sister, sister, save my life,
Binnorie O Binnorie,
An I swear I'll never be nae man's wife,
By the bonnie mill-dams of Binnorie.'

And on it went.

And then I sang her my favourite, *The Strange Banquet*.

'Cook Laurel would have the Deil his guest,
And bid him home to Dinner.
Where fi end never had such a feast,

Prepared at the charge of a sinner.
He called for a puritan poached,
That used to turn up the whites of his eyes.
With a hey down down, a down down.'

I sang her *The Stepmother's Cruelty.*

'*O then bespoke the scullion boy,*
With a voice both loud and high,
"If that you would your daughter see,
Good sir, cut up the pie."'

And then my mind went blank, and all I could think of, as I watched her lurches grow fiercer, was *The Ballad of Queen Jane*, which I could not sing because it is about a woman who dies while birthing a child. So I sang *The Twa Sisters* again.

'*He's taen three locks o her yellow hair,*
An wi them strung his harp sae fair.

And then bespake the strings all three,
"O yonder is my sister that drowned mee."'

At the end of the ballad, the dead sister appears before the one who murdered her, conjured up by a travelling harp player who has taken some strands of her hair to string his harp. She points her finger at the murderess, her sister, and the sister is taken away.

When I finished the song for the second time, the room was quiet. The tiny, lumpen, teaspoon-sized creature that slid from

Marie Eliza was wrapped and stitched into some scraps of linen they found in the wardrobe, by the girl who had been mopping her brow, and Marie Eliza lay staring at the ceiling, blinkless, a strange, vacant expression on her face.

She rolled her head towards me. Her eyes were ringed blue, her face a grim chalky white, and she said in a very calm voice, 'That is a curious song indeed, the one about the sisters. I should be pleased if you taught it to me.'

6

YOUR FATHER TOOK HER HOME in a chair. The play
was cancelled, tickets were refunded, silver tokens given
out, and the Maut Ha took the brunt of the crowd as
they poured into the night, wanting something in return for
the pleasure they'd had cut short. The following night the girl
who had mopped Marie Eliza's brow took the role of Lucy
Lockit, and the play resumed. I continued traipsing up from
Newhaven to sell my oranges.

It was some ten or fourteen days after Marie Eliza lost her
baby, when a cadie came to the theatre with a note for me.
You will not believe this Cecilia. You will scoff from the
comfortable memories of your upbringing, but I had never in
my life received a note before. Until then I wasn't certain that
any of the men who scurried around the theatre and its
surrounding closes, carrying these precious little missives, even
knew I had a name.

To see my name — Isobel Duguid — written down in ink
that bloomed at the edges of the letters, on that coarse, thick
paper was a strange thing. Of course I could read my own
name, even then I knew my letters passably well, but I could
not before remember seeing the sounds spelled out like that,

like notes on a stave, like a cipher, a stamp of recognition that I existed.

It was sealed with a round red bead of wax, that I suppose looking back was probably rather grubby, though at the time it seemed fine and it made a beautiful sound when it separated from the paper, between a suck and a pop. Standing with my shoulder pressed to the splintering stage, tallow smoke in my nose and my greasy apron covering my brown dress, I wondered what it would feel like to receive letters every day. What should I do with them if I did? Oh, if only I had known. I hoot now to think how I chuck my letters out of the window (that's what I did to yours Cecilia — did I tell you that? If I kept them all I'd have nowhere to sit down in my parlour).

The note read something like this:

Dearest Isobel,
I meant it when I said please come to teach me your ballad about the sisters. I lodge on the Netherbow, not far from the theatre, first turnpike on Fountain Close, second floor. I am indoors most afternoons before the theatre. I am recovered now, and I thank you for the part you and your music played.
Your servant, Marie Eliza Herz.

Your servant.
My music.
The part your music played . . .
Music.

146

Here was Edinburgh, opening her arms.

Where I was from, there was a woman who made the ale in the village, and she sang songs while weeding her garden and brewing her beer. She lived beside the stream, and she was always there, gathering buckets of silty water, singing. In fact, I might have heard *The Twa Sisters* from her. It might not have been Mrs Rixon at all. In the country, music belongs to everyone. It is there at a dance, or it is piping through the town on pageant days. It is in the mouths of the women who launder clothes, the men who drive carts over the lumpen, rutted paths. It is something you do to divert you while you perform your real task. You do not stop to listen to it with reverence, or kick up a stink when the singer you want to hear doesn't appear. Even the man whom I believe may have been my father had to clean the horse shit from the Earl's boots when he was not playing his fyfe and drum.

My music.

Here in Edinburgh, everything has an owner: houses, horses, ideas, words and music. You can put your name next to it, write it down and it becomes yours.

In your mother's letter, I scented again that thing, that thing that didn't have a name yet, but that I had smelled when my face was pressed in the crook of Jas le Corbie's neck.

I had expected more grandeur of the Herzes' flat.

He was, after all, director of the Edinburgh Musical Society, leader of the Playhouse orchestra. I fancied they must have maidservants, that she must take Chinese tea, and have a wig room where the hairdresser set her powder in the evening. I fancied their house was stuffed with Japanned furniture, that the silk curtains sighed, and the sashes of the windows gasped as they were opened. I had seen his finery, seen it embroidered all over his body. And I had heard the music he played, which was refined to my ears. But musical notes cost less than gold or grain here, and the Herzes lived in a second-floor apartment in Fountain Close, overlooking the garden of the Marquess of Tweedale, who lived in a house neither they — nor I — would ever afford.

If Marie Eliza opened the rotting sash (that did not gasp but creaked) and craned her neck, she could just about see into the Marquess's medlar orchards and covet the things he grew.

I knocked that afternoon, on Marie Eliza's door. It was painted a blush pink, streaked with a film of black from the fish-fat sconce in the filthy turnpike.

The door was opened by a girl in a dark velvet gown, braced wide by panniers. A veil rose from the back of her head, gathered in bunches and held in place with an enormous Spanish comb. The dark of the turnpike shadowed her face, and yet she looked so grand, so still and funereal that I thought there must have been some tragedy which had befallen the family, and I made to retreat. But she leaned into the gloom, peering at me. The fabric of her dress crunched, and she said, 'Yes?'

I had to stammer, 'I'm sorry. Mrs Herz sent a note for me.'

The girl stood aside. She twirled her gloved hand, mockingly. Little actress. I crossed the threshold, passing her — unnerved but still clutching the confidence your mother's letter had given me — and I noted her strong smell of old cloth and incense, not unlike the costumes in the actors' green room. From beyond a doorway further down the hall, a quiet, swift tinkling of spinet keys floated on the air.

The girl led me down a narrow hall, where piles of sheet music were stacked carelessly, and half-bits of instruments, pipes, pegs, bows, the bells of horns, skins of drums, lay in piles. Rosin had left its sticky dust on the side tables, and splashes of dropped black ink sprouted on the floor like mould. The girl led me into the parlour, which overlooked the close. She glided like a ghost in her gown. I stood in the parlour doorway.

Marie Eliza was bent over the spinet by the window, the light casting a cloud of suspended dust around her. Her burnt-sugar hair was piled on top of her head, chestnut and silken, held in place with wooden combs, very unlike the white wigs I later saw her wearing on stage. Her neck was a golden brown, and her cheeks were flushed with concentration, eyes piercing critically her fingers as they moved up and down the keyboard. She paused to scratch a charcoal pencil mark into some paper she had spread across the top of the spinet. She did this again and again, oblivious to us standing in the doorway. She would play a while, interrupt her melody, cut it off sharply, scratch a line and start it again. It was odd and disorienting, like living the same moment repeated over and over again, with different endings. And yet when I think of it now it was a rare thing, to hear aloud these inner workings of her mind, her thoughts audible; interrupted and begun afresh.

Suddenly she started.

The music stopped abruptly. She leapt to her feet. 'You came. Isobel.'

I couldn't quite make out her tone. She made no effort to cross and greet me, and I felt embarrassed, that perhaps I should not have come after all, that she had not expected me to, that her letter had not been sincere, or that I should have sent a note in return first.

The room seemed all of a sudden very empty without her music. She laughed awkwardly and I breathed out.

'Are they surviving without me, at the Playhouse? What do you think of the girl playing Lucy Lockit? Is she better than me?'

I kept my voice light, disguising my nerves. 'Is this why you wished me to come? For a spy?'

She looked bashfully down at her dress. I couldn't help but stare at her flat belly. 'I am only joking Isobel. I wished you to come so I could thank you. Your song was the best medicine I could have had that night.'

'Are you well now?'

She didn't answer but gestured for me to take a seat on the divan, which I did. There wasn't another chair in the bare parlour, aside from a child's rocking horse, so she scraped her spinet stool across until it was opposite me and sat down there.

'I am as well as can be,' she said. 'The child was given a parish burial. It is all we could have done. But I have to return to the theatre as soon as I can. It's a luxury to be unwell. As you can see, we don't live grandly.' She glanced around the room.

I didn't know what to say to that. Words jammed in my throat. It was true. She had no harpsichord. She had a scratched spinet they rented along with the rooms. No Japanned furniture, just a divan that was moth-eaten and covered over in blankets to hide the holes. It was one of the darkest rooms I have been in. Only a blade of dusty sunlight cut across the spinet, and even that disappeared when a cloud passed over the close. The Herzes were buttoned tight to their opposite tenement neighbours — an apartment close enough to string a line of washing to.

She had no study in which to compose and later I learned that while Wenzeslaus played the fiddle at all hours, enraging the neighbours, he himself had no tolerance for noise of any kind when he was composing — including the noise of her spinet playing, or their young son — so frequently he went to the coffee houses or elsewhere in the city (he didn't always say where) to compose instead.

They had been married less than a year, but there was a child in the house who was nearing two.

She saw my awkwardness. 'Angelica, fetch us some wine from downstairs will you? You will drink wine?'

It was barely two in the afternoon, but I will drink wine at any hour. I nodded. She gestured to the girl in black, who curtseyed facetiously and disappeared. I heard the front door slam.

The divan smelled spicy and mouldy. A draught was coming up through the floorboards, making the small selection of glassware arranged on the mantlepiece rattle.

Marie Eliza saw me gazing at the window. 'If you peer far enough around the courtyard, you can see orchards, the Marquess of Tweedale's. He has a hothouse and it's said he is trying to grow a pineapple, though it makes him bad tempered because so far he has failed.'

I laughed. 'You can buy one for a shilling in Newhaven, fresh off the ship.'

'Is that where you're from?'

'I stay there.'

'Every day you go back and forth to Newhaven? You should take a room here in the Town.'

Just like that. It was true I was tired of the smuggler. I no longer had any fancy for him and the smell of mackerel in the house was beginning to make me nauseous each night when I returned. But — notwithstanding his mother, who still called me 'The Lassie' — there were things I liked about my lodgings there. I liked being able to step outside and breathe the salt air, and to see the sun break free from behind the sea at dawn. I wasn't yet quite certain of this Town and its gloomy soot, and its rats, and I wasn't sure I'd find a place as large as the smuggler's or with a girl to clean it, like he had.

'Anyway,' Marie Eliza said. 'You know men. They want to know how things work. They want to take things apart and put them back together and see them grown from their roots. They want to be in charge and bring life into the world. Even if it frustrates them.' She sighed.

I didn't know what to say to that. There was a small silence.

'Did you like what I was playing?' she asked. 'I am trying to compose something for the benefit of the Charity Workhouse on Briston Port. You know it?'

I did. Poorhouses, workhouses, almshouses have always caught my attention, and not in a pleasant or even a passing way. For me they are places of caution and terror. You won't understand this Cecilia, but they are impossible not to notice when you have grown up knowing you are always within a hair's breadth of ending up in one.

'There is a benefit concert,' she went on. 'The ladies of the choir are going to sing.'

'The ladies of the poorhouse have a choir?' This surprised me.

She nodded. 'They sing regularly at Greyfriars kirk. A public concert. It's good for staving off temptation to sin, so they say.' Her voice trailed off and she peered towards the door, as if impatient for her wine. I was very aware of a cleft between us that I was incapable of crossing. Had she invited me here from obligation, to sate her conscience? Or was there some other reason?

I fidgeted. 'You write music then, as well as sing, Mrs — Herz?'

'Call me Marie or Eliza.' She smiled and blushed. 'Or Marie Eliza. Just not Mrs, I don't care for it. And we're friends, aren't we Isobel? Izz? How can we not be ... ?' She swallowed and looked vaguely around the floor. 'I do compose, yes. I try. It's not easy. Wenzeslaus goes to the coffee house. He has his places, his hideouts, his salons. I spend my afternoons here.'

I was about to ask her why she spent her afternoons here, when she could just as easily go to the theatre or the coffee houses herself it seemed to me, when the girl in the black gown returned with two cups of gooseberry wine. She planted a small pile of coins on the mantlepiece at the side of the room, slamming them down on the wood, then stood in the corner by the door, watching us.

The wine was tart as a whip, but it warmed my stomach. We sipped in silence.

'How do you compose?' I asked Marie Eliza.

She looked curiously at me for a second and smiled. 'You mean how do I compose in my head? Or how do I manage to compose, being as I am a woman, in a town where women do not compose?'

Once again, I felt the cleft. I felt as if I were being outfoxed, the way I did when Jas le Corbie took the things I said and deliberately misunderstood the meaning of them, or ridiculed them. 'I mean both,' I said, feeling myself blush. 'How do you decide which notes are to go where, and how do you record them?'

She looked as if she was about to laugh again, and I felt queasy with shame and wished I hadn't come, with my callow questions and greenness. I wished I had stayed walking up and down the High Street, or gone to look at the castle pipers with Meg and Jeanie. The blood began to throb in my cheeks.

But then Marie Eliza's stare became earnest. 'I don't actually know. It isn't something I really think much of. Sometimes they appear in a pattern, a rhythm, sometimes in a melody in my head. And then I write them down the way anyone does, on staves, those lines you see on the music sheets.' She hesitated. 'How do you learn the songs that you know?'

The way anyone does.

'I listen to them. I hear the music and then it's just in my head, it's there for me to sing.' It had never occurred to me there was any other way.

'But how many times do you have to listen before the tune is fixed in your head? If it isn't written down?'

'It's never written down,' I said. 'The tune is never fixed. I could sing it differently a hundred times. It's how I feel when I'm singing it. I know the tune, but if I forget a bit, I make that up. Then maybe something will make me want to hold a note longer this time, to go up, down, if I'm feeling the game

154

of it, to put in a wee different touch. But it will always be the same in some ways. It's just that everyone has their own way of singing a ballad. If you were to copy another's you'd be — well there wouldn't be a life to the song.'

Marie Eliza sipped her wine. She stared at me silently. Her eyes washed over my face. The stare was so forceful it was like soft fingers, pulling down my eyelids, raising my lips, examining the things hidden inside my body. What was she thinking in that moment? Was she thinking; ah here is a girl who is interested in me? Or was she thinking; ah here is a girl in whom I am interested? And if so, was she interested in me in the way of a curio she could collect, or in the way of an idea she could learn? I don't know if I ever found out.

'Go on then, I will try your method,' she said. 'Sing it to me, and I'll listen and see how much I remember.'

I was conscious of the girl in black, still standing in the doorway of the room. She had a potent presence. She didn't feel like a maid — she was too haughty — but I didn't really know what else she could be doing there. Anyway, I sang *The Twa Sisters*.

When I finished, the girl in black spoke, and I jumped.

'Was the big sister hanged? At the end of the tale? Was she hanged for the murder of her sister?'

'I— I don't know,' I said. 'I think so.'

'Don't mind Angelica,' Marie Eliza said. 'She is morbid. She is only interested in a story if it ends in death.'

'For that is life,' the girl said solemnly. She watched to see my reaction. I was busy trying to place her accent. It was neither Scottish nor English. 'My mother was placed into a nunnery,' she said suddenly. 'For lunacy.'

I didn't know what to say to that. She had that trait some young people possess, of wanting to shock you, and I didn't want to either show her I was shocked, or embarrass her by not being shocked.

Marie Eliza sensed my discomfort. 'Our guest doesn't want to know about your mother Angelica.' She turned to me. 'Angelica is Wenzeslaus's daughter. From his first wife,' she explained. 'She came from Spain to live with us.'

'Ah,' I said. And then I added, 'My own mother was a witch you know.' And I laughed. It was the first time I had told that lie, and they both laughed, and I liked it. In that strange triangle of women, there was suddenly a weird power; an unholiness, as we voiced our common strangeness, the strangeness of our mothers.

'I suppose the ballad does end rather abruptly,' Marie Eliza muttered.

She looked about to say something else when a shrill wail came from down the hall.

Angelica stared at Marie Eliza.

'Go and get him, will you?' Marie Eliza said.

Angelica waited a moment. Her expression soured. Her lips pursed. Then she stood up straight, crossed her arms and left the room.

Marie Eliza was frowning at her lap. She looked up, shook her head, and shrugged. 'I'm trying but I can't do it. I can't keep it in my head. I have the first line, but if I think of the words, the second phrase of the melody eludes me. The thing is, Izz,' — she realised her joke and giggled; a soprano laugh — 'I can't learn songs that way. I think I have to see them written down. I was brought up on music, you see, but I could read it by the time I

156

could speak, and it's twisted my senses a little. When I sing, I have to be able to see the dots dancing in my head. You see?'

I nodded and sipped my wine. I had no idea what she was talking about.

'Perhaps.' She hesitated. 'If you were to come again, and I were to hear you sing *The Twa Sisters* a few more times, I could try to write it down. Next time. Will you come again? Or better—' she spoke quickly, as the wailing drew closer from the hall — 'perhaps you could sing your ballads to an audience? No, but that is too much of a presumption. What am I thinking? I am putting you on the spot.'

'An audience,' I said. I perked up all of a sudden. My pulse began to drum. I began to imagine myself in her costume, her paint; standing before those beautiful theatre backcloths. I thought of the women of the poorhouse, in the choir of Greyfriars. If they could sing in concerts, why not me? 'At the Playhouse?' I asked. I must have sounded eager. She looked past my shoulder towards the door.

At that moment Angelica came back into the room with a squalling child in her arms, a toddler boy in a white nightgown. He stretched his hands out towards Marie Eliza, and I couldn't help but notice the blood quickly drain from her face, like someone had taken a knife to her throat. But she held her arms out and took him. 'Tommy Tucker, there there, it's all right,' she soothed, cuddling him close to her, rubbing her nose through his hair.

He was a sweet-looking thing. Curls of sugar brown like hers, cheeks of cream and rose; little putto, a cherub. I held out my arms, and he eyed me suspiciously. He balled up his little fists and scowled and rubbed the sleep from his eyes. I nodded to encourage him, and after a little cooing from Marie Eliza he crawled across from her lap onto mine. Promptly he began to piss from beneath the fabric of his white gown onto my skirts.

'Oh God, I'm so sorry,' Marie Eliza gasped, rushing to retrieve him. The warmth soaked through and onto my legs. Angelica ran to the window and Marie Eliza rucked up the little boy's nightgown and together they dangled him out while he finished his fountain. There was an angry cry from below.

She pulled him back in and they closed the window.

'It's all right,' I said, hastily, trying to make them both feel reassured. 'There are only a few specks on my apron.'

Marie Eliza frowned at the fist-sized stain. 'I don't think we have any water here at the moment. Angelica? Grab a rag from the kitchen.'

'It's no matter,' I said. 'You're near enough the fountain. I'll rinse it on my way home.'

Marie Eliza looked pained. Tommy wriggled in her arms and she gave him a sip of her gooseberry wine. He screwed up his face. Angelica laughed.

'I think I might need to procure some food for this little billy goat before Wenzeslaus comes home,' Marie Eliza said. 'He teaches Lady Monboddo singing on a Tuesday. Will you come again, Isobel?'

I didn't want to let her forget her promise. I was still dreaming of singing with the echoing sound of that stage, the wooden cocoon, the ship's belly. 'You believe I could sing at the Playhouse?'

Angelica suddenly snorted.

Marie Eliza's face became stricken. 'No, no, Isobel. I meant . . . I meant in the streets. You should sing your ballads in the streets.

You would make a pretty penny with the strength of your lungs. I've heard others who are not a patch. Oh God, Isobel, I'm so sorry if you thought I meant—' She kept on rambling, about laying down a handkerchief for pennies, about the hours when the lawyers were abroad when I could make the best money — it seemed as if she was trying to scramble over whatever embarrassment she might have caused.

I felt my face burning, and took my leave as graciously as I could, staring down at my torn leather shoes shuffling along her cluttered hall as she led me towards the door. She stood, balancing Tommy on the bundle of skirts at her hips, while I stepped backwards into the turnpike stairwell.

'I'm very sorry again,' I said, 'about what happened to you at the theatre. Your child will be in my prayers. Let it never happen again.'

She looked past me for a second into the darkness, then cast a glance at Tommy. I don't know what drove her to say what she did next, whether it was a moment of impulsive candour, a desperation to paper over the humiliation she had caused by giving me a sudden token of her intimacy. Or whether she needed to confess to someone and I was the safest bet for a spilled secret. Whatever motivated her, she lowered her voice. 'Isobel, I took tansy that morning. They say if you do it before the quickening it isn't a sin.'

I could hear my breath slow down. I tried to keep my face plain. 'I understand,' I said.

'It's not a sin, is it? You said your mother was a midwife.'

'Stepmother,' I murmured.

She looked at me, searching my face for something. I could have withheld my absolution then. Spitefully taken the wound she had given me and parried it with a counterblow. I could have told her it was not for me to judge, that only God could decide in the end, left her with the terror of that suspended, unresolved thought. But instead I shook my head. 'No, it isn't a sin.' What good would it do to punish her, just to quell my own hurt pride? Besides, it was what I believed. I did understand. I understood well.

'Come again, my friend,' she said. 'I like your company. I trust you.' Leaning forwards, with the child in her arms, she reached across and squeezed my hand. Her own hands were pale, soft, the fingers long, the nails elegantly shaped. I thought in that moment that we might be made from different clay. Then I realised what a foolish thought that was. She had simply been preserved better during her time on earth.

I was still cross with myself, over my misunderstanding.

'I will come again,' I said. 'And I will teach you *The Twa Sisters.*'

She closed the door.

Passing Parliament Close at dusk later that day, I asked a chairman where I could stand to sing, and he pointed me to a spot opposite the Tolbooth, next to St Giles.

If the walls of this gaol were glass panes, I could see it from where I sit now. I put down a handkerchief, near to where a clutch of clerks and guildsmen were abroad and bartering.

I sang *The Twa Sisters*, and I sang it loudly. Where did my voice come from that day? Where had it been hiding in me? I did not know, but it came out bold and deep and I felt the vibrations of the song warming and trembling my body as it coursed through it, up through memory, into the lungs, the trumpet of the mouth, the chapel of the skull. And I discovered for the first time that insubstantial but toothsome grip of pleasure that comes in the pause when you finish a song, just before the audience begins to clap.

In the middle of the crowd there he was, grinning, clapping loudest of all, with his long fingers balancing his obscene pipe, Jas le Corbie.

7

PIECE BY PIECE I removed myself from the smuggler's house. I took with me my comb, my nightgown and my horn spoon. I took my linen stays, a scrap of a shawl that had some of Mrs Rixon's embroidery on it, and a pot of rouge I'd bartered from the doxies for a couple of oranges. My soap I left, for it had taken on the stink of the fish-house, and I left my prayer book there too, for I no longer saw use for it.

I lived from then almost exclusively in Jas le Corbie's Cowgate lodgings, and when he was gambling on the cockfights or at cards, I slept in his greasy bed with the quilted blanket made by his mother, that he never washed. In the mornings I listened to him pace back and forth on the floorboards of the small, thick-walled room, smoking his thin pipe, the smoke seeping out from between the woman's legs, along with his thoughts, which he muttered aloud.

Jas spent his days in the university halls, and his money in the coffee houses. On Sundays he would visit his mother and father who lived down the Canongate and they always sent him home with cooked meat and fruit puddings and cakes in a basket, which I'd wolf as soon as they were in my sight. Jas didn't eat much anyway. He smoked and he drank and he thought.

In his tenderer moments he would tell me he liked my name. 'Izz,' he would murmur, scratching the skin below my ear with his chin. 'Your name means you exist. You are. It is.' Perhaps I should have told him to fuck off, that I was not an idea he could dream up, and I was not an 'it'. But back then I didn't have the tongue I have now. And I needed a bed to sleep in. And also I liked him too in these moments, when he was pensive and wanted to share with me his thoughts.

Other times when I asked him to tell me what he was thinking, he would say he was working through some problem of philosophical matter, the like of which I would not be able to grasp. If I pressed him, or chided him, or spat back a response, that his thoughts would never help the labourers who built his house or the midwife who would bring forth his children, he would adopt his smirking look, and before long he would have turned me over and fucked me until we could neither argue nor think anymore.

Then he'd make a note of it in his diary: 'Tuesday, AM. Fucked the questions out of Isobel.'

Every time he bent me over or climbed atop me and rucked up my skirts, he would scratch out a note in this diary afterwards, a hard-bound ledger with swirls of ink on its cover. Sometimes I read these notes; they were always brisk, in his spidery hand.

'Tuesday, PM. Did Isobel, standing up this time, against the back wall.'

'Thursday, AM. Did Isobel twice, once ran at her while she touched her toes, and then again, with her legs splayed open on the writing chair.'

'Sunday, AM. Gave Isobel a thunderous hammering. She is soft as a jam pudding.'

I didn't know what his plans were, if any, for this poetry, or who other than him was ever intended to read it. It was as if he wanted to record his carnal activities because to him nothing was real unless it was written down in a book. But it made me uneasy, being scratched into paper in this way. I didn't like to think of one day others reading about me through his eyes, the way people read about Lady Macbeth and the Wife of Bath. I didn't like the idea of them forming ill, poisonous opinions of my part in Jas's life.

I began to investigate ways in which I could keep my womb from his seed. I frequently stole pennyroyal from the Physick Garden by the old loch, and drank it in a brew, for it was not unpleasant and even had a mintiness to it I enjoyed sometimes. Tansy I tried a few times but it made me sick, and rue I could only stand if I swallowed it down in a stolen tincture of Jas's good whisky. (This he kept under his bed in a plump green glass bottle for when his friends came by, etching the bottle with a pen knife every time he took a nip to make sure I didn't drink it while he was gone. I did drink it though, and I filled it up with dregs of black cork or sometimes leftover gravy from a pie, mixed with water, and he was none the wiser, so he can't have been as much a connoisseur as he took himself for.)

I can see him now, even in the corner of my straw-strewn cell: standing, leaning against the wall of his dark room, rats rustling under the bedframe, among his discarded books, his etched whisky bottle chiming as it rolls around, sweating still from the heat of the gaming table he has been at in the basement. His apartment overlooked Candlemaker Row. It stank day and night, of wax and fish fat. But it was close to the university. From the window, I used to be able to see the spires as they pierced the stillness of the night.

8

GUIDO GUADAGNI came to the Playhouse on a Friday.

Wenzeslaus had the orchestra gathered before the rehearsal. 'Don't call him a castrato, they don't like it.'

'What about capon?' The trumpeter laughed.

'What about goose?' 'What about eunuch?' The clarinet player and the flautist put their instruments to their crotches and waved them around. They looked over at us orange girls, over the lip of the orchestra pit, to see if we would laugh with them.

'Can we call him Molly?' The gamba player twiddled the lace on his wrist cuffs.

'Can we call him Flop?' The timpani player clutched his privates.

'You will call him *Maestro* Guadagni if you value your purses,' Wenzeslaus said. 'He is here at the invitation of the Musical Society, and we are lucky he has time in his schedule to give a concert here.'

'Does he have a gap in his calendar?' the clarinettist asked. 'Does he have a space, somewhere, for us to fill?'

'You'll see,' Wenzeslaus said, quietly. He knew what they did not, then. He knew.

But like most men, there is so much to divert them in the outside world, that while they are busy looking out, they don't bother looking within.

The ladies in the boxes were alert. Their senses were pricked. I felt as if I had seen their movements before — the small noises they made — in birds, foxes and cats.

Their smiles were taut, their fingers strained. Their cheeks were poised, their eyes were still. Their backs were arched, their skirts quietly restless and the scent of their powders carried in the air, jasmine, rose and heat. It was collective, and it was contagious.

I caught it, the erotic wave, rippling from box to box. It hit me like snuff. The auditorium seemed all of a sudden as though it had opened its roof to a heady, pollenous summer, though it was barely May. The hall was vibrating with a noiseless hum, like the murmurings of an early evening garden, which are not caused by buzzing insects, but by the flowers probing their stamens into the air, lifting to raise the scent from the petals.

All this, and he hadn't even entered the room yet.

In the quiet of the theatre, the sound of him carried from the wings. How does a person devise such a sweet way of moving, of breathing, of murmuring? His breath was musical. His clothes were cut so precisely to his body, that they made slicing shimmers when he moved. The fabrics he wore were rich; the lace ruff rippled, apple blossom at his throat. The faun-hoof clip of his walk pierced the air, and when he stood still in a room his fingers absently brushed the downy black froth of his moustache, making tactile sounds.

City gossips were quick to label him 'dazzling', 'dashing', 'tall', 'fair', 'dark', 'slender', 'strapping', 'blindingly beautiful', but it was not his looks that marked him. It was never only the way he looked.

Guido Guadagni was the first castrato I ever heard.

I gaped when I heard his first note. My heart parted. There were whispers of disbelief lining the hall when he opened his mouth and the first pale, piercing ribbon of beauty came pouring out.

He sang *Ah Can I Think of Days Gone By*, by Thomas Welsh, and then *Ombra Mai Fu*, by Handel. He sang some Italian songs, and then he sang *An Thou Were My Ain Thing*, which was a song I'd heard sung in my village, though never like this.

Thuds ricocheted round the hall as ladies fainted in the boxes. Skittles toppling.

'Why is he so dark?' one of the orange girls whispered.

'He is half Moor,' Jeanie replied.

'Is it true, there is nothing in his breeches? Nothing at all?'

'No, that's not true at all. They say it makes the cock bigger. It doesn't stop growing, the way a normal man's does, because there is nothing else to make space for within the codpiece. Look how tall he is.'

'Imagine a man who would fuck you all night but never make you with child.'

And the orange girls, coarse as we were, we sighed for him too (though we did not drop our baskets of oranges like the ladies did their fans, because we could not afford to lose them in a fit of sensual abandon).

When his performance was done, he bowed deeply and his periwig pigtail flipped over his shoulder, and the tip of it, along with its black velvet tie, grazed the stage. He padded into the wings, and as he came down the steps at the side of the stage a great mob surged at him from the pit. We orange girls were caught in the middle. We found ourselves pressed backwards. We stumbled into him as he passed. He smelled of neroli, of an expensive draper's, he smelled of a dusk garden, of pomade and cinnamon and rouge. Meg reached into her basket, thrust out her arm, and presented him with an orange. He looked down and his lips curled into a smile. She let out a small whinny, like a horse, as he touched her fingers, and afterwards she wouldn't shut up about it for hours. He tucked the orange away next to his breast, then escaped through a side door. By the time the crowd breached the exit he was gone. Edinburgh closes serve their purpose. Try hunting a stag through the Old Town. You'd never catch it.

9

I SANG BALLADS EVERY DAY. I came to know all of the ballad singers that traded on Edinburgh's setts and dirt paths: the political ones who crooned for money; the lassie who sang laments of days gone by with a handkerchief at her feet; the man who strode up and down the Netherbow, slurring toasts to the 'bonnie lassies'; the 'Nainsel' from the Highlands (actually he was from Fife, but he wore a kilt) who carried a jester's bauble and made himself the butt of jokes for coins. He was smarter than he gave off. It was he who told me to be wary of men with their notebooks out, that there were some printers' mates who would pull out their fists, reach into the air and steal your very words, then put their names to them and trap them in a book. And to think, Cecilia, I too thought him a fool, like the crowds, and paid him no heed.

By sidling up to chapmen on execution days, I broadened my repertoire of ballads. I learned the *Final Confession of Bessie Row*, the *Dying Words of Hector Crowther*; I could recite the *Lamentations of David Dobie*, tell you all about the *Murder of Betsy Smith*, or *Daisy Dickson's Fear o' the Hangman*, or the particulars of the *Liberton Tragedy*. Although I did also learn that if I didn't want to end up with a thickened ear from a blow, I should take care not to sing my new songs beneath the noose where other singers had staked their pitches. I have a scar on my left breast the size of an egg, from where a woman, who had accused me of stealing her pitch, pinched me hard.

I was in the Maut Ha, drinking a glass of strong black cork, sating my stomach and exercising my teeth with some bony chicken feet before the play began, when she summoned me again. It must have been about six weeks after the first time. (I had not, despite telling her I would, dared to knock on her door of my own accord.)

She sent a note to the tavern. Again, I experienced that intense sensation of my own existence, looking at my name written down, touching, picking open the wax.

> *Dearest Isobel,*
>   *I hear you often, even in my house, when you are at Parliament Close. The wind carries your song, and when you sing The Twa Sisters, I throw open the casements and I listen to capture the notes.* (Did she really? Even at the time I think I doubted this part.) *I have many of them now, but would you do me the courtesy of coming around again, so I can learn the rest?*
>   *Your servant, Marie Eliza*

She had begun another sentence but scribbled it out.

There I was, her mistress again. *Your servant.* There must have been a part of me that couldn't help but doubt the rush of her enthusiasm, but there was also another part that could barely keep my hand steady as I drank the rest of my beer. I didn't know what I was afraid of, or excited by, but I had the feeling once again of being pulled across a threshold, into another world, another half of the city. I swallowed the dregs of my glass and immediately traipsed the two or three closes up the High Street to her turnpike.

As I climbed the stairs I could hear raised voices. They grew louder as I approached her door.

I knocked, and the shouting stopped. Muffled words from inside. The door opened abruptly, and Angelica stood there in her heavy black skirt again, her mantilla high on her head, winking jet sparkles shoved into her hair at random. I had not heard her footsteps approach the door, and wondered if she had been standing there, hovering, waiting to escape. To my shame I had been just about to crane close to eavesdrop. She caught me with my shoulders hunched forward, my neck dipped. I stood up quickly and brushed down my skirts. I showed her the note Marie Eliza had sent. She read it thoroughly, like a guardsman, before opening the door to let me pass.

Marie Eliza came rushing out of the parlour and threw her arms around my neck.

'Izz,' she gushed. 'You came. I have been bereft, knowing I could only hear you but not see you.'

I was stunned by the force of her embrace. She smelled strongly of rosewater and black tea. I wondered what she meant; why she could not see me, since she had a pair of legs and I sang outside in public spaces. Then I saw her bracing her stomach as she pulled back.

'I have not been well,' she said, turning her eyes down. She was pregnant again. Not very far along, but she had the sickness, I could tell by the way she held herself, stiff, grimacing. She gestured for me to follow her into the parlour.

Wenzeslaus was there, standing by the window. He was staring out into the gloomy close. He didn't turn around to greet me. It was the first time I had seen him not wearing his wig, and his hair was a greasy brown, tufting around his head. Now and then he scratched and pulled at it. He didn't look at all well either. The atmosphere in the room was sour.

'Wennie,' Marie Eliza said carefully. She pronounced it the German way, 'Venny'. 'This is Isobel, from the theatre. You remember her.'

Wenzeslaus barely glanced at me. He looked extremely morose. He went back to staring out of the window and said murmuringly, 'I fear something terrible is about to occur.'

Marie Eliza glanced sidelong at me. 'My husband is a little disturbed today. He is struggling to compose. He finds Edinburgh dark and noisome. It is not good for his creative mind.'

I absorbed this. I felt frozen. I didn't really understand what I had walked into, or why they had opened the door to me if they were in the middle of a quarrel. It felt as if she was making an effort to feign normality whereas he didn't care.

He was muttering something to himself.

'What's that my love?' she asked.

He spun around. 'And you forgot to mention,' he said tartly, 'that it is a city run by cabals of guildsmen and masons and puritans looking for a reason to hamper you, looking for a reason to silence your work and shut you down.' He went back to staring out the window.

'We were invited here by the Edinburgh Musical Society, at St Cecilia's,' Marie Eliza explained calmly. 'Only Wenzeslaus is struggling to compose the latest piece they have commissioned from him, for their Friday concert.'

He spun to face us again. 'Do you want to share everything of our lives with the orange seller?' he spat. 'Or is it that you invited her here to sabotage me? You have no idea of the loose tongues in this city. How do you know she won't go away and tell one of her cadie friends and it will be all over the city within the hour, that Wenzeslaus Herz has lost his mind and can no longer compose. Is that what you want?'

'Wennie ...' she said again.

'It is *eating my mind*.' His eyes flamed. 'I cannot *think*. My head is pressed between two stones. It's a kind of torture, a pain. This, this foggy, stinking city, watching over your shoulder. It is suffocating. It is eating me alive. You know I can't compose without air. I just can't do it ...'

'It was the same when we were in London, Wennie, the same in Vienna. In Verona, in Prague you couldn't compose either—' She began raising her own voice.

I panicked then, at being hemmed into their small parlour while they bickered, and it struck me to say something helpful to try to defuse their tempers. There were a multitude of pieces it seemed to me that Wenzeslaus could have played at the Musical Society concert instead of having to compose a fresh one. I said, 'What about that piece the ... the, you know, the *musico* sang, at the theatre? The Scots one. That fine air.'

The atmosphere suddenly turned, like milk in the sun. I thought perhaps I had used the wrong word, that my pronunciation of '*musico*' had insulted him.

But he stared at Marie Eliza, his finger pointed at her. '*He* will ruin us. They brought him here to replace me, you know that, as Musical Director of the Society. They are sneaking around behind my back, plotting and I'm not even gone. He is the talk of the town. What shall I do? Shall I cut my balls off too?' He began to shriek, in a high-pitched fever. 'Shall I cut my balls off and preen and prance and sing like a merry little girl and perhaps then I will have no need to compose music for all I need to do is turn up on stage, strutting like a capon and trilling like a goose and all Edinburgh will fall at my feet.' He capered hysterically for a few seconds. I was terrified. I thought he would dash his head into the wall or throw something. Suddenly he stopped. 'You know he is Lady Douglas's new singing teacher? I bet you do already. That's money we no longer have.'

'Good riddance,' Marie Eliza murmured.

'You don't understand, you have no concept of how we live, of how things come about, of how the things we have are paid for. *These people*, like them or not, pay for our rooms. They keep us in concerts and we must keep them in music. It's a devil's bargain. I won't have it. I can't. I can't.'

'I don't know what you want me to do, Wennie.'

'I cannot just — *this room* was supposed to be for my peace. Here. To compose.' He clutched at his cropped hair again. His fists balled and he turned to look at her. 'But I'm not the one who has been composing here,' he said quietly. 'Am I?' He looked at his feet, which I saw then were stockingless. With his hairy toes out, he looked oddly like a fighting cock. I felt a little sick.

'What are you saying?' Marie Eliza pleaded. 'We need somewhere to sit, Angelica and Tommy and I. This is our parlour. We need somewhere to rest. You have the coffee houses to go to.'

His voice dropped to a hiss. He no longer seemed to realise, or care, that I was there. 'Tomorrow is the first rehearsal. And if I have nothing for them to play, then there will be nothing for people to pay the society to hear and I will lose money. Do you understand? I will lose money. *We* will lose money. We will lose our rooms. We will lose our fine parlour that you use to sit in, with Angelica and Tommy and your orange seller callers.'

'Please, my love.'

Wenzeslaus was not a large man, but he was muscular, and when he was fired up there was a seizing of those muscles; you could see it in his neck, his fists and his naked calves, and you could smell it on him, a smell I recognise, a warning scent like an animal about to bite.

Marie Eliza's voice was quiet, but there was a chill note to it. 'I'm very sorry about this quarrel Isobel,' she said. She took a step closer to him. 'What are you asking me, Wenzeslaus? Are you asking me to give you my motet that I've been working on, for you to offer to the Musical Society as your own?'

He swallowed. When he spoke, he was more subdued. 'You seem to have no problem composing in this room, that is all. And I just can't do it. I sit and stare into space and the keys don't perform for me.'

'Wenzeslaus, it's for the women of the poorhouse.' She forced him to look her in the eye. 'You know that.'

'I will never ask again.'

'You have asked too many times already! It's too much.' She sighed and sat down on the divan.

I stayed standing, fidgeting, petrified to open my mouth.

'What will I say to the women?' she said. 'The women waiting for their motet, for their benefit concert?'

'What will I say to our patrons?' he replied. 'Those men you disdain. Those men who keep you in dresses and cloaks and rooms?'

'Rooms like this?' She threw up her hands.

Now he came away from the window and his heavy tread rattled the floorboards. He knelt down and grabbed her chin. 'There will be no room like this, Marie Eliza. There will be no room. Just an upturned bucket and a hurdy gurdy and a pig that knows the works of Shakespeare and a travelling fair where you can sing ballads.'

She gasped in horror. It went straight through my throat.

I had a nausea then that travelled through me, a very sad and painful feeling that I had seen something true about her, that shattered any illusions I might have been quietly crafting to myself that we were equals as friends.

I made to leave quietly, but Marie Eliza stood up. She flung out her hand and grabbed my wrist.

'Wait, Izz,' she said. 'I want someone to be here. To listen to whatever bargain he makes with me.'

I stood still. She didn't seem to have noticed that her horror of singing ballads in a fair had insulted me.

She said, 'I have a bargain for you, Wenzeslaus. Listen to this. If I give you the motet I have been writing for the poor-house, then you must let me write an opera, a full-length piece which *you* will secure to open the Canongate Playhouse season in October—'

He opened his mouth.

She ploughed on. 'I *know* you are booked to direct next year's season.'

'It's impossible,' he screeched. His hands went back to clawing his head. 'We likely won't even be here, unless they increase our retainer from the Musical Society.'

'We will be here. You know it.'

'In any case, this isn't London. Operas here are hard enough to drum up subscriptions for. They'll get shut down by the fucking kirk even without it being an opera by a—' He turned back to the window. There was silence.

'By a woman? Is that what you mean? An opera by your *wife*,' Marie Eliza said bitterly. 'An opera by Signora Herz will not summon the crowds? An opera by a woman is even more immoral and ungodly and risible than one by a man's hand. Is that what you mean to say? Wenzeslaus? And yet your wife's work is good enough for you to pass off as your own to the Musical Society, when it suits you.'

He crossed to her and knelt at her feet. 'You are a wonderful woman. I cannot fault you as a wife. You bring joy to me.' He looked up at her, earnestly seeking her gaze. She withheld it for a few seconds, then eyed him cautiously. I saw a flicker pass over her face — of something. Memory? Tenderness? He squeezed her hands. 'You are an excellent mother. You must take comfort in that. Not all women can seed babies at the rate you can. Is that not enough for you?'

Her gaze turned cold. 'Oh yes, my womb is splendid fine,' she said.

'You are being sarcastic my love. Why be so cold?'

'Then why aren't you content to sit by the hearth with Tommy and Angelica? Nursing your natural instincts, instead of sitting in the coffee house trying to think about what's possible? Trying to express everything that gurgles and churns inside you, that you see in the world, in sounds? Why should I be content with the output of my womb instead of my mind and my soul?' Her voice had risen and was trembling. 'Anyway, if I were to give up composing, who would drag you out of the mire when the muse fails you? You need me to compose, Wenzeslaus. You need me. For once, let the compositions then be known as *mine.*'

Wenzeslaus stood up and went back to the window. He dragged his finger down the pane, making a tooth-chilling squeak. I could hardly bear the silence that followed, the echo of that grating sound. Eventually he murmured. 'What will you say to the ladies of the poorhouse?' He didn't look at her. 'If you give me this piece?'

She sighed again. 'I don't know. I will give them something I composed last year, a motet I was working on when Sophia Mary died.'

'You were writing motets when Sophia Mary died?' His head snapped round. His red-rimmed eyes were brimming. Oh to see the indignity of that jealousy in his eyes. He cared not for the mention of his dead daughter, Sophia Mary, he only burned with curiosity, with a need to know what work his wife had been creating at the time.

'I needed something to do when I was lying in, waiting to give birth.'

He stepped back, still staring at her. His eyes were narrow with disgust. 'You were composing while our daughter died inside you?' His implication was clear.

'Yes I was, Wenzeslaus. I needed to use the pain while it was eating me fresh.' She put her hand to her head. She looked as if she might be sick.

He stayed scrutinising her for a few moments. 'Very well,' he said. 'Give me the motet. Write your opera. You can have your time as a moth in the flame, and you'll see how it comes back to burn you when it's time for opening night.'

He crossed to the doorway and slid his bare feet into buckled shoes. Then he left, still wigless, still stockingless, slamming the door behind him.

10

Tommy began to bawl from down the hall.

Marie Eliza raised her hand to her brow. 'Angelica. Can you fetch some milk from the grocer? Or better, take him down to see the chickens at the poultry market? He likes them. Please. Could you do that?'

Angelica drew a sharp breath. She folded her arms, grating the taffeta of her dress, and left the room. I heard her softly cooing down the hall, her voice rising and falling. Tommy's cries trailed off. The front door shut and the noises faded down the stairs with their footsteps.

Marie Eliza sat with her head in her hands. Her voice was muffled. 'I do not mean to take my anger with Wenzeslaus out on her. She is only his daughter.'

'Is it true about — her mother?'

'The nunnery? Yes.'

'Is she mad?' I asked.

Marie Eliza snorted softly, sadly. 'She is frenzied. She was an actress. Now she writes poems to the ascension, treatises on ecstasy. She does it incessantly. Says she can't help it. She says it is God's will.'

'And that is the sign of her madness?'

'Something happened to her on the stage, which she does not speak about, that changed her. And now she has a need to purge herself. Is she mad because she writes? Possibly. Am I mad for wanting to compose music? Probably.' She lay back, tossing and patting the cushions around her as she wriggled to get comfortable.

I took her question at face value. 'I don't think you're mad. Probably quite tired, with the baby.'

She laughed and looked at her stomach. 'You are funny Isobel. You cheer me. I did not mean to have you arrive into that. Whatever that was.'

'I'm sorry,' I said. 'I should have gone away.'

'I'm glad you didn't.'

There was a part of me that was still smarting from the gasp she had made when Wenzeslaus threatened her with singing ballads. I didn't have the appetite or the language, though, with which to describe what I was feeling to her, so I left it there, festering in my breast, in the hope it would wither and die.

Besides, Marie Eliza's own expression was horribly melancholy, contorted.

'It doesn't matter,' I said truthfully. 'I've heard worse arguments.' It was true. Couples often bickered in front of Mrs Rixon when the woman was about to begin her lying in. The bigger houses weren't so bad because the man was never there. The middling ones were the worst, as the man tried to interfere.

Marie Eliza smiled ruefully.

'What will you do about the poorhouse benefit?' I asked.

'I will make something up.' She propped herself up with her forearms. 'Perhaps I will arrange *The Twa Sisters*. Though it's hardly appropriate, is it? Women of sin singing about murderesses and betrayal. Ah well, perhaps I'll finish the other motet, like I said.' She leaned back again, closing her eyes. I could hear the low grumbling of her stomach beneath her stays. I thought about what she had told me about the tansy, and wondered if she would take it again.

'Shall I sing it to you again. *The Twa Sisters*?' I asked.

Marie Eliza stared at the ceiling for a second or two. 'Actually, I should like a walk,' she said.

'A what?' I thought I had misheard.

'A walk.'

'That's what I thought you said. But why? To get where?'

'Have you ever seen Duddingston?'

'I have not,' I said.

'Shall we go there?'

I was a little confused as to why we were going to spend our energy walking all the way to Duddingston and for what purpose, but Marie Eliza seemed set.

She reached out her hand and I pulled her up off the sofa, and she picked up her husband's justacorps that was lying tossed aside on the spinet stool and threw it around her shoulders, and off we set.

11

I DO UNDERSTAND CECILIA, that times are what they are, and people do take walks for pleasure. I have even tried the same myself from time to time since the day I went with your mother to Duddingston. But you have to understand that when you are accustomed to your feet being a wagon for getting you from place to place, for heaving you from the cottages of Newhaven to the throng of the High Street, or to carry you on your escape from your village lest you be smothered and stung by its briars, then the idea that you would walk for pleasure is indeed a strange one. Of course there were many indications that your mother and I were from different worlds, but this notion of sprightly idle time which one could spend meandering through parks while employing the goodwill of one's stepdaughter to mind one's child was, to me, one of the starkest.

Nor had I ever yet ventured yet into that place called the King's Park, that sits to the southeast of the city, a mountainous green fist on the skyline. I'd heard tell by my fellow ballad singers and loiterers of Parliament Close that the King's Park was a grim place, where bandits could take you by surprise and empty your purse and slash your throat. But once we had escaped the Cowgate and crossed over into the scrubby heather that bounded the park, to my surprise, it was not like that at all.

The air was clean. Small flies, wasps, bees and sparrows flitted and buzzed around us. We saw no bandits, but drovers, day trippers, girls collecting wild thyme, and shepherds with their black and white dogs at their heels. That was the difference, I was to discover, between nights spent exchanging frightening stories around burning tar barrels in the Cowgate, while Jas le Corbie bet his pennies on jacks and clubs and fistfights, and days spent wandering the city, when one had the leisure to not be hard at work and could see its beauties for oneself.

It was so idyllic in fact, with the sheep grazing on the hillside, that I felt a sudden pang of homesickness for my village. But what would I be doing there? Churning butter? Bearing children?

Marie Eliza talked about her childhood. She had been born in Edinburgh. Her mother was a miller's daughter and her father an Italian violinist, brought over, like her husband had been, by the Edinburgh Musical Society. Into a land of candlelit concerts and late night, cobbled together feasts and wine-in-lieu-of-payment she had been born. Into Handel and oratoria, and arias, afternoon salons, discussions of the merits of opera seria, motets and madrigals, *ridottos* and other words she took patience to explain to me.

Her love of music was refined, cultivated as a rose bush, always tempered, never spinning out of control, even when it was fiery. She had learned to read music before she could read words, and she could play the violin, though she would never have shown it publicly, for she had also learned the rules of being a woman in a refined city. But she sang from an early age. Always in drawing rooms, always by candlelight. She was trundled out in her satin dress and sash, after supper, after the croquetas and the panforte and the muscatel had been passed around, at the behest of her parents' friends and patrons, to hushed audiences waiting to delight at hearing the little cherub girl sing in Latin and Italian, of broken love, of the Glory of God.

She loved the music of Pergolesi and Corelli and Gluck and other men I hadn't heard of. She loved Monteverdi and Barbara Strozzi and she became animated when she spoke of Strozzi who had lived in Venice a hundred years ago, in an apartment that overlooked the same canal Marie Eliza and Wenzeslaus's apartments had overlooked when they were married. Strozzi, Marie Eliza said, had composed many arias, beautiful songs, but never an opera because she was not permitted to. Venice was a city that tolerated vices but not freedoms. This was a fact Marie Eliza would return to again and again, worrying at it like it was a scar. It gave her great pause but also great pride, I could see even then, to imagine she might be able to cap the achievements of her heroine, in this her new home; a city of possibilities.

We passed through the gates of the King's Park, and the grasses grew longer and wilder. It was an overcast day — a classic Edinburgh day, muted blue sky with grim flashes of pewter — and the dew was freezing on my ankles. But she didn't seem to mind or notice.

By the time we reached the loch my feet were in shreds, as numb as if they had been crushed by the witch pricker's boots. I was puffed out, wheezing coal smoke and dirt from my lungs. She on the other hand seemed brightened by the walk.

We stopped. The loch was glassy and silver, mirroring the clouds.

'Go on then,' she said. 'Sing.'

'Here?' I thought she must be joking. I laughed.

'Why not? There is air for your lungs, a sky to catch the notes. What more do you need? You have an audience.' She grinned, pointing at the swans who were slicing the glass of the water as they circled the loch.

Exposed to the stiff grass, the sheep, the hares, the crows, and the rust-coloured crags looming in the distance before us, I felt horribly conscious of myself, of what this open space had the power to do to my voice. It would swallow it. Or worse, it would scatter it. There was nothing to contain it. The words would go tumbling into the limitless air, and where would they travel, and where would they end up? I had a terror of the exposure. But she was waiting so expectantly.

'Go on,' she said again, quieter.

I began quietly murmuring the melody of an air.

'Louder. There's no one around. Come on Isobel, sing!'

I stopped and took a chill breath. I sang the first verse of *The Twa Sisters*. I stamped briskly, awkwardly. The turf dampened my beat. It felt strange, almost illicit, as if I was an interloper and was doing something I had no business doing.

'Louder,' she cried. 'This is your world, this is your city!'

It was. It was my city. It was mine as much as it was hers. I knew it just for that second, and I sang with my grit and my soot and my rasp and my croak. I sang the Old Town out of my chest, pushing out the grime, labouring it free, ugly as it was, harsh as it was, beautiful in its ugliness and harshness and rawness, and I roared for the dead sister at the moment she accuses her murderer. My voice poured out into the wild sky, accusing the hills, the cawing corbies, the swans on the loch. I sang the song like it was mine.

The ballad hovered in the air for a long time after I had finished. It made a shivering cloak around the pair of us, with the wind carrying its memory like the echo of the sister; dead as a viol, still raging to be avenged.

I wondered then, as I wonder now, how much truth there is in that ballad. Not in one sister murdering another, for murder has been part of life for as long as we humans could walk or fall in love or lift an axe; but in the act itself being impossible to conceal. That it must, someday, force itself back into the world through somebody's voice. For secrets cannot stay drowned, the way bodies cannot. They are light as air and they will always bloat and wash up.

I could feel Marie Eliza's excitement beside me. I could feel her swallowing the song, taken by its force. She was panting, as if she had been running, as if it were she who were singing. Your mother loved music, Cecilia. She felt it in her blood and on her tongue like no one else I've known.

My eyes remained fixed on the loch. Two swan cobs were circling, wings lifted as if they would fight. I peered forward into the pewter mirror until I could see my face. Marie Eliza took a step towards me, and in the reflection of the loch she appeared over my shoulder, enormous in the rippling waves. Just in that second my heart froze. My senses left my body and I felt a powerful grip of terror, as if she might be about to push me in, like the elder sister in the song. It was so strange and potent that I remember it as if it were yesterday, because I was so very afraid of the way her face looked in that loch.

But then our reflections disintegrated, as one of the cobs raised his wings, lengthened his neck and launched his bite at the other. My senses returned, my rational thoughts.

Marie Eliza startled me by saying, 'Your voice is bold, raw. You sing this tale as if you were every woman in it. It is something I could never hope to capture.'

12

SHE TAUGHT ME HOW to hollow my chest, to send a note soaring; how to change the tone of sound so that I did not have to shout until I was sore. She taught me how to slow a note, when to pause, the value of the rest. *Minim rest, quaver rest, semibrieve rest.* She used the Italian, words that felt more of their meaning than their English counterparts. *Fortissimo*; loud. *Piano*; soft. *Melisma*; melody the note while holding the same word. Words she had learned from her father; words that sat in her mouth as easily as sun, water, heart.

She talked about the beauty of *The Twa Sisters'* music, about how the intervals between the notes created the melancholy. About how lingering on the middle of the phrase — '*to be their wooer*' — or changing the pitch slightly could add menace or sadness. She dissected it, took apart its organs and presented it to me, open and pulsing.

I said I did not ever think of such things, but only of the soul of a song which you could not see or describe but which was passed heart to heart. That was how a song stayed with me.

'Then you must have a very dark heart,' she said. 'If you were taught this song and it stayed.'

'Perhaps I do,' I said.

With her that day I felt the further prising of that opening of the world that was talked of by Jas, but which I had not yet been able to grasp. I was growing, I was learning. The fingers of my mind stretched towards the sun, and she gave me a glimpse of a possibility to become something other than I was, or that I had expected to be.

We hiked up the high path from the loch, ending up on a road with only a few sheep drovers. The wind was so strong it felt like sea currents, and there she told me about the opera she would write.

It came spilling out of her, in feverish clashes of words with the wind. She shouted it over the air's roar, and it seemed as if she was divesting herself of a lump of something hard and tough that had been building in her body for a long time.

'It will be called *The Swan Murder*,' she yelled. 'Your ballad has given me the key. Isobel, I don't know what I would have done if I hadn't met you.' She shrieked to clutch my hand as a savage gust whipped her.

I could have stopped her then.

I could have stayed her in that freezing whirlpool and told her that it was true the ballad was not mine, but nor was it hers and she mustn't take it for herself. But I knew the truth, which is that ballads are everyone's to take. If they belong to no one, they belong to everyone. And I did not know on whose behalf I should be affronted by her caging it in music written down, but the ballad's itself, which seemed to me very silly.

How do you make a barter for ideas and words? How do you decide their fair worth? She had stood and sung with me, at the loch. She had taught me how to howl to the birling clouds, how to compete with solan geese, and I was afraid of her taking these things away from me if I challenged her about taking the story from the ballad.

'I will begin writing straight away. You heard Wenzeslaus, didn't you? He cut a bargain. He cannot go back, now you have heard him.'

I wasn't sure how much currency my word carried, but I had heard him. I told her so.

Further down we passed a cairn of stones, littered with forget-me-nots, dog violets and dead daffodils, crisping. It had a haunted beauty, and I asked what it might be, thinking it was probably a shrine to Mary Queen of Scots or some forgotten figure.

She said, 'Ah this. It is for a woman who was murdered, a few years ago now, but not many. People still remember her I suppose and bring flowers. They add stones to the cairn. She was lured here by her husband and he beat her to death. You see Izz? In Edinburgh, you are never more than ten feet away from the site of a murder.' She smiled, and leaning gently against the pile of stones, took a brief rest from walking.

The thing that still gnaws at me in the night is that she knew this, and yet what came to pass still came to pass. Or was it because of this that it came to pass — does murder not, in fact, act as a repellent to us all, but instead simply breed more murder?

13

W E DREW WATER from the cistern near the old abbey and drank it and let it refresh our raw throats. And then we relieved ourselves behind the palace walls. Marie Eliza let out a peal of laughter as she hitched up her underskirts. Hers were clean and made of cotton, while my linen one was washed to greying, the threads scrubbed fragile and thin. Her skirts fell back to earth with the heaviness of theatre curtains, while mine wisped like laundry in the breeze.

We began to walk back up the Canongate, but as we drew near to Playhouse Close, we were pulled into the surge of a travelling crowd.

The closes were spilling out onto the High Street. Apprentices in leather aprons came striding out of barber shops and ironmongers, and even the rushed patten footsteps of the gentry were echoing down from the turnpikes of tenement lands into the swell. Sash windows were being yanked open. The air was thick with slurring songs and chants.

Marie Eliza clutched my hand.

I hadn't known it was a hanging day. I glanced at Marie Eliza. She looked suddenly petrified. The Royal Mile was rammed with bodies, and the crowd lurched and hissed, banged walls and tin cans with sticks and kitchen spoons. It was full of something; a brew of noise, rage, sanctimony, terror.

We were pushed about, side to side. I tripped into Marie Eliza.

'I hate this,' she hissed into my ear. We couldn't get anywhere near the entrance to Fountain Close. The tide of the crowd was against us.

'She is with child!' I cried, but I was armpit height to a cluster of sweating, aproned men and my voice was drowned.

I was telling Marie Eliza we should try to plead with one of the Town Guard to escort us home through the crowd, when I heard her shriek. 'There! Look. She has Tommy!' She began to pull me into the middle of the throng.

A man in a tartan cloak knocked his beer cup into my ear, trickling froth down my neck. Some stinking guildsman with a crimson nose spat tobacco on the ground in front of us. As we were swept towards the Tolbooth I realised we were being sucked close to the centre of the fever; the prisoner was about to be brought forth.

Marie Eliza had me by the wrist, pressing forward through the crowd with her child in her sight, head dipped into the humid bodies. Up on the Lawnmarket people were leaning out of windows. The Luckenbooth doors spilled onlookers.

Then I saw them too; Angelica and Tommy, a flash of black lace gloves and rose cheeks.

Angelica had Tommy in her arms, lifted high over the crowd. She was bobbing him up and down. Each time his little face rose above the sea of heads, he laughed gaily. The black lace made strange flowers of Angelica's hands, clutching Tommy's chubby body.

Marie Eliza was near frantic by the time we reached the West Bow. 'Tommy!' she was screaming. And he had seen her too now, and now when Angelica tossed him up he caught the gust of his mother's voice and was confused and began to howl.

The crowd flowed down the West Bow and at last began to jam into the mouth of the Grassmarket. As soon as we had stopped, Marie Eliza pushed aside butchers in bloodied over-alls. I saw her kick a dog that skidded under her feet. I followed the path she cut.

She knocked into a chapman, selling ballads of the condemned man's last words. His sheets cascaded out of his hands and down onto the filthy cobbles.

'Hoor! Bitch!' he cried after her. I bent to help him gather his sheets back up. They were sticky with straw and mud, and I pocketed one for my troubles. He didn't notice and thanked me for my help.

She was ahead of me now, but she cut a brisk path and I could follow her wake.

Then a hushing — a wave of gloom — broke over the crowd. I could not see what they were looking at, but I heard in the silence that fell, the distinct tread of the condemned man's feet creaking up the scaffold steps.

I wondered what he had done. There were soldiers present and for them to have been there it must have been heinous. The assassination of a Judge, or a Laird, or a Redcoat? Was he the instigator of some seditious conspiracy, who would look contemptuously on the crowd he had drawn to watch him die? Would a glimpse of his evil face stop me in my tracks? Would his crime have scarred his expression forever? Would he look like a dragon? Would it freeze my blood to watch such a monster hang?

I thought of my mother and was suddenly sad. Had they turned out for her in such numbers?

Marie Eliza seized Tommy into her arms and wept. 'Why did you bring him here?' I heard her cry to Angelica. Tommy was bawling. Several children were. (Although some were not crying, but laughing and throwing pigs' bladders.)

Angelica only shrugged. 'I have longed to see a hanging, but Papa won't let me go.'

'With good reason,' her stepmother screamed.

I still had in my hand the printed sheet I had stolen, and I looked down at it now and saw a crude woodcut of a young man in farm clothes, brandishing an axe above his head. It was striped in gouges and the printing ink had bled. I looked back up at the scaffold. The condemned man was visible now, staring ahead. There was nothing proud about him, nothing monstrous. He looked feeble minded, simple, scruffy, impulsive. He looked as if he couldn't fathom what was going on. He looked as if he wanted to thump the hangman, whatever the consequences. He looked as if he had been told — by a chaplain or by a kind turnkey — to stare straight ahead, don't look at anyone or anything, focus only on the horizon, hold your head up high, die like a man. They placed a sackcloth hood over his head and bound his hands with rope.

I read the first few lines of the broadside verse. Even back then I knew that seldom were these final confessions sold at the foot of the gallows true. But sometimes they had a grain of truth, taken down in haste at the Tolbooth door.

I, Peter Macauly, do solemnly repent,
That I took my sweetheart, from heaven sent,
When I found the lass was big with child,
And that her virtue I had defiled,

I bad her meet me in a wooded glade
And struck the life from her with my blade.

Peter Macauly dropped.

The cheers of the crowd drowned out his choking. I glanced at Angelica.

She was gazing at the dying man — her eyes wondrous, her face cast as if the Lord's light was shining. A shiver ran through me.

Marie Eliza grabbed Tommy's head and buried his face in her bosom, so he couldn't see. She turned aside. She clung to Tommy for life. She wrapped her arms around the back of his head, kept him pressed to her as if she would press him back inside her body. She waited, biding her time until they could escape.

I felt sad for Peter Macauly. When he was a boy, did he know how his life would turn out? He jerked and he twisted and his shoulders twitched one after the other towards the rope constricting his neck. I don't even think he was conscious during this dance. His body was just clutching at some kind of survival. When he was a young lad running through the fields or the closes, did he ever think that this was how it would end, in front of the Edinburgh Grassmarket crowd, keening and growling and baring their teeth for his strangling? Did he know that he would be cut down by the anatomy students, his body whisked away and chopped up, opened in a public dissection room, his blood all drained into a basin? Was that what he had imagined for himself?

When I glanced back towards Marie Eliza, I saw she had left my side and was picking her way back up the West Bow, through the crowd.

Angelica trailed behind them, a vulture on the tail of spoils.

I was alone in the crowd and I felt restless. I didn't know what to do.

A few moments after the spectacle ended and Peter Macauly's dance ceased, the crowd began to disperse, until after a while there was space to move and the stink of bodies wasn't so close. People headed back to work.

The taverns had thrown open their doors and some folks were now heading off to drink. The chapman whose ballads had spilled took his post at the bottom of the scaffold, with the melancholy body of Peter Macauly dangling high above his shoulder. The hanged man's feet were within touching distance, as the chapman began selling his broadsides, spreading the criminal's tale before his blood was cold.

I stood for a while, listening to the sound of the market traders as they set back up, listening to them soothe their animals and unfold their tables. The sheep were calm but the pigs knew something was up and were squealing.

I did not like the sight of Peter Macauly hanging there. I wanted to turn away too, like Marie Eliza. I wanted to go back up to the Netherbow.

But I was not Marie Eliza.

I spied an empty patch of ground near the mouth of the Cowgate, and so as not to compete with the chapman, I put down my handkerchief there, and I began to sing.

I used the words of the printed sheet in front of me but the tune of *The Strange Banquet*. After three or four rounds looking at my sheet, I had learned most of the words to *Peter Macauly's Final Confession*.

I didn't even notice when the sun began to set and they cut him down. One second, I turned my head and he was there, a black silhouette against the row of fire torches lining the battlements of the castle. The next, there was an empty space, a small tuft of rope, the only marker left of his terrible crime.

Some drunk men stopped to clap me along, and Gingerbread Jock danced a jig, and the market wives were feeling generous so I made bawbees enough to sum three shillings in a single hour. I took a break to swig down a bit of tuppenny that a barkeeper brought me in a tin cup, and struck up again, as the market men went home and the gamblers came out.

That was when I saw a figure I knew, leaning against the wall of the Lucky Middlemass tavern, listening to me. He was lithe and spry, and I recognised him straight away, for he stood out from the crowd. But it was not Jas le Corbie this time. It was Guido Guadagni.

14

I TRIED NOT TO FEEL SHAME for what my performance was to him, this singer whose celestial voice I had heard at the Playhouse, who even now had wax dolls fashioned in his likeness and sold for sixpence at the Luckenbooths.

I told myself to think of the number of people who had stopped to listen to me. They were entertained. They had clapped and danced. I counted the number of pasties and chicken legs I could buy with the farthings and bawbees folks had dropped into my hankie, the number of nights I could stay in lodgings that weren't Jas le Corbie's room. I tried to think on whose day I had brightened with my grim tune.

But after I finished my song, I did not sing again. The few stragglers who were clustered, hooting me on, dispersed. I had made four shillings and a few stray farthings. I bent down, gathered up my handkerchief, tucked the corners together, and – willing the damp of the evening to cool my blushes – put the money into the bosom of my dress.

I told myself: *I have heard him sing, now he has heard me sing. We are even.*

I started to walk away, but he beckoned me over. 'You. The orange seller.' He had a cool, pure whisper; a voice that seemed to land in my own throat, making my neck tingle. He was tall, neither slender nor broad, but he was imposing. There was a stillness to him. He did not swagger. He stood like a statue while the city moved around him, like a sailor with good sea legs on a listing, rocking ship. There was something very quiet, very focused about his presence.

'I did sell oranges once,' I muttered. 'But I don't anymore.'

'You know her, don't you? The woman who composes. She is married to the angry violinist. I have seen you.' He stared at me. A gaze that gripped even as it was soft. What a strange, feminine, virile, strapping man he was: a brawny, elegant woman with a soldier's bearing. He was wearing rich fabrics, a rose-pink velvet waistcoat with mustard embroidery, a sage green silk coat. His hair was pomaded white and pulled into a loose pigtail. He wore no paint and his skin was soft and brown. 'You are her *ragazza*, her girl.'

I bristled. I did not like that phrase — *her girl*. I did not like him thinking that. 'I am not her girl,' I murmured.

'Where does she live? Can you carry a message?' Now it was he who blushed, and he looked at his fingers, twiddling a folded letter.

I knew then what he wanted from her.

Why did I hesitate? It was not morality. I did not care about the slight or betrayal of Wenzeslaus. Nor was it jealousy. I was not stupid enough to think I could have Guido Guadagni for myself, even if I wanted him. I was not so foolish. But I did not want her to have him either. She had too many things already.

I nodded silently, anyway. He handed me the letter, a sixpence alongside it, pressed against his thumb discreetly.

And so it began.

15

AFTER I DELIVERED her that first letter from Guadagni, I began going back and forth daily between her lodgings and the Maut Ha, where he had his post delivered.

She had been confused by his first letter. She had taken the sealed paper from me with a smirk, a faint amusement, a fondness almost, reading it in front of me with nothing to hint to its contents.

She bid me wait on her dusty divan while she wrote her response at the spinet, and when she handed it to me (no sixpence though), she had a coquettish swagger in her hips and I saw a little glimpse of the woman she might have been before she met Wenzeslaus and embarked on her merciless Catherine wheel of pregnancies.

His letter, it turned out, had been no caddish summons to a tête-à-tête, but an invitation to her to perform alongside him at St Cecilia's Hall, with the Edinburgh Musical Society. Of course I was curious — I still thought from time to time of the Italian fiddler from the ship at Leith — and of course I had no expectations that in my blue linen gown, with barely two shillings to my name, I would be granted access even into the Laigh Hall. But I stood outside below the stonework of the oval room that night, and I listened. I stood in the Cowgate, with my back to the cold wall, and I heard their voices wrapping around each other like ivy, dipping and slicing, horseflies dancing in the sky. Their voices came tumbling down one side of the wall, serene and cool, while across the road the shrieks and caws from the cockfighting basement made a strange, clashing duet with them.

He was bound to her through music then at first, Guadagni. But I know too it cannot have escaped her notice that many of the women in Old Town Edinburgh coveted him.

And then gradually, note by note, note by note, I watched as he began to fill the cup of her consciousness, so that after a while when I came to deliver these notes to her she barely acknowledged me at all; only as a conduit — 'there you go Izz, thank you'. She would hand over her latest missive before retreating to hide, and wait for me to come back with its echo.

She grew serious, quiet, then silent. Mute. No room left in her thoughts, no place in her soul for friendship; it was only him. He spread like wings in her mind, supplanting everything. If I did see her, she would look into my eyes but her gaze would be placed far back in her head. She lived for these letters, and Guido Guadagni took root, a tree planted in her soul.

One day I went to Fountain Close, and she didn't even come to the door, or call to receive me. Angelica insisted she was indisposed.

Then the next time she was 'composing'. The next, Wenzeslaus was at the spinet and the house must not be disturbed. When Angelica said that word, 'disturbed', she stared up and down my new green gown, that I had from a cheap draper in the brightest fabric I could afford, a linen dyed with nettles. I couldn't see what was disturbing about it. But then I also couldn't see the appeal of dressing like a widow when one was barely past her menses, and would have told her as much, had I not been so 'disturbed' myself by the sight of her.

It came as a surprise to me then, when I was one day singing in the Cowgate, halfway through *The Stepmother's Cruelty,* and I saw two eyes behind a black velvet mask, peeping at me from round the corner of Robertson's Close.

It was a round mask, a *moretta,* the kind you have to bite to keep in place, which keeps — they say — the tongue out of mischief.

The eyes sparkled in the black moon face.

A velvet hand began to stretch its fingers around the corner of the harled stones. The fingers parodied a gesture of seduction, they twiddled in the air, then the index finger lifted and beckoned. I laughed. The hand flew to the face, patted the velvet cheeks. The face looked here, then there, then fell into a pantomime of modesty and lasciviousness, raising a hand to its brow, covering its lips, licking its fingers. I stopped singing and laughed.

She didn't see — though I did — the man approach from behind while she was busy miming a faint. He grabbed her by the hips. She shrieked. I ran forward. The mask fell from her mouth, and I saw it was Marie Eliza.

Together we wrestled the man away. He was just a drunk in a butcher's apron, with punch on his breath. I bit his arm. It tasted of rot. Marie Eliza slapped his face and he staggered back up the close. I could feel her heart hammering through her dress. She was coughing.

'I didn't mean it to turn out that way,' she said. 'I have an invitation for you.'

I bent down to pick her mask out of the straw. I was breathless from the fight, and she was still panting from shock.

She dusted the muck from her mask with her gloved hand. 'I wanted to invite you to the pleasure garden masquerade. I don't know how it will be. I have never been to an Edinburgh pleasure garden. Cold, I suppose, compared to Vauxhall. But there will be costumes, masks, fireworks, punch, roast hog, sweetmeats. You'll come, won't you?'

I gathered up my handkerchief with the pennies. I was surprised but at the same time not surprised at her gesture. She could be silly and theatrical and generous when she wanted to be, and there is a seductiveness to that kind of person that is impossible to resist. And she meant it too. She meant the invitation; she meant the thank you. It had been her whim to put on her wig and mask and gloves and come to find me to make me laugh and win me back.

She watched me tuck the money down my sark. I tried to be discreet and quick. She waited patiently, then took my arm. 'Thank you, Izz, for carrying the messages, from ... I couldn't bear to have a cadie, you know, the gossip in this city ... You are very discreet, and you are kind.'

'Your baby's growing.' I nodded at her belly. She was still wearing stays but she had loosened the laces. I could see the beginnings of a bulge.

She followed my gaze to her stomacher. 'Yes, big and healthy. But — thank you Izz. That is what I came to say.' She didn't want to talk about the baby. Only Guadagni.

'Think nothing of it,' I said.

'Let me repay you with a ticket to the Pleasure Gardens. Please. And a habit too. We can borrow them from the Playhouse wardrobes.' Her eyes were alight, waiting.

She saw my hesitation. I couldn't help but feel, after my misunderstanding about singing at the Playhouse that first time, that there was some trick in this, and that if I opened my mouth I should say the wrong thing and feel regretful and sore.

'Come on,' she said. 'Come with me. I will sing my newest arrangement, which I want to be a surprise for you, and Wenzeslaus will play his fiddle, and perhaps if I drink enough punch you shall even see me play the violin! Guadagni will be there, as I am sure you know, from his latest *communiqué.*' She studied my face, smiling.

I said nothing. I felt insulted that she thought I would read their letters, but I couldn't find the words to contradict her.

'Would you not like to hear me sing? Are you not curious about my latest arrangement? Come on Izz, if you do not come, I shall die.'

She couldn't help herself, could she? *If you do not come, I shall die.* Did she believe that? Even as a metaphor? Sometimes I think it must have been exhausting to live in her head, to live with the amount of fervour she had for everything. Rushing through there like an unstoppable torrent of feeling, of uncontained passion. But sometimes, I also think, perhaps she was just insincere.

211

'I'd be very grateful to accept a ticket, and a habit. Thank you.'

I took her arm and we walked up Robertson's Close until we reached South Bridge.

I had not known Guadagni would be going, of course, because I did not take the liberty of reading their *communiqués*.

Yet.

16

THE EVENING OF the Comely Gardens masquerade was a soupy July dusk, the lanterns moist and heavy with mist, the air scented with a sensual pollen. There had been a light rain just before we arrived and everything was wet, the heads of roses and irises and foxgloves bowing with pearls of water, the grass slippery and squeaking underfoot. A waiter stood under the doocot arch offering a tray of sherbet ices, which had melted as the rain dropped into them. The midges swarmed in dense clouds and this made the patrons dance in very singular spirals, waving their fans around their sticky glasses of hock.

As I walked through the crowds I saw women with swans on their heads, ships setting sail in their wigs. There were delicate fabrics, and unicorn horns and velvet masks that concealed the eyes but not the lips.

For my costume I had chosen from the actors' room above the Canongate Playhouse the gown of a duchess. I wore a wide-hipped mantua in ivory silk, embroidered with weaving ivy on the skirts, and a cage of panniers beneath it, as heavy as cannonballs. I wore a white lace mask across my eyes, and I felt marvellous. I couldn't stop swaying my hips, for the weight of the dress was like nothing I'd felt before, and the sensation and the sound of it stroking the damp grass was so very pleasing.

Marie Eliza had come as an orange seller. She looked like a painter's portrait of an orange seller: beautiful, but with too many petticoats, too pale and smooth a bosom, and her bonnet was too dainty. She had painted her face artfully, with a gentle sheen of lead white and pearl powder, dampened her eyelashes and brows with charred cloves to slick and darken them. She had rubbed a little soot into her cheeks for the effect of grime, along with her rouge. She looked nothing like me or like the other girls at the theatre, but I don't think that bothered her.

I was strolling with her through the chilly shrubs. 'What did happen to the women of the poorhouse?' I asked. 'Were you able to write them a new motet, for their concert at Greyfriars?'

She sighed peacefully. 'I did. It was an incredible evening. It was majestic Izz. The light was perfect, the skyline from the kirkyard was magnificent, and inside the kirk the voices of those women were so powerful. It made me think for a second.' She stopped and faced me. 'I wondered if one could atone to God for one's sins through the beauty and power of music. That if you commit some wrong in your life it does not matter, if you pay the bargain off to God through creating glorious homage to his grace. What do you think?'

I had the feeling she was not asking me at all, but appealing to me to agree. 'If that's the case,' I said slowly, 'with my tunes and voice, I'd better brace myself for the warmth of hell.' I laughed.

She didn't.

I stopped laughing and nodded. 'It is an elegant idea.'

'It is, isn't it?' she said earnestly. 'I want to be a rational woman; and I dislike the kirk, you know Isobel, I'm not a kirk woman. But when I feel music, when I hear it, I believe there is a way to encounter the divine. What else can it be but God, in music?' She looked at her feet. The dew and grass had stained the hem of her skirt with green smudges. 'But then I spoke to a man who is a scholar at the university, after the concert, and he said there is no such thing as God, that the beauty of music goes to prove it, for all the wonder of creation comes directly from man. He said the beauty of the voices of the poorhouse women goes to prove there is no such thing as sin. Only unfortunate behaviour. Sin is a confection.' She stopped walking.

We were in a bower of pear trees with the beginnings of hard little teardrop baubles on them; roses twining the pear branches, drooping with the late afternoon's drizzle.

'Do you think that's true Izz? That there is no such thing as sin?'

'I think,' I said slowly, 'the question is not whether sin exists, but what counts for sin. The women you speak of are poor, not sinful, yet the kirk calls it sin because they sell their bodies. Does the kirk not question why they sell their bodies? And what of the purchaser?'

'Yes I agree.' She nodded energetically, but she was still frowning as if the problem bothered her deeply. 'But if there is no sin, then there can be no atonement, and atonement is the most wondrous thing of all. It is a marvellous thing to be able to give grace. I don't want to live in a world without forgiveness.'

It is a marvellous thing to be able to give grace. Is it, Cecilia? I am thinking on that, even as I write to you. Every day, every word in fact.

I could have said then to your mother that it is a fortunate thing to know what grace is, because surely some have never felt it, and must wonder why God or society has forgotten them. I wondered if the poorhouse women — even as they sang and their voices ascended in the glory of the Greyfriars kirk, on such a picturesque night — had felt the same grace that she had felt hearing them sing her words, knowing that after the concert was finished they had to go back to their regimented beds, their tough sack dresses and their punishing work. But I did not ask this.

And then she said, 'Oh, what do I know?'

We walked for a while, arm in arm in silence. I asked, 'And Wenzeslaus? The Musical Society concert — the music you had intended for the poorhouse women, that you gave to him — what of that?'

'What of it?' She gave a little shrug. 'It's his now.'

Did she really believe that was it? She said it nonchalantly but the briskness of her tone belied her. 'Have you done that for him before?' I asked cautiously.

She plucked a crimson cherry from a tree, then laughed as she spat it out. 'Sour! Yes. In Venice. At first it was fun, exciting. I don't know — the thought that I was behind his music. In chapels and palaces when people clapped, well, it was my secret. He was my mask. They thought they were clapping for him, but really it was for me, and to know that gave me a thrill. But now I do not like it so much. I do not know why it has changed. But it has. I want my music to be mine.'

At that moment we were disturbed by a rustle in the cypress behind us.

A man in a domino habit, long to the ground, wearing a raven's feather mask with a pointed black beak, was parting the branches. Marie Eliza shrieked, then began to giggle. She raised her own pink mask, which she had on a stick lying idle in her basket of oranges, and covered her face.

'Do I know you, orange seller?' the raven breathed.

It was Guadagni. He couldn't disguise his accent.

'Do I know you, raven?' Marie Eliza countered.

'I shall peck at your oranges.' He bent over and began a frantic burrowing of his hard shiny resin beak in her basket, tumbling the oranges onto the ground. She squealed and scrabbled to pick them up and he bent down to help her. When she stood up again, she was breathless. She leant on a tree, and looked as if she might be sick. I had forgotten about the baby and I think she had too.

Guadagni stood, picking with a nail at the skin of an orange, apologising profusely in Italian, and she replied in Italian, and they conversed a little, while I stood stiffly, the broad dress I wore not concealing the awkwardness I felt.

'Shall we hear some music?' he asked in English, offering his arm to her. She had left the basket of oranges at her feet and as they walked away, I saw they did not intend to take it with them. I picked it up, making sure all of the oranges were gathered back up, and I hung the basket over my arm.

I followed Guadagni and Marie Eliza towards the doocot where the orchestra, led by Wenzeslaus, were playing. It was past dusk now. The cushats and doos were coming home to roost, and the musicians were competing with a soft chorus of cooing sounds, strange melodies that chimed in and out of their orchestral march. I liked nature making its presence felt on the music, as if reminding us who learned the art first. It made me think of standing by the loch, singing.

We all waited for Wenzeslaus to draw the orchestra to a close. Everyone clapped politely. I turned my head to Marie Eliza, but she was suddenly nowhere to be seen.

You understand Cecilia, it was not curiosity that drew me to seek them out. But there was nothing else to do, and I knew no one, so I wandered through the mizzle, my wig weighing me down as it became damp, the powder beginning to clot and run down my neck. I idled my gaze over this bench, down that box hedge maze to see if I could glimpse where she had gone to. I sat down on one half of an S-shaped love seat in a bower and picked the skin off an orange and ate it, which was something I could never normally do when I had a basket of them to sell.

I heard rather than saw them.

Her laughter was light and small at first. Some words in Italian. Unfolding like ribbons. Lilting, rising. Muted by the breeze. I heard the very distinct sound of fingers grazing over threads, the pluck of bodice laces, the scratch of crocheted cuffs stroking each other, the tumble of fabric, the silky hiss of feathers. Then the path of a thumb pressing flesh, dragging across skin, a sound soft and long like brushing leather, swift, slow, then stopping.

I heard her sigh, and the deep click of eyelets being unhooked, knots being tugged and picked; the rasp as long laces were pulled through metal holes. I heard the brush of hair against palms. She laughed, like she had been tickled. He mumbled an apology.

I froze, entranced. They were concealed just behind me, within an orchard of pears. Shielding them was the rose bower in which I sat, deep blush roses just beginning to bud. I couldn't see them and they hadn't noticed me on the love seat.

Now the noises grew, and I heard skin being shuffled from cloth, wriggled free, a small gasp of relief. Then the suck of wet lips and breath; small, clipped kisses. She moaned. Her pleasure came out like a song. What was he doing to her to make her make that sound, this half-man, this castrato?

I could not help but think then of the brisk way Jas lifted my skirts, his smirk. The way he cleared his throat as if preparing to give a sermon. He kept his eyes tightly closed during the act. I kept mine open, for I was often bored, and it gave me some kind of fun to watch the faces he pulled as he took his pleasure.

'Wipe yourself up Izz, that carpet's from the Levant.'

He had entered her now, the castrato, I could hear it, with his fingers or his tongue or maybe his cock. Her timbre changed. Her throat was open, the sound lifting upwards, as if she had her head tipped back. Then the pitch of her voice became suddenly muffled, as if his hand had stopped her mouth, and I heard the graze of nails scraping skin and hair.

She released herself.

I had never made that sound for Jas. Any pleasure I took from him came afterwards, while he was writing in his book, when I had to furtively finish myself off, and be quiet about it. Once he caught me and the look of amusement on his face put me off the act for some weeks.

I listened to the sounds of Marie Eliza and Guadagni's copulation among the pear trees for a while, and then when I'd had my fill of it, I went back to watch Wenzeslaus conduct his orchestra in the doocot. I could not feel sorry for Wenzeslaus, because he had stolen the motet she was writing for the women of the poorhouse. But there was something crushing and pathetic in the look he gave her when she reappeared, flush-faced, alone, rushing to the doocot. It seemed she had missed her cue. Again.

As soon as Wenzeslaus spied her, he opened his arms wide, grinning, guffawing. 'There she is!' He seized her by the waist, and in front of the straggling crowd and the tired musicians, pushed her against the arched wall of the doocot, and planted on her lips a long, firm kiss. A strangled gasp caught in her throat. Her eyes were pinned open. She tried to laugh it off but I could see she was horribly embarrassed by the display.

The crowd of onlookers clapped, some gaily, some politely, and there was merry laughter.

Wenzelsaus handed Marie Eliza a violin, and they played a duet together, a fast, lyrical piece, the threads of their melodies competing and overlapping. When they had finished, and the audience were cheering, Wenzeslaus clutched Marie Eliza's hand, raised it into the air and with a choke in his throat said, 'Ladies and Gentlemen, behold my wife. My wife, my wife!'

Everyone applauded. Marie Eliza looked as if she wanted to flee. But she was trapped there, in that tiny space, another baby in her belly already, hemmed in by their two crossed fiddle bows — hers and Wenzeslaus's — like pikes. She was hemmed in by the contract they had signed with the Edinburgh Musical Society, and by the other, deeper contract, that a wife signs with her husband.

Believe me Cecilia, when I say that I wanted nothing more at that moment than to run to her and liberate her, to take her hand and ferry her back along the rows of fruit bushes, back towards the clandestine rose and pear grotto where she had sounded so happy only minutes ago. Where she had sounded so free. I wanted that for her. I wanted her to be happy. I felt in that moment as if she *deserved* her freedom.

But that was before it all turned.

'Now, my wife will sing.'

Wenzeslaus stepped aside and raised his violin. He played a short, melancholy solo.

The hairs on my skin sprang rigid with recognition.

She began to sing.

She was singing *The Twa Sisters*.

'He's taen three locks o her yallow hair,
An wi them strung his harp sae fair.

And then bespake the strings all three,
"O yonder is my sister that drowned mee."'

My face, beneath the lace mask, began to grow so hot it itched. She sang it beautifully. She sang it like I had never heard it sung before or since. She sang with the melancholy notes of fate on her tongue. She sang finer than a nightingale.

Were it not for the rage, the uncontrollable rage battering at the armour of my rigid duchess stays, I would have fallen at her feet. Angel voice, music of glass. She sang as if she herself was the murdered sister, resurrected as the harp made of flaxen hair and bone. She sang practised and perfect. She sang as I have never, nor will ever sing it. She made the song sound refined. She was refined. In harmony with our age, which is of refinement.

When she finished, the air was charged and silent. It was as if we had all been cloaked by a spell. She kissed her fingers, all ten of them in turn, and extended her hands towards me. 'Dearest Izz, who taught me that beautiful ballad.' She was smiling fondly.

I dug my nails into the piece of belly that lay between my stays and my duchess skirt, tender, covered only by a thin shift. I dug until I heard the linen threads break, my skin split.

17

I BEGAN OPENING THEIR LETTERS, with a candle and a draper's pin.

Mia Bella Maria,
My ears are empty without the sound of your voice.

My darling Guido,
Your words are tinder to my stomach . . .

Mia Bella Maria,
I can bear it not a second longer without the smothering velvet of your breath.

My Guido,
Last night I could not sleep for in the night I imagined you came to me, your perfect form, your skin on mine. I should be ashamed, but I am not, to say that as I lay with one hand across my mouth to still my cries, I placed my other hand— I'll spare your blushes, Cecilia, you were, after all present in certain form, during this pageant.

Mia Bella Maria,
You are the music in my heart and you ring with each step I take.
I will come to your dreams every night.

My Guido,
When I feel the beats of your spine under my fingers, time disappears. There is no man, no woman, we are something different . . . For those precious moments, we are full of one thing only; grace.

Mia Bella M,
I cannot breathe without you. You are home to me.

On and on they went . . .

My G,
It is as if a ghost has taken up residence in my body. Our love is holy for it is a glory without the chains of marriage, the terror of childbirth. When my heart weeps for what became of your body, my soul cries out that without that mutilation, you would not be you. I wish to cut off something of mine, that I too can be made strange, and we will exist only for each another.

I was an impeccable cadie; always prompt, always knowing where each of them could be found, wasting no time in delivering the missive from lodging to land, theatre to concert hall, pleasure garden to kirk (I'm lying, your mother never went to kirk). Though Marie Eliza never offered me anything for my

224

troubles, Guadagni without fail paid me a couple of bodles a letter. I became good at prising open the seals without cracking them.

Why did I do this, open their letters? What was in it for me, to pry inside their lives?

Well, tell me this Cecilia — are you still reading? Have you skipped ahead yet to the part where you discover what role I played in that which you accuse me of? Or are you, like I was, too eager to step inside the heart of someone else for a while, to dream of what it would be to be them? I was, in many ways, entranced by the life your mother led.

But she had stolen my song.

And now I wondered what I could steal from her.

18

Mia Bella M,
You must leave him. I can bear it no longer. I don't know
what I will do if you do not.

Sweet G,
Have patience. After the opera, we will travel to Naples. I
will arrange passage from Leith. After that night, we will
live as one.

19

I STILL SANG AT PARLIAMENT CLOSE and in the Cowgate. But I could no longer hear the notes of *The Twa Sisters* on my own tongue without thinking of them in her mouth. Many nights I would go home to Jas's rooms without a penny, and let him bestow on me a nip of his good whisky and drone his revolutionary thoughts until he was ready to tup me.

'Fucking you, Izz, is like the taste of a clootie dumpling when you've been starved all day. I should write that down, I think it's good.'

Jas liked to debate his ideas with his friends, who were also scholars. Sometimes I would be allowed to stay, feigning sleep in his bed, under the quilt his mother had stitched, while he and his friends smoked tobacco and ate mussels they had bought from a woman who had hauled them on her back from Leith.

The flesh of woman was a favourite topic in Jas's intellectual circles. They made mysteries of us. Our flesh on their tongues became an idea, a substance about which they could debate the virtue.

Were women pure? Was there purity in sin? Could there be anything but purity in something that felt so like the quint-essence of ecstasy? Was there any virtue in a diseased woman?

If sin became visible, through disease, then how could sin be only a theoretical idea? If a woman's hymen was pierced with fingers, was she still virginal? What was virginity, and did it increase pleasure, or was it an idea, and if it was an idea, then was it not possible for an idea to become tangible, if translated from the mind to the body, from the theory of pleasure to the physical reality of it?

Jas had a society he went to, the Pigs in Wigs, and to his delight had recently been made Chief Boar, which meant he was entitled to give a Maiden speech.

He chose for the subject of his speech, *The Transgressive Virtues of the Edinburgh Peasant Woman in the Hands of the Philosophical Man.*

'Would you stand naked on the table while I recite my speech, dear Izz? My darling Izz, my Izz that *is*, my earthy beautiful Izz? Would you stand, like the goddess of the soil, while I give worship to your stout body, your unadorned flesh, your yielding strength?'

'No.'

'Please Izz.'

'No.'

'I'll pay you.'

'Fuck off.'

'You'll be famous among scholarly men, who are the best kind, and if you are lucky, they might write about you.'

'Can I sing?'

A hesitation. 'No.'

'Then no.'

'Perhaps briefly, you can sing. But it will spoil the illusion, Izz.'

'Then no.'

'Do you want to go back to living with the smuggler at Newhaven, Izz? I will take away your books, I will never teach you another word. I will keep my ideas to myself and never let you eavesdrop at the lectern of my bedroom when my friends are round for our vigorous debates. I will take back my quilt and my ink and my pens and I will cast you out into the Cowgate, where they do not write about women like you in *Ranger's Guide to Edinburgh Ladies*. I have something you want Izz, as much as you have something for me.'

What a fucking palaver.

Standing in the middle of that table, in the Lucky Middlemass tavern, Lucky herself averting her one eye from behind the bar, because she'd seen it all before, and humiliation no longer had the power to move her. All the while Jas le Corbie dissected the panegyrics written about women in the *Edinburgh Review*, scoffed at ladies who were painted as 'celestial', 'dainty', 'pale', who were compared to flowers and angels. He opined on the honest beauty of the peasant woman, the unadorned purity, on the semantics of purity itself (was it an essence, or the reduction of matter to its barest soil?), all the while pointing at my nipples, mons and arse.

At first I closed my eyes, but then I opened them, because I wanted to see their faces, gathered round the long rectangular table, their bloodshot whites, their snuff-pocked noses, their gouty fingers, the egg and beer on their cravats, the pudding penises in their hands, as they tugged away, trying to get a dribble over the edge of the gouged-out cow horn that they passed — man to man — for the purpose, which was an essential part of membership of this thinking salon.

231

I did begin to sing, despite my bargain, but when I began they all talked over it, chattering like magpies, and my voice was drowned. I gave up after just one verse of *The Twa Sisters*.

I went back to Marie Eliza then, because although she had stolen my song, she did at least listen to me.

As an appendix to this chapter Cecilia, Jas got the gout, then died of syphilis in about 1780 (I forget the exact date). He is six feet under now, in the Canongate Kirkyard, his parents having buried him in their vault, much, I'm sure, to his atheist dismay. He never got round to having his diaries printed, so his ideas have all gone to the grave with him.

20

I HAD BEEN PLAYING CADIE CUPID for Guadagni and
Marie Eliza for over a month when, climbing to the top
of her turnpike one day, she flung open the door herself
and ushered me inside.

She looked exhausted. She led me into the parlour and
flopped backwards onto the divan. The parlour had not been
cleaned. The corners of the room were clustered with grainy
balls of dust and hair and the windows were streaked with soot.

You could see that the baby was growing; you were growing.
Her dress was starting to bulge. She always had the sickness,
and she had it the whole way through her pregnancy this time.
We used to call you the vomity babe, Cecilia. I sometimes
wondered if these lurches and seizes and turns she felt would
rub off onto her music, in leaps and beats and crashes.

I studied her, to see if I could find some indication of the
woman she was in her letters, whose mind was soaked in love.
She looked tired. I supposed she was good at concealing parts
of herself, as indeed we all are. And she'd had much practice,
deceiving Wenzeslaus too.

I watched her recline on the sofa. I sat on the spinet stool.
She was looking at the ceiling. But as I stared at her, I saw her

crafty eye drift downwards and lock onto mine; she thought I wasn't looking and as soon as we had caught one another's gaze, hers flitted back to the ceiling. 'Isobel, I don't know what to do. I need someone to help me and thought perhaps you could suggest someone. You know, your scholar? Your student?'

The very idea that Jas le Corbie was 'my scholar' sat as ill in me as a slug in the stomach.

She stared at me now. 'You know the one?'

'I do know him.'

'Your sweetheart.'

'There is not much that is sweet about him.'

'Then your lover.'

'If you must.'

'Do you think he would make fair copies of my libretto for me? I have not the time, Izz, to sit and copy it out five times. I still have to finish the second sister's aria, the love duet, the ballad at the end. I could—' She looked around her; her gaze paused on the filthy spinet. 'I could find some way of paying him — we could, I mean, together, I'm sure. Men are very pliable really, or persuasible at least.' She grinned weakly.

I knew what she meant. You will say that my suspicions were too grotesque, too fanciful, too quick. But then Cecilia, you have never been a poor village girl in a city where society is cleaved in two. There was — there is — a very clear social contract in Edinburgh, and as luminous as those brilliant minds are, they still need people to do their dirty and menial work, to cook their meals, launder their clothes and see to their needs. But I was damned if I was going to wash Jas le Corbie's stinking shirts or offer him more baroque sessions with my cunt so that she could have her opera written out by him.

'I'll copy it out,' I said.

She could not keep her face from looking stunned. I don't even think she tried. 'You?'

'I can write.'

Her mouth moved, but no sound came out. Then, 'But of course you can,' she said. 'I only meant not to trouble you. But — you can write in a fair hand, Izz? The printers around here you see, they fuss so, and the singers are so very particular of spelling and clarity of line, it's not that I don't trust you, but just that a scholar . . .'

I leaned across the spinet keyboard and took from the music stand a sheet of the thick paper on which she was writing her score. It was the same paper she used when she wrote those luxurious, creamy letters to me, that I loved to pop the wax on.

I heard a strangled, stifled grunt from her as she saw me seize the sheet of paper, and take up her quill that was resting in the inkwell on the stand. But then she sat back again, undisguised curiosity spread — catlike — across her face. She watched me.

I rose and took from the table beside the spinet the first book I came to. *Memoirs Concerning the Portuguese Inquisition.* (It was one of a number of Angelica's pamphlets on religion and torture.) I opened it at a random page, sat back on the spinet stool and leaning on the music stand, I copied out the first line I read:

'Mr Collier, in his historical dictionary, cautions that Fox was a careless writer who gathered his accounts from people who could not be trusted. In fine, Queen Mary was much the most _tender and merciful_ of the whole race of the Tudors.'

When I had finished I passed it across to her. As I did so, I began to realise the craven callowness of what I had done. I was a performing pig in a fairground. I was the pig that pointed its nose at a board of alphabet letters to spell out the name of Shakespeare's plays. I was so eager to show her that I was more than she believed I was, and that desperation made me feel soiled. She hefted herself forwards and took the paper. Her eyes skipped from left to right and back again. She looked up at me.

'It is good,' she said, plain faced. 'Very neat.' Then she nodded and said quietly, almost to herself, 'Do not you agree, every woman should have means to divulge herself with words, even when she wants no one to hear her?'

When she wants no one to hear her.

I believe she was probably talking about her letters to Guadagni when she spoke thus. But I have thought on those words of hers many times since, for they seemed strange to have come from a musician, surely someone whose life is dedicated to making sound that others hear. But perhaps she was also talking about her reasons for composing as opposed to performing. It was never enough for her, just to make music. She wanted to create it, she wanted to know that it would echo through the years, surfacing in other places and times.

And now, sitting here with some time to think more on it, I think Cecilia, she was right. Sometimes we are not ready to stand on a scaffold and sing the truth out loud. Sometimes it is better to write it quietly down. And sometimes those around us are not ready to hear it. After all, you turned your back on me. You threw me in the Tolbooth.

Are you listening now?

She said to me, 'I can pay you less than I would a scribe, something like sixpence a copy — is that all right?'

236

Something I was less quick at back then — though it is thankfully no longer the case — was adding numbers in my head. Sixpence times five seemed to me an adequate number of coins. It could not take me so long, just to sit and copy out words that were already there. (How wrong I was. It took an age. It took every minute of every night for the next two weeks.)

But even though my numbers were poor, some residue of mercantile spirit I'd had from the smuggler was still with me. What did I want? What did I really want from her? I thought on that for a moment. 'I'll take a part in your opera too,' I said.

I expected her to laugh. I was braced for it. My whole body was stiffened for the blow. It would have been nothing strange to me if she had deflected me the very same way she did about singing in the Playhouse. But she just spread a smile, a great beaming one, and said, 'I was thinking to ask you the very same. I do have a role in mind. Well, well, Izz, this has been a productive afternoon for us. Do you see what happens when two ladies such as us come together to create?'

21

EVERY SOUR FEELING I had felt for her evaporated on that afternoon. Suddenly I became stuffed so full of hope I thought I would suffocate. It took less than a second for the picture to build in my mind; me, that stage, that Canongate Playhouse wooden stage, the noise of it, my skirts kissing the boards. Lairds in rough silk; ladies in satin in the boxes. Anopera!

When later I walked past the coffee houses and heard the students and the professors and the advocates arguing, I did not feel the cleft of the divide between myself and them so keenly anymore. I did not go home to Jas that night. I stayed all evening in a tavern near Goose Pie house, and I danced a wicked jig with Lady Agnew, who likes to drink with rough women, and Jeanie the orange seller, all of us cavorting with jugs of black cork in our hands.

Observing Marie Eliza pull the bloodied thread of that opera out of her, word by word, note by note, I thought that it was not unthinkable that one day I might write down my own ballad.

Then the afternoon arrived when Marie Eliza told me she had the libretto ready. I was to make five copies. Every night in Jas's room, after singing in the Cowgate, I scraped and blotted my way carefully through the letters, trembling lest I mistake a curve or a dot, and ruin the meaning. I hid the papers under Jas's bed, a sheet wrapped around them to protect them from the rats, or from Jas's prying eyes, for I didn't know what he would say if he knew I was doing this. And besides it was my work, not his. I didn't want his questions or his scorn.

The sixpences from Marie Eliza never materialised. But it was not gold I was after anyway. I was eager to know which part she had thought of in her opera — for the Canongate stage — for me.

I finished those five copies of the libretto for her. Three of them she took with her to the Playhouse. One was given to the printer above John's Coffee House. I doubt it's still there and I don't remember the man's name.

The fifth copy she kept at home. She kept it carelessly on the spinet, even after the events of that night which I will call here The Doomed Incident. And when the time came for her coffin to be lowered into Greyfriars Kirkyard, you will thank me for telling you that it was I who dictated that the libretto and score should be shrouded and interred in the grave too, so that I should take comfort in always knowing where it lay — lest, of course, it be lost.

ACT III
THE SWAN MURDER

1

CECILIA DROPS THE PAGES she is reading; wispy, tawdry sheets, penned on Tolbooth ledger paper in Isobel Duguid's grimy scrawl. If she was ever *very neat*, as she claims Marie Eliza said to her, the habit has been lost. Her eyes squeeze shut and she battles with the tears she wants no one to see. She clenches her teeth until the pain in her gums is too much to bear. She sinks to the floor. The emptiness in her palms, where the pages had rested, is like the hole that has pierced and stretched her heart ever since she was old enough to know what love was.

Cecilia can barely breathe. She has fed tea to that woman. She has the imprint of her monstrous dress on the bolsters of the rented sofa.

She picks up the pieces of herself, and, as she has done hundreds of times before, gathers them together until she is whole again.

She climbs the stairs. They are too narrow for the bulk of her formal skirts. She brushes along the upper landing and into the large front bedroom. Though it is the biggest of the bedrooms in the house, Mrs Abercorn does not sleep in it. Mrs Abercorn does not like to sleep overlooking a street. The sounds bring her nightmares, of thieves and bludgeoners, of people being cudgelled in the night. She and Mr Abercorn share the more modest back bedroom that overlooks the tiny knot garden. Leaves and hedges bring her peace.

In this cavernous front room everything echoes.

An interloper would notice at once that there is no bed, that there is scant furniture, save a travelling trunk and a bare mahogany bench pressed back like a church pew against the opposite wall. There are no rugs or carpets. The drapes at the window are muslin and they let in the light and the cold.

In the corner furthest from the windows, there is a large, square cabinet. It fills the corner alcove, as high as the ceiling, wide as a pig pen. A minor-key lowing is coming from within the black wood.

'Angelica, you old demon!' Cecilia calls out. 'Get your cloak on, we're going to the graveyard.'

The singing stops.

Closet doors, blood-brown as a confessional, rattle as they slide open on their metal tracks.

A figure shuffles forward, out of the gloom.

The eyes are invisible. Angelica is wearing her blackest veil. There is no way she can see out of it, and she has no candle inside her little travelling hermitage. Cecilia cannot remember the last time she saw Angelica's eyes. Do they even exist anymore? For all she knows the mad old woman has gouged them out in a fit of religious fervour. Angelica lives in the dark in her confessional. The box is a chapel of sound alone.

'It's buried with her. Her opera is in her coffin. Fetch your cloak. What are you waiting for?'

The veiled head droops. Angelica's voice is dry and cool. 'How are you planning on extracting it from the earth? Shall we bring a garden trowel?'

'You're the one who makes pacts with devils. Can't you find us a resurrectionist?'

The hood remains still.

Cecilia loses her patience. 'People dig up graves all the time in this city!' she shrieks. 'Ask anyone on the street, they'll tell you.'

'I do not make pacts with devils, as well you know.'

'Fine, you do not make pacts with devils. And it's perfectly normal to live in a box singing psalms all day. *This is my mother's opera!*' Cecilia's rage reaches screeching point.

She thrusts out her arms to strike the penitent crow. But Angelica has turned to wood; she is immovable. Cecilia's hand freezes before it touches her. She goes to strike her again. The same thing happens. She cannot touch her. And again. But the fourth time her fist comes down on Angelica's shoulder and she is suddenly overcome with a cold, penetrating dousing of guilt. It is as if she has been plunged underwater, as if a hand has reached down and grasped her by the neck. Song explodes in her head, voices from nowhere, harmonies filling her skull, blocking out all other sound, and all of a sudden she wants to throw herself at Angelica's feet. 'I'm sorry,' she weeps. She clutches Angelica's gown. 'I'm so sorry.'

How did she do that?

Angelica places a gloved hand on her half-sister's forehead. 'There there,' she says. 'Come, get yourself dressed. We shall pay a resurrectionist. But ... I want to warn you, to prepare yourself, for what we might find.'

She shuffles backwards into her wooden box and emerges wearing a thick fox fur muff.

Sniffing, wiping her tear-stained face, Cecilia climbs to her feet.

2

THE TWO RESURRECTION MEN are shadow-eyed creatures. They exist, like the fruits of their profession, under the ground. They skirt the canals, scuttle in cellars, disappear down turnpikes that lead beneath Edinburgh's seven hills. They ferry things forbidden through vaults to people who will pay for them. They turn dead flesh into chinking gold, and they drink black porter, and feed off rotting pies, because they are cheaper.

They have no lantern for they can see in the dark.

They have no ladder for they can scale walls.

Angelica, tall and robust in her muck-skimming cloak and fox muffler, vaults her small half-sister over the kirkyard wall and drops her in a rosemary bush. She climbs over and appears before Cecilia without so much as a smear on her pristine black robes.

It is raining, and the two women clutch each other as the cold saturates their hems and creeps through the leather of their shoes. The men have made good progress. They are already four feet deep. Their sweat rises, sharp. They work like beetles, never tiring. Angelica has promised them a reliquary from Venice for their troubles, containing, she says, a toenail belonging to the Magdalen.

'Jacobite shite,' one of them spat.

'We can sell it,' said the other.

They got on with the task.

Angelica shrugs. She doesn't really care about the fate of the Magdalen's toenail, whether it is cherished by the men or sold. It will be out there still, somewhere in the world. Even if it is destroyed it will still exist. It will still exist because she has chosen to believe it to be so.

Cecilia thinks she will freeze or drown before she looks on the buried bones of her mother. She wonders if the sight will make her sick. Or will there be something still left in the face, in the skull, some wisp of herself she can catch, like in a mouldy mirror, that will make her fall in love?

The men dig.

'Hit wood,' one of them lows.

Then, the ordeal of prising the lid off the coffin. They are not used to dealing with such old caskets. Most of their commissions are for freshly laid bodies. Here the nails have rusted. The wood has welded fast. No one has a pick.

'Oh just smash it!' Cecilia cries in a fit.

'Keep your fucking voice down,' the resurrection man hisses. 'If you're begging to be taken to the Tolbooth there are easier ways.'

Eventually she hears the creak. It is diabolical. It is like the rageful shriek of a ghost who has been confined too long. It seems to echo round the graves. It is the worst thing Cecilia has ever heard. It is the sound of betrayal, of trust being severed.

Then, silence.

One of the men grunts.

'What can you see?' Cecilia says, in a small voice.

Angelica clasps Cecilia. She strokes her hair.

'Come and take a look for yourself,' the resurrection man says.

Cecilia breaks from Angelica's grasp and takes a step closer. Her feet slip and slide. She must not fall into her mother's grave. She must not. She could never climb free again. It would eat her. It is a great monster and she would be bound to sail in its stomach forever. She leans forward. She can see nothing at first. The pitch black is even darker down there than in the rest of the yard, shouldered six by three by six feet of muck.

The resurrection man mutters something. He lights a stub of candle with a flintlock, holds it low. Its glow is shielded by the depth of the grave.

Then Cecilia sees what they see. She hears the fluttering as the wind catches it.

A sheaf of papers, rustling against wood, spinning, echoing. Echoing in empty space.

There is no body in there.

No clothing. No bones, no hair, no jewels.

There is no body. She begins to shake.

The terror Cecilia feels at that empty space is like nothing she has ever felt. It is like staring into a mirror and suddenly seeing no reflection. It is like picking up a book she thinks she knows and finding the pages have turned blank.

There is no body. A howling inside her.

There is nothing in there but bare, rotten wood, clumps of wet muck and a sheaf of paper. The sheets are moulded and blackened and corroded by dirt, parts of them scarred and stolen for the feasts of insects, covered by blankets of fungi.

Still trembling, she takes the pages, cold between her fingers. She takes them as delicately as if they were hot blades. She stares keenly in the small glow of the resurrectionist's candle, peers, scours the smeared and mouldy lines. It can only be fifteen or twenty pages long. Of the remaining ones, only a handful of words are left undestroyed on each page. It is written in a hand she recognises, a hand that is not so *very neat* after all.

Do those foxed and rotten sheets contain the death knell of both her mother and her father? Do they contain the cipher to the murder of a castrato, one so inflammatory she had thought it would set fire to her hands to hold it?

She tries to read it again, and again, and again, tries to prise more words from the corroded pages. Whatever it was, it has been transformed through time and decay into something else.

T e Sw n

Mur r

                                        A spinet,

Evelina   *wig*   *Cassandra — the younger —*

          Twa

               drapes   *fall away to reveal*

                                   Cassandra's

Cassandra

                    not

               your luminous tongue.

Evelina   sister.

Cavatina

Cassandra   love.

          a secret, torturing

One minute   a swan

The next,   fire

          a man hanged

     split   her heart with a knife.

                                   stagehands with fans

curtains billow.

Cavatina

                                      stone

                      glass   mason

Recitative

Cassandra   I do not   want stone for my heart.

                   stranger   fleshmarket,

                 lifeless ducks

       with a pick, prised the chambers of my heart,

       won't say his   Tongues wag.

Evelina   Fie!   Talk is harmless.

Cassandra Words murder!

Duettino

   I dream of   water,   hearts   canals   Venice.

   Safe   nothing real, nothing wrong.

   for us to be so close a devil could not slice a knife between us.

Act II

Earl of Niddrie -   *hot house.*

Recitative

Grow, wretched pineapple.

                       wife

And yet.

           hot at the poultry stall. My hands   touching

cool feathers   she brushed my coat   I could not breathe.

Aria   my moonlit lover

Two sisters   only one love.

My betrothed

   would

birth children until she died. Three, four, five strong babies.

               birthing,   strapping babes! Until she died!

       this fountain pool. Tell me, of the two faces you see,

           which is for my heart?

A pause. Reprisal?

my night beauty and I

dream of

bones

But when she laughs

the

green waters of Venice.   mine. She is mine. She is

A Ballad Singer clamours the railings   *in her arms a baby wailing*

Penny for the last words of the hanged man,

reeking hag

Wait.   the city,

babes.

The love

Ballad Singer My eyesight is poor. Some gold would help me see.

gold chain

Ballad Singer runs

Hag of song!   Stop thief!

old Nor Loch, lapping. Moonlight. Swans

Evelina emerges   *hides*

    Bohemia.

                                          Prussia.

        our faces and names belong to no one,

            only love.

Recitative

Cassandra   He comes.

Evelina   I   hide.

Master rides   *a small pony,*

Duettino

Master   Moon woman,   shield

ourselves from hell.

    from the port of Leith to

    Venice   masks, hide our faces, become another.

              walk   the city forest.

The moon shifts   his face

Evelina

claws herself

    Drown me   witches   live in you.

                         rats at my feet.

    Magpies

      cast by a hag. Pluck my eyes   block my ears

      This mire   summoned this sight

    And now,   I see   everything

          In flames. The bricks blackened, eaten.

      evil thoughts   kill

              beneath my feet.

Act III

Cavatina

Master   *again. He paces.*

Master

    open the cavity   peer at the heart.

          restless clockwork of the soul.

Recitative

Evelina   my love, you are honest as glass.

Master   Glass changes shape when   washed by water.

              Could you love a man who loved another?

                  I could love a man who fed   his heart lightly

                                                  did not burn to cinder.

                  I could love a

              shield to protect his wife

Evelina   You destroy me.

Master

                  bracelet and a dagger).

Aria

                                              monster   me.

                                  Know you broke a woman in two.

              nothing but my spinet, my sister and you.   serpents.

                        chorus sings 'Binnorie O'

Evelina takes out the knife.

        pushes Cassandra's body into

                                    adders' teeth?

    Or is it hell?

    body floats away.

Evelina flees.

Intermission

hornpipe   *fiddle.*

Act IV

      Beggar Jeannie

animal bones to carve.

        long

      love   a man   hawking songs. To Fife

                        He gathers

    from the ploughmen,   tanners   fishwives,

      bones I forage   to sell in the closes of the Old

  Town.

dead   *swan*

Recitative

                       pale mermaid?   tongue cut out?

                                hidden in this swamp?   the

city that glimmers in the minds of   men.

                crimes, of passion   gore,

                all rise one day.

     I will   a token

              From your robbed heart music will spill,

plucks   *three feathers,*   *takes*   *a tooth*

Niddrie's Palace.

    waving   *crowds.*

Ballad Singer crosses   *baby still in*   *arms,*

    (*aside*) Is she an omen?

             feast   feast,   feast

All is restored.

this holy couple.

dancing.   *clarsach*   *three feathers*

Chorus   no blessing like song.

now, look upon my magick harp.

three feathers of a swan, its

tooth

Spirit of Cassandra   *on a cloud*

trapdoor enough   A thunderclap?)

Bless this house. Bless   my father

silent part   can find no suitable bass)

Bless   my lost love.

bless the sister who

left me to drown.

Cassandra's filthy breast   pig's blood in a

handkerchief).

Bless

the girl who gave me back my stolen song.

O Murderess!   You

believed love was soft. But I knew

it mirrored hate. So love   for sisters too.   perhaps

the only true love I have known   .

kisses   *Evelina crumples weeping.*

the curtain falls   *two sisters.*

Izz,   a fair copy   before opening night.

3

CECILIA PUTS DOWN THE PAPERS. She is safely back in her Young's Street parlour, her feet in a basin of warm water beneath the slender-footed writing table. Outside the window the street is chill, pewter, colder and quieter than the teeming soil of the kirkyard. Percy is upstairs, snoring, Angelica back in her box doing God knows what. She has scrutinised the pages three times, repeated its strange poetry over and over to herself.

She was hoping to feel something; love? Her mother wrote this piece while she was inside her belly. Can she feel the words in her flesh? If she looks hard enough, without her eyes, can she conjure up the hidden, eaten ones? Where have they gone? She wants to slice open the bellies of the ants that have gobbled her mother's words, to scrape away the mould and examine their stomachs with eyeglasses. Or are those words already inside her, imprinted onto her, because they came from inside her mother at the same time she was growing? There is so much talk of love and passion in there, and yet Cecilia cannot *feel* anything. She cannot feel what she is desperate to feel. She cannot feel what love to her mother felt like.

Would she know that kind of love if she felt it? Is love passed on through the womb? Or does it have to be passed through the eyes, and through the mouth, through the soft noises made in sleepless nights, through lullabies and touch, through stroking fingers and carrying arms?

The thought bewilders Cecilia. It smothers her. It is like with these pages she has been promised a cave of riches, but just inside the opening of the cave there is a hole, and she has tripped into it, and it is black and blinding and never ending. Is that really all that is left?

No, but that is not it. There is something else there. Tucked behind the final page, folded into a quarto, there is a single scrap of score. Cecilia unfolds it. Cecilia can read music the way her mother could; as if it were words on a page. She scans the melody once and recognises the tune of Isobel's murder ballad, *The Fiddler's Wrath*. Whatever Isobel considers Marie Eliza to have stolen from her, she has performed her own theft in return.

Cecilia puts on her cloak again, and walks in the dawn light back to the Tolbooth. On the first floor of the building, behind the cross bars of the window, open to the brisk sunrise of the Royal Mile, she sees the shape of Isobel Duguid. She is sans wig now, haggard in her filthy mantua with its snapped whalebones and lopsided bodice. She has a lantern on the table, streaking smoke up into the cell, and still she is scribbling furiously away.

ACT IV
CARRUBBER'S CLOSE

1

M Y DEAR CECILIA,
    I do not believe it takes a scholar's beady eye to
    see that these lines Marie Eliza composed were
an indication of the turmoil in her own mind. She was trying
to choose between her two lovers. The stodgy verse that opera
is made from — fire and water and witches and bones, moons
and such nonsense that would have shamed a beggar bard —
all that was the sign of a woman whose feelings were so
extravagant she couldn't think properly.

You will be lucky if the rats have digested it, Cecilia. It will
spare your eyes. If I were to have eaten her words, I likely
would have thrown them up. But the rats around here are used
to living on the disgorging of other people's stomach contents,
and they have stronger constitutions for it than I.

It was a fiendish arrogance of hers, in my opinion, to make
herself the Master in her tale — oh yes, that is the character she
represents, whether she intended it to be obvious or not — with
her husband and lover as the twa sisters. To set it all here in the
Old Town and to talk of riches and palaces and glass bellies and
swans. It is enough to vinegar one's eyes. Were the words of the
original ballad not enough for her? Was the setting of that song

that had served so many people not fanciful enough? But what do I know? Who am I to cast my judgement?

She was still convinced then, that Wenzeslaus was good for her. He had given her children. He had given her a life of music. The power of two musicians combined was more potent than one alone and she never would have had the access to the stage or the salons in this city if she were without him. He was held in good standing in the Edinburgh Musical Society. Her father approved of him, which itself was worth a thousand kisses from a lover. And though he had a habit of stealing her compositions, had he not also set the stage for her to have something she never could have imagined; to have her dream of an opera brought to life in the Canongate Playhouse? Can any woman be blamed for a little ambition?

But he kept her pregnant, and even a fool could see she no longer enjoyed his caresses or his company.

Were she to have eloped with Guido Guadagni then, could she have been happy? Could Cassandra and her glass belly and her moon kisses and her Venice canals have triumphed in the end?

I am not asking you this with the power of hindsight, but I could see even then that your mother had a choice between passionate love and sensible love.

And she feared that one would stab and drown the other.

She was terrified that one of her lovers would, in the end, murder the other.

2

ONCE THE LIBRETTO WAS DONE, as summer drifted to a close and the date of the opera drew near, she became feverish. Every time I saw her she seemed more and more terrified that Wenzeslaus was intent on stealing parts of her opera, on making up pretences for needing her to give him fragments of this part of it or that; an aria, an over-ture — a commission for an assembly, a Musical Society concert. One day she summoned me by letter to Fountain Close. Angelica showed me into the parlour. Marie Eliza was lying back on her divan, leaning against a pile of tapestried cushions, a wooden board planted across her lap. Her scores were all in disarray, and she was scowling at some pain in her belly that was troubling her.

'Are you well, Marie Eliza?'

She started at her name. She stared at me. After a pause she said, 'I am not.'

Her hands rifled through the scores. 'He has asked me for an oratorio, that he can pass as his own in a private concert. He knows I have no time to compose it. He wants me to give him something from my opera.'

'Say no.' The solution seemed simple.

'But it is money, Izz. Money for him is money for all of us. I cannot say no.'

'He can write it himself then,' I told her.

'He cannot,' she snapped. 'He says he cannot and if he says he cannot then he cannot. I cannot make him compose. I cannot force him to write. I cannot do anything about that but give in to his wishes.' She sighed.

I didn't know what to say.

'And I am to host a soirée for the board members of the Musical Society.' She closed her eyes. Another cramp in her womb.

I knelt at the couch. 'How is the baby? You can still feel it move?'

She bent double. 'I feel it move constantly, Isobel. It never stops moving. You know about these things, Izz. Is it – is it all the ... activity with Guido, that has made the baby mad? Are these things true?'

My mouth hung open, for I did not know how I wished to answer that. But at that moment Angelica brought in Tommy by the hand, holding a little tin whistle in his other fist, that he was blowing short shrill bursts on, very pleased with himself. Marie Eliza clutched her brow. She let him crawl onto her knee and blow his whistle in her ear a few times, and then she kissed him on his nose and said, 'You must go with Angelica now, my good little billy goat.'

Tommy looked crestfallen at his exile. But he didn't cry.

'Don't take him to the fleshmarket again,' she said to Angelica. 'He had nightmares about the sheep's heads last time.'

Angelica bundled Tommy up into her arms, and made a joke with him that she was counting his eyes and found seven on his face, to distract him as they left the room. She shot Marie Eliza a look as she closed the parlour door.

Marie Eliza's head was in her hands again. I peeled her fingers from her face. 'You must focus on your opera. That is enough to sate your mind. And it is what you desire, which is best for both you and your baby. That is all.'

'But Wenzeslaus—' She let the air from her lungs.

'But nothing.'

'I don't know what to say to him.'

'Then say nothing. But provide him with nothing. The opera is yours.'

I cannot say that I had no interest of my own in this. Her opera, as you have heard tell, was to be my ticket to the Canongate stage, and she still hadn't told me what part I was to play, though I thought it likely to be Cassandra the Younger Sister who is murdered. But I also did believe it was in her best interests to channel the focus of her mind, to stop it from jumping around in a way that would excite her and risk ruining both pregnancy and opera.

She seemed to retreat inside herself for a moment. Her thoughts were already in disarray and when she spoke again, it was of this dinner she was to host. 'He complains of the noise we make drowning out the music in his head, but how am I to compose, when my head is full of boiled mutton and possets of lemon? Composition is impossible when all I can think of are curd pies and pigeon dumplings. I must prepare the food myself, because we have no money to pay a cook, and I must discover how to pay for it or beg for credit at the grocer's. I would rent a room at the Fortune Tavern but we could never afford it. They must come here.'

271

She glanced around the parlour, casting her gaze into the corners where balls of soot and dust twitched like mice in the draughts. She looked down at her scores again. 'He will take my music. He will. This is his plan, to occupy me so I have no time to make it good. He is determined I should fail at this. He would crawl inside my mind to ruin the thing if he could.'

She clutched the scores of that opera close to her belly, as if it were another child of hers. She was terrified of Wenzeslaus stripping it meticulously, finger by finger, bone by bone, aria by aria, mutilating the shape of something she had made that was beautiful.

If this seems to you like vanity on your mother's part, if it appears frivolous or histrionic in the face of her more pertinent responsibilities — such as her children — ask yourself this: why does Percy Abercorn wish so fervently to publish his own book?

Come to think of it, why did you marry Percy in the first place? It wasn't for his intellect, was it? His luscious looks? I don't think so. His taste in waistcoats? No. It was your ambition to be wife to such a man, with all that it brings. Is a woman's only permissible ambition yoked to her choice of a husband, knotted to the fecundity of her womb, or are we allowed to wish for that thing the students in their frock coats, in coffee houses, earnestly, loudly demand as they try to re-shape the world; that urge that cannot be tamed inside our bodies but is determined to burst from us, the power to enter rooms and have our ideas heard, the power to have our thoughts put down, in books, in stone, the right to hold the attention of another person, if only for a few seconds?

Ambition is only tawdry when it is unrealised.

I understood her desire to have created something of her own.

My name is not printed on my ballad, even when it comes stinking fresh from the press. If my ballad is ever printed in a book (and I'm not including your husband's), it will be called *A Traditional Edinburgh Ballad*; you see if it isn't. It will belong to no one but those who cry it and those who listen to it. We are the hidden architects, the secret, sulphurous sounds that weave their way into your thoughts. We build morals, climb into your bones through your ears, and hand you your history. And yet you will never know our names.

Your mother, even as she stole that song, she lit the kindling for my own ambition. She built my thieving, deceitful hands.

3

I TOLD HER I WOULD GO to the grocer's and the pâtissier and I would collect everything she needed for the soirée. I am not much of a cook now and I wasn't then either, but I would help her as best I could. I would play maidservant, and while I cooked and prepared the parlour, and Angelica minded Tommy, she could focus solely on composing her opera, and then composing herself for the Musical Society Board.

Angelica and I dragged the applewood table from the kitchen through to the parlour and positioned it before the fireplace, with enough room for chairs on all sides. The Herzes only possessed three chairs, two in the kitchen and one in the bedroom, and so we amassed these in the parlour and went downstairs to knock on the neighbour's door. An old music dealer lived below them and was amiable enough to help us heave up the spiral turnpike four of his own oak chairs from his dining room. We found a bedsheet in the Herzes' spice chest and Angelica pressed it with the hot iron onto the table. Marie Eliza we moved, for the time being, still on her divan, beneath the window, with her spinet beside her in easy reach and her board of scattered papers on her lap.

I visited Mr Jamieson's on the High Street and chose some bread, two shovelfuls of macaroni and a jug of cream. When I asked to put the bill on the Herz account, they said the Herzes had bad credit, so I took the liberty of charging it to the Edinburgh Musical Society, hoping they wouldn't balance their ledgers until after the soirée. Then I went to the fishmarket and asked the fishwife what she could give me for sixpence. She offered me a bucket of lively partons that were vexing her by scuttling from their container. At the Maut Ha, I told them the Canongate Playhouse was sponsoring a soirée at the Herzes' and could I beg a barrel of brandy, a demijohn of Portuguese wine and some Malaga sack? They let me. My face was good there, if not my credit. They even threw in the end of a dried neat's tongue which was starting to sour.

I arrived back at Fountain Close later that morning, laden down with my baskets and paper packages, conducting the strapping cadies with the booze up the stairs, ready for my turn as cook and servant for the benefactors of the Edinburgh Musical Society. I had been via the poultry market and the fleshmarket too and I had some good scraps for soup, a skinned deer's head and a couple of plucked pigeons.

I was determined to keep my cheer, and I had already decided that once I had the parton pies on the fire and the pigeon soup on the boil, I would boldly ask her to tell me which part I was to sing.

Wenzeslaus eyed my arms as I bundled past him down the hall. 'What is she going to make?' There was no one but the two of us in the hall so I answered him myself.

'Parton pies.' I met his stare. He looked confused. 'Crabs. They're very good.' I rattled the bucket. He shrank back against the wall. It was a recipe Mrs Rixon had made for me dozens of times, boiling the little blighters, scraping clean their flesh, mixing it with breadcrumbs, stuffing it back inside them and poking them over the fire until they blistered and smoked. I loved it. The crack and hiss was the best bit and it even made me sweetly sad when I heard it nowadays, for it made me miss my Sunday afternoons with Mrs Rixon.

I was going to make pigeon soup with macaroni, and neat's tongue hash, and I hadn't decided what I could do with the deer's head but I could always fling it in the soup if nothing else, and since I had no skills to turn my hand to posset or pudding making I planned to make poor knights for dessert, which was also one of my favourite things to eat — though I seldom wanted to waste the wine on soaking them if I was paying for it myself, and I never had cream in Jas's lodgings. I was quite excited to play cook.

'You can't feed the Edinburgh Musical Society soup and poor knights, 'Wenzeslaus shrieked. 'And what is this crab nonsense? The house shall smell like burned fish.'

I heard Marie Eliza's voice carrying from the far side of the parlour. 'Why don't you cook then Wennie?' Though she sounded distant, as if she was still concentrating on her score rather than on me, those words cheered me. Wenzeslaus stomped off into the bedroom and I laid down my bucket of partons in the kitchen (covering it with a plate) and went through to the parlour.

Angelica and I had done a tolerable job of sweeping up the worst of the dust and straightening out the throws and the cushions. The divan where Marie Eliza lay was still a disaster, but the spinet looked neat and the light was shining on it nicely. It looked like a clean artisan house, perhaps a minor craftsman's or a shopkeeper's — not as fussy or furnished with goblets and trinkets as the smuggler's had been, but better than the squalor Jas and his university friends lived in. The fire was burning in the hearth for once and we had wiped the soot stains from the panelling so you could see the lovely creamy colour of the paint on the walls.

I watched Marie Eliza for a moment, as I had done from the parlour doorway that first time I visited. There was something magical about watching her compose, just something about the concentration in her face, something I liked to watch. She had strapped Tommy to her back with a piece of strong linen to keep him out of the way while Angelica and I cleaned. He was swatting at her face, pulling her hair and sneaking his fingers into the outer corners of her eyes, trying to get her attention. I could see she was working hard not to be frustrated at him, while at the same time her concentration sought to cut through these distractions.

Her hand would float up above her head, quill still in her fingers, and she would gently take his palm and place it back by his side, then return her pen to the board. Then she'd do it again, and again. All the while she was entranced in some melody she was humming, or singing, testing on her own voice. Sometimes she paused and sang a line over her shoulder to Tommy, and he leaned forward and his putto face swelled into a smile as he enjoyed a fleeting hold on his mother's gaze. Then she'd go back to absently twitching her head out of his grasp, submerged in her own thoughts. It was a strange dance, a strange, incongruous combination of things, the music in her head, the child on her back.

'Marie Eliza,' I said.

She looked up. She was so deep in her opera that it took her a second to return to the room and focus on me. Tommy bounced up and down on her spine and she winced.

I blushed and couldn't find the words — it seemed too audacious to me then to think of asking things for myself, from her of all people, now of all moments. But there may not have been any other moments to ask. I pulled myself together and from somewhere said, 'What part did you have in mind for me, for your opera?'

She continued to stare at me, as if the question had confused her. Tommy probed his tiny thumb into her nostril. She let her breath out sharply and pulled his hand away, vexed.

A lump of panic formed, that perhaps she had forgotten about promising me a part at all. But I was certain all would be well when her memory was jogged so I went on. 'I should like to begin practising, you see,' I said. 'It does not matter if you have not the music written in full. If you play me once the spinet line, I can remember it. You know my memory is perfect for tunes.'

She was silent. Still staring. I feared I had made her uncomfortable. Her breathing sharpened. She bent double. Tommy lurched forward on her back and cried out.

'Marie Eliza.' I crossed to the divan and hooked my hands under Tommy's armpits. I wriggled him out of the linen binding. He was squirming and crying, reaching his hands towards Marie Eliza.

'I need to lie down Izz,' she said, sliding back down onto the divan. She lifted her knees as far as they would reach towards her belly and rolled from side to side. She was gasping for breath and her skin was clammy. I balanced Tommy on my hip. By God he was a strong child, and he whacked me and screamed as he tried to pull away.

'Shall I fetch you some wine?' I raised my voice. I was alarmed for the baby. 'Do you need hot water?'

She rolled some more, clenching her eyes, then she seemed to recover a little.

'Is it coming?' I asked. Tommy calmed down and settled on my hip. When he was quiet I put him down and he toddled towards the spinet and began to fiddle with the legs.

Marie Eliza held her breath for a second, then let it out and shook her head. 'It has passed.' She breathed again. 'I'm fine. I think perhaps the baby did not like something I ate.' She laughed lightly and wiped her brow. 'You are doing such an excellent job of preparing the food. And looking after us—' She glanced at Tommy. 'I don't know what I should do without you. I need to lie in the bed. I need to sleep a while before they all arrive.'

I helped her to her bedroom and into the bed they shared — all of them, save Angelica who slept on the kitchen floor. Wenzeslaus was in there standing at the window, staring down at the close, but at the sight of us he came and helped me heave her into bed. He stroked the damp hair from her brow and asked if she wanted wine. As he left to fetch some from the kitchen, she began muttering about how she was behind on her scores. She should have cast the opera by now. They should have been underway with rehearsals. But the aria she had given to Wenzeslaus for his private student meant she had to write another tune for the scene where the two sisters sing about their lovers.

'Shhhh,' I said, propping her up. 'Don't think of that. Have some rest before the Board arrives.' Wenzeslaus came back with a wineglass of warmish Malaga sack and she took a few sips.

I was terrified that if the Board saw her in this state the rumours would spread that she was indisposed, and it would cast doubt on the opera. The subscribers would pull out. The Playhouse would insist it was cancelled.

Wenzeslaus did not share my fear. 'See what happens my love, when you think too hard?' he said, continuing to stroke her hair. 'It is bad for the baby, all this composing. My angel, look at you, my poor angel. You are feverish. It is doing you harm. Why don't you forget all about it, at least for a short time.'

On and on he soothed her, leaning over her, until I felt a discomfort at their intimacy, the way I had done at the Comely Gardens masquerade. There was something eerie about it; too bright, too enthusiastic, almost sickly. It was the way he touched her, clutched her shoulder. The way she leaned on him. The pitch of both their voices. Did they love each other? Or did they love *something* about the other? And was that thing the same thing that had drawn them together in the first place? I never felt uncomfortable spying on her with Guadagni in this way; only with Wenzeslaus.

He sat on the bed and held her hand. 'Why don't I tell them you are indisposed? That I must let you sleep on.'

She shook her head stubbornly.

'I think some rest is all you need,' I said. 'I will take care of everything. Give your mind a chance to lie still and empty. Do not worry. You will be fit by the time they arrive.'

I could feel Wenzeslaus glaring at me. I would not meet his eye.

I settled her among her cushions and went back into the kitchen and began heating water to boil the crabs. I clattered around with their copper pans and fish kettles and china bowls. I fed the fire with coal.

As I worked, I could not keep my mind from straying to thoughts of her opera. There were three parts in the opera for women — the two sisters and the bone-collecting girl, Beggar Jeannie — and they were all substantial, and would take practice to perfect, even for a proficient singer such as myself. I fancied the part of the younger sister, for though she died halfway through, her resurrection was the most dramatic moment in the piece. I had seen the machinery the sailor men had rigged to fly actors and actresses down onto the stage from on high, or to lift their souls up on crescent moons or clouds, and I wondered if this was what they would use to fly the ghost of the younger sister onto the stage at the moment she returns to accuse the older one. I fancied her costume would be gossamer and had seen some beautiful skirts and pastel-coloured stockings in the green room that I had my eye on. I was excited that there would be a pony in the pageant, for I had never seen a pony on the stage before and the idea seemed very dazzling to me.

Even if I was given the part of Beggar Jeannie — the least prominent in some ways — there would still be much to enjoy; in the simplicity of her song, her gestures, the lugging of the swan's body from the trapdoor. What on earth would they use for the swan? Would they have to kill and stuff one? I wanted to know all of this. I wanted to begin rehearsing so I could live out the next act of my life.

I helped myself to a glass from the Malaga sack barrel, and it gave me an idea. I went back to check on Marie Eliza. She had fallen asleep and was moaning lightly between snores. Wenzeslaus had retreated into the parlour; I could hear him pacing, nervously rearranging the plate and glassware.

I propped Marie Eliza up on her pillows, and whispered to her that I would take care of the Board, that they wouldn't notice she was even slightly off colour, that all would be well. I went back into the kitchen.

Into my cauldron of skinned deer head, neat's tongue and pigeon, I poured half a barrel of sack.

4

I STAYED IN THE KITCHEN as they arrived. I heard the tempered tread of their footsteps on the hall floorboards. Four men. Backs were slapped. Greetings given. Questions posed. A little rabble of competing jollity. Wenzeslaus's voice rang out, too joyous, too strained, as he ushered them one by one into the parlour.

Then I heard her gay laugh; like a waterfall. She had emerged from the bedroom and she was chattering away, her voice rising and dipping, gushing and accepting compliments with grace.

I ferried dishes back and forth from the kitchen to the parlour, while Angelica sat before the hearth and played with Tommy. Wenzeslaus brought out a clarinet for him to blow on and he puffed and screeched and held it and banged the table legs and they all chuckled and leaned down and ruffled his hair and said 'what a celestial sound' and 'what a little maestro', before Marie Eliza discreetly took it away from him again.

The parton pies all disappeared and the spiked soup was sinking down a treat. I almost dished out the whole pot when I refilled the tureen for the second time.

Midway into the dinner I could hear them from the kitchen, begin to burp and slur their words.

Marie Eliza came shuffling through. She wore no slippers and her stockings made a silky hissing — a breeze in the bulrushes — as they grazed the flagstones. She had a fine lace fichu around her shoulders that I had never seen her wear before, and she had styled her hair on top of her head. I could see smears of rouge on her cheeks and smudging her lips. 'Izz, they have agreed to sign our retainer for another year. Oh I could kiss you. I couldn't have done any of this without you.'

She embraced me tightly, the bulge of her belly pushing me backwards. She carried a glass of wine in her hand. Some of it splashed cold into my hair. As I pulled away from her, I thought that perhaps now I had her attention I could ask her again about the opera. I took her hands. 'Say nothing of it. It was my pleasure. But tell me, what part is it you want me to sing in the opera? I have been driven mad imagining.'

She sank the rest of her wine and her cheeks blazed. Her smile was full and she looked happy and rested. 'Oh, it is the perfect one for you Izz.'

'Which? Tell me, which? Is it the younger sister, or the bone-collecting girl, Beggar Jeannie? I fancied I was not old enough for Evelina, the murderous one, and that perhaps you wanted to sing that role for yourself, for it calls for such control, such tempering of mood, such power beneath the sweetness, which of course you have in you.' Such craven words I used.

At that moment the kitchen door flung back, crashing against the whitewashed wall, and a burly man came stumbling towards the hearth. I remember he had a tiny lick of custard from the poor knights staining his ruffle, which my eyes could not help but fix on.

Marie Eliza flung out her arms to stop him from tripping into the hot black iron door of the oven. 'Oh, Mr Ogilvie.' She steered him back. 'How on earth did you lose your way? This is the kitchen, don't you know. It is no place for a gentleman.'

Mr Ogilvie had a ruddy, drunken look about him, spiked tufts of iron-grey hair creeping out from under his periwig, big hearty lips that looked as if they were used to the whisky glass. He waddled a few steps towards Marie Eliza, his silk shoes skidding on the flagstones. She dodged him deftly. 'Is it more wine you wish for? Or punch? There is some in the parlour I believe.'

'It's a fine thing for a woman to have penned an opera, don't you think?' He reached out his arm and clutched her about her waist. I could do nothing, though I saw her eyes widen. 'Deil fine,' he said. 'You're a talented lass, aren't you?'

'My husband has good faith in me,' Marie Eliza murmured. 'He values my compositions.'

'Your husband is a lucky man,' he said.

'And I think if you wish he will play for you this afternoon. If he hasn't drunk too much sack.' I heard her light laugh again. She succeeded in squeezing herself free from Mr Ogilvie's grip. But he placed a hand against the wall, blocking her exit from the kitchen. I don't suppose it mattered to him that I was there, if he noticed me at all.

'I was fancying,' he slurred, 'what would make the occasion of your opera even more of a celebration, would be to have a *ridotto* before the opening night. You know, a masquerade? Make a ball of it.' He leaned closer. 'Let's do it how the Venetians do it, shall we? Don't you think?'

Marie Eliza smiled and looked down at her glass. 'I could wish for nothing so extravagant.'

'Why not?' Mr Ogilvie threw up his arms. 'It *is* a strange fancy for a woman to have written a whole opera. It is. But for that we must celebrate. Let us celebrate with a carnival.' He dropped his voice and leaned close to her again, his whisper loud but conspiratorial. 'You know I have given a great sum towards its subscription.' He stood up again. 'Here in Auld Reekie we are progressive people and we value the contribution a woman can make to discourse and culture.' As he said it, I saw his fingers drift almost absently close to the perfumed curls at the back of her neck.

I had a flash memory of her then, howling on the floor of the Canongate Playhouse dressing room. And I understood the intention of his call for a masquerade. Blackened, lamplit Edinburgh closes. Great cloaks concealing forms. Masks hiding faces.

At that moment a man who had lost his justacorps and wig, with shirtsleeves rolled up to the elbows and great bushels of hair at his ears, poked his head around the door jamb, knocking Mr Ogilvie off balance and making him stand up straight again. 'Did I hear mention of a *ridotto*?' he said. 'A fine idea.' He wedged his way into the cramped kitchen. 'Yes, let us all dress up, not only the players. We shall be masked and birl the nicht awa.' He jigged forwards and tried to embrace Marie Eliza, but Wenzeslaus had, by now, also squeezed his way into the kitchen, behind the wigless man, and now he coldly retrieved his wife's pregnant body from the wealthy patrons' clutches. My question to Marie Eliza was forgotten.

'Wennie,' she said, pointedly. 'The Musical Society are most excited about my opera and they are talking of a *ridotto*, isn't that a marvel?' I saw in her eyes then not the panic of the victim but the gleam of the opportunist. She could handle her way around these men, and even knew at times how to play her husband, and I could not help but feel a stab of admiration. 'They want to make it a huge occasion, because it *is* a huge occasion, isn't it? Mr Ogilvie himself has donated generously to the subscriber fund.'

I saw Wenzeslaus's glare flash on Mr Ogilvie. The board member, drunk as he was, for a second looked cowed by the secret he had shared with Marie Eliza, which she had just gaily betrayed. I didn't know then whether he had been truthful or not about his contribution at the time, but he was certain to have to dig into his pockets now. 'And while we are on the subject,' she went on, 'we must have a horse for the opera, must we not? I saw one once on the London stage and it is so majestic to see a horse with a rider on it, singing their heart away.'

'My love,' Wenzeslaus started to say. 'We have discussed the horse. It is not practical.'

'Oh there must be a horse,' Mr Ogilvie cried. 'Yes, give her a horse!'

'Oh she shall have a horse.' The wigless man joined in with the vulgar joke. They laughed and clutched each other's arms, and I had to steer the wigless man away from the soup pot, as he began unbuttoning himself.

Behind them both, Wenzeslaus stood watching their capering in his cramped, meagre kitchen, his arms folded, his legs slightly apart that way he stood, proud. He turned his gaze on me and narrowed his eyes as if this were all my doing.

I decided to seize the opportunity. 'And tell me now, friend,' I cried loudly at Marie Eliza, 'which part I am to sing in your opera.'

The laughing men fell silent.

'Is it the younger sister,' I went on, 'Cassandra, or Beggar Jeannie? I like that one very much, in fact she is very like me, I can see from when I copied out your libretto. I can stand the suspense no longer, tell me.'

Marie Eliza's face clouded. She saw the questioning looks of the men. 'Oh, this is Isobel Duguid. Yes, she is also a singer ...' Her voice trailed off. Mr Ogilvie glanced at his friend, then gave me a hesitant bow, half-facetious, half-curious. I wondered if he was trying to place me. I was sure to have seen him passing by Parliament Close.

'But—' Marie Eliza took my hand. 'Oh Izz, no not the sisters, no nor Beggar Jeannie.' She smiled fondly. 'It was the part of the Hag — I mean the Ballad Singer — that I had in mind for you.'

I felt dizzy.

I became suddenly aware of the silence in the tiny kitchen.

'You know,' she went on, filling the discomfort with her gaiety, 'the Ballad Singer, with the baby in her arms, who rattles the garden gates and drops the broadside, then she steals the Master's gold chain and runs away. It is a marvellous part, so very important for the story.' She gabbled away about it, in exactly the way she had that time before, where I had thought she had been inviting me to sing at the Playhouse. I felt my heart shrinking again.

'I think you will do a wonderful job of it,' she cried. 'I can't think of anyone more perfect for the role. It will be so authentic to have a real ballad singer playing the Ballad Singer. And how exciting to have your debut upon the Canongate stage. How many orange sellers can say that they have sung, not in the pit, but on the boards? Are you delighted, Izz? I know we will have such fun. Will you say yes?'

5

A T THAT MOMENT, CECILIA, I wanted to upturn the remnants of the boiling soup pot onto your mother's feet.

The *Ballad Singer. 'Hag of Song.'*

I was too ashamed to show my rage.

I feigned delight. 'It is perfect, yes. I could have wished for no more.'

At my enthusiasm, the tension in the kitchen cracked and the two Musical Society board members beamed at me and chuckled to each other. 'You will do very well, I'm sure,' Mr Ogilvie said, nodding.

'You will be splendid.' Marie Eliza gripped my hand. 'You have the coarse voice already. I cannot wait. You could practise now. Sing it to me, she has a line you know. It's a very important one. She sings, "My eyesight is poor, some gold would help me see." Sing it.'

I looked at the two men beside us, still beaming and watching. 'I couldn't.'

'Don't be shy. Remember the loch.' Her eyes were bright, expectant.

With reluctance, I sang the line.

'Louder Izz, you can do it.'

'But—' I gestured to the two men.

'Forget about them. They are drunk. Just sing.'

I don't think they heard her. They didn't flinch. Wenzeslaus had a ghastly look of scorn on his face. My eyes on the bubbling soup pot, I bellowed, the words catching like thorns in my throat. 'My eyesight is poor, some gold would help me see.'

Marie Eliza clapped and squealed as if I were a fool at a fair. 'I cannot wait to share you with Guadagni and the rest of the cast.'

She ran, skipping from the room, her belly all of a sudden light as a silk balloon. When she returned, she had the remaining two members of the Musical Society Board, one in each palm. Bemused, their cheeks scarlet and shiny, their coats and waist-coats unbuttoned, shooting glances at one another, they all crammed into the hot, tiny kitchen. Marie Eliza directed me with her eyes and stood back.

I sang softly, 'My eyesight is poor, some gold would help me see.'

'No, Izz, like you did a minute ago. Loud, raw, with feeling!'

I sang. I had nothing to lose. My dignity was bubbling away to slime with the soup. 'My eyesight is poor, some gold would help me see!'

She made me caw that line again and again, and again, until her mirth was slaked so hard I thought she might give birth on the hearthstone.

'My opera,' she said gaily, over and over to the board members. 'She will be in my opera.'

6

I SHALL SAY I DID REGRET pouring all that sack into the soup. The vomiting of the Board of the Edinburgh Musical Society began soon after that, into tureens and chamber pots and whatever was to hand. Chairs were called for, and they were sent swaying down the turnpike, singing snippets of old airs and arias that clashed with each other. I heaved another pot of watery puke over to the sash and flung it out, crying 'Gardyloo' into the close.

Marie Eliza, perspiring, ruddy, brim-full of joy, came waddling back into the kitchen. She stood against the door jamb. Neither of us saw her husband approach until he was right behind her. She flinched as his face appeared over her shoulder. 'My love,' he whispered. 'Must there be a *ridotto*? It is going to be difficult enough to put on an opera of that size, on that stage, with all the costumes and mechanics you wish to use, and with the kirk men watching. You know they hate masquerades even more than plays and operas. They're not going to tolerate drunk people running up and down the Canongate in masks.'

She flinched from his grasp. 'Mr Ogilvie suggested it.' She smiled. 'You said yourself he's the treasurer. He pays the bills. He has subscribed privately to the opera, and we must please him. If a *ridotto* is what the Board and the subscribers desire, then they must have one.'

'But how will it work? Are the orchestra to be masked too? I can't play violin in a mask. And the players?'

I pretended to concentrate on sloshing out the plates that had been brought back to the kitchen for washing. The water in the bucket at my feet was fetid and my hands were coated in a thin film of cold grease.

She considered this. 'Perhaps they can take their masks off to play. But they must be in their costumes. Oh it will be so joyous, and such an occasion. And you must let the board members worry about the kirk. I don't intend to trouble myself with it.' She picked up a half empty glass, sniffed it and sank it. 'All we must think of is making the opera as great a success as can be. Perhaps if it is *such* a success, we could think even of — a season in London? Or Bath? Or Venice?'

I couldn't help but think of her letter to Guadagni. *I will arrange passage from Leith. After that night, we will live as one.* Was she still considering running away with him? Or had the conversation with the Musical Society Board changed all that? Or was it possible that she held the two different paths in her head at the same time, even believing in some strange realm that she could tread down both of them?

'You have drunk too much wine my love,' Wenzeslaus said.
'I have not.'

'Yes you have, I saw you with the Malaga sack. And just now, you finished off that glass.'

'Never you mind that glass. I am parched with thirst. This entertaining is extremely drying on my throat and the fire is lit and—'

Their argument faded as they moved off together into the parlour. Angelica came into the kitchen with Tommy. His arms were laden down with yew branches. I deftly bargained them away from him for scraps of a poor knight, before he had the chance to suck on the poisonous berries. I had no idea where he had got them from.

I was tired of the Herzes, and it was hot in their kitchen. But Angelica had disappeared into the bedroom and Tommy had been left next to the open fire on the range, so I coaxed him into my arms and took him to the parlour.

They were both sitting in silence; her on the divan, him on the spinet stool. Wenzeslaus saw me and gestured for his wife to get up from her couch to fetch the child from me. I could see from his face that whatever had passed between them had made him even more unhappy than he had been in the kitchen. Marie Eliza heaved herself up and took Tommy, but as she wrestled him from my hip to hers, his leg swinging over her full belly, she whispered, 'Wait by the door,' in my ear.

I nodded, gathered my shawl from the kitchen and padded down the hallway. I waited, listening to their voices snap quietly at each other. She appeared after a minute, fumbling in her pocket. She snatched a glance at the open parlour door before pulling out a letter. 'Please,' she said.

I pushed the letter away. 'You need to think of your opera. Finish it before you see him again.'

'Just once. Please. I'll die if I don't see him.'

I'll die if I don't . . .

She had said that once, about me, too.

'You can see him at rehearsals.'

'Not like this,' she whispered. Her voice was strained. She reached into her pocket and pulled out a bawbee. Her eyes were plaintive. She closed my hand around the coin.

I could have said to her then, 'Look to your children.' I could have said, 'Madam, is it not enough that you have a husband, an opera, a child, a pregnancy, but that you need a lover as well?' I could have said, 'Madam, you are a serpent and your appetite is too much. If you keep craving to swallow life at this rate you will one of these days eat something you love.' Would it have made you look more favourably on me, Cecilia, if I had said those things? Am I the judge of your mother? I am not. Should I be?

The truth is Cecilia, I really can't remember whether I cared about you in that instance or just about Marie Eliza's engulfing appetite for everything, and how irritated it made me. I cannot separate my own objective morals from being prejudiced by those very personal vexations, and so I shall not try. I shall only say that I did nothing. I took the letter.

Feeling sick with myself — for the way the afternoon had ended, for taking the coin, for the grubbiness of the whole situation — I pocketed both letter and coin without another word.

7

THEY GREW CARELESS, that was the trouble.

There was one night when I was passing down World's End Close and I tell you I heard them. They had scaled the wall of the Marquess of Tweedale's garden and they were in his apple orchard, pressed against the trees. She was a vigorous, passionate soprano, and if the Marquess of Tweedale himself wasn't listening in, sating his own lust on the freely given song of her ecstasy, then he was a fool who missed a trick.

They had become brazen in public too, touching each other in the street, teasingly, outside the Playhouse after a rehearsal, or as they walked up the Netherbow towards Fountain Close. She would tenderly wipe a smear of paint from his cheekbone or pluck a powdered curl free from his wig; he would clutch her waist, lightly nip the top of her arm. I'm telling you the truth, Cecilia. People were beginning to talk. At the fountain, at the draper's, at Parliament Close. Even Jas's friends knew about the 'hoor and the capon'. I believe they both thought the guise of his freakishness and her pregnancy was enough of a bluff to a society that never would have credited it possible one be attracted to the other.

Was it that, after all, which drew them together? Was it simply that he could tup her all night and never get her with child, or was it that she saw a sadness in him as there was in her – they were both locked by their bodies, confined, destined to do only that thing that was carved into the destiny of their flesh? Was there kinship there then, that their thoughts, their minds, their ideas were seldom listened to, because no matter what they sang or played or created, the men of the town would always look at them through the frame of their bodies?

I have felt that way too.

One night, around about seven or eight o'clock, after the Friday concert at St Cecilia's had disgorged its patrons into the Cowgate, I came upon them, clasped in some intimate conspiracy behind an old bread cart, from which a woman with a child huddled in the folds of her skirt was selling burnt scraps.

I was not following them, of course. But they were only spitting distance from the entrance to Jas's lodgings, so it was impossible not to notice them when I had my key in the turnpike lock. She froze when she caught my eye. She had the good grace to look sheepish, to see to her dark cotton skirts. Her back was against the wall, the bread cart standing between them and the main street, barely concealing her from the waist up. Her legs were spread wide, she was slouching slightly, the belly protruding. He had an awkward grin on his painted face. I murmured a greeting and continued unlocking my door.

Then I noticed from afar Wenzeslaus approaching. He was roving down the main street, with his arm hooked around a young man's neck, in a brotherly fashion. This fellow I recognised as one of Jas's scholar friends. They were deep in conversation, Wenzeslaus gesticulating to make his point with his free hand.

Before I had the chance to even turn back to her they stopped and fell silent, and I saw that Wenzeslaus had glanced up the lane and seen Guadagni and Marie Eliza. There was an agonising pause as everyone stared through the stinking gloom at one another — the scholar fellow at me, Marie Eliza at Wenzeslaus, Guadagni and Wenzeslaus at each other — as if we were in some slow and sulphurous underworld.

She dropped Guadagni's hand. Time slowed further, at the sound of their warm skin separating, peeling apart from each other, the small suck and hiss of their clothes detaching from their entanglement.

Wenzeslaus knew.

I can summon those sounds again, agile in my mind now. I can conjure up all the noises of Horse Wynd that night. Jem Barbary's fighting cocks screeching in their baskets in the basement behind us, the bread-woman's child crunching open-mouthed on a crust, the stones and straw under our slithering feet.

Wenzeslaus stepped forward with his palms open and seized Guadagni by the lapels of his coat. He glared into his eyes. My breath stopped.

He pulled Guadagni into an embrace. 'My good man! Chaperoning Marie Eliza through the Cowgate.' He thumped Guadagni's back.

'I was hungry Wenzeslaus,' Marie Eliza said flatly. 'I was craving bread. The smell was too rich for me to ignore.'

Wenzeslaus still had Guadagni's palm gripped in his. It was like a horrid mirror of the brotherly embrace he had given to the student. His other hand was on the castrato's burly shoulder. He was not letting go. But he was staring past him, at his wife. She was holding onto the wall for support.

'You were hungry?' He paused. 'My poor darling,' he said, nodding towards the woman selling burnt and mouldy crusts. 'I must buy you one.'

I heard her swallow.

'I am sated now, Wenzeslaus. It was a passing fancy.'

'Nonsense. My wife will have what she desires. It is always the way, isn't it?' He dropped Guadagni's hand and laughed.

The student laughed too, but catching his eye, I could see he could make neither head nor tail of this exchange.

Wenzeslaus strode over to the old woman's cart. He selected the foulest, most blackened crust he could see. Its edges were scalloped with ash and there were pock marks missing from where it had fallen in the muck, and been picked clean. 'I think this piece should do you,' he said. 'Mind and eat it all. I would not want you to feel faint on your journey up the hill. In your condition.'

'Perhaps,' I said, 'you should accompany your wife back home instead of attending to the cockfights. I believe that is where you were headed.' I looked again at the student and back at Jem Barbary's basement.

Wenzeslaus barrelled towards me like a musket ball, his finger pointing. 'You. Hold your tongue.' He was a terrifying man when he was angry. I could see the tremble in his jaw, the whites of his eyes, the force of his stare. His whole body was braced for violence. I recalled our first encounter: him striding up the stairs of the theatre, his violin scroll stabbing me in the kidneys.

He turned from me now, threw his bodle at the bread woman and picked up the rancid piece of dough from her tray, then came at Marie Eliza with it. It was long and thin and deformed.

'Here is your crust, that you craved,' he said. 'I would watch you eat it all.'

'Wenzeslaus—' Guadagni protested.

'Perhaps if you do not, you shall be too sick to compose the rest of your opera, and it will have to be shut down.'

'It is composed,' she spat. 'If it were not for the aria I had to give you last week—'

'Eat the bread!' he roared.

Guadagni took a step towards him. Guadagni was a larger man by six inches, breadth and height, but he did not have Wenzeslaus's viciousness, and he also knew his place against the Playhouse Musical Director (though not so much as to have left his wife alone). He looked from Marie Eliza to me to Wenzeslaus, to the student, who was affecting now not to notice the spectacle.

Marie Eliza nibbled gently on the crust. I watched her crunch and swallow. She began retching. I could not bear it.

'Let me take some.'

'You would take the food from my pregnant wife's mouth?' He pointed at me. 'No. She eats it.'

On that night I saw the determination, the iron will, of Marie Eliza. I could not have swallowed that fetid crust, but she took it all, piece by piece, and she held her husband's gaze as she did it. That was how much she wanted her opera.

'Will you walk me home then Wenzeslaus?' she asked. 'Or did you have something else to attend to? Some urgent gambling away of our household fortunes to amuse you?'

He cast his eye briefly over his shoulder towards the mouth of the Cowgate. Then back to her, and then to the glowing entrance to the cockfighting den at the side of the close. 'The capon will walk you home,' he said. And he disappeared inside.

8

'I HAVE A BAD FOREBODING, ISOBEL,' she said.

We were in the theatre. It was the middle of the afternoon and a few members of the orchestra had been rehearsing with the singers, while the old sailors from Leith hacked bits of wood into scenery. They had built a mechanical puppet swan — not a very good one but pasted in papier mâché and real goose feathers — that could be moved about between the floorboards by someone standing in the bowels below the stage. They had painted linen curtains with tall grey stones and fashioned the castle rock from a tower of chimney pots covered over with slate sheets. Now the seamstresses were poking pins into the waists and rear ends of sopranos; the pit benches were a mess of strewn coats and wigs, bits of lace and pannier frames. I loved those afternoon rehearsals. I loved the sound of Guadagni's voice practising in an empty theatre (he was to play the Master in the opera), soaring through the wood. I loved seeing the fragile mechanics of the opera knotted and hooked together. I loved it all.

Marie Eliza was struggling to walk now, her bump was so large. More than one singer and musician had told her that day that she should not be at the rehearsal, that she should be lying in, which she took in good grace, but which I knew was a thought she would never entertain.

'He is plotting something. I know he is. He is calm in the house now, but he barely speaks to me, even over the breakfast table.'

'Hold your nerve,' I said.

She breathed out. 'I don't know. I don't know.'

'What don't you know?'

'The last thing I want to do is tempt his anger.'

I swallowed, thinking of the crust of blackened bread.

After the musicians had packed their instruments back into their velvet-lined cases, and the scene painters had moved everyone off the stage so they could begin turning Newgate Prison from *The Beggar's Opera* into the Nor Loch backdrop, she sat down on a bench in the middle of the pit, wheezing hard. I fetched her a glass of small beer from the box office and watched her gulp it.

The sight of her swan throat that afternoon, tilted up towards the theatre Gods, the gulping noise she made as the beer slipped down, sticks in my mind. She finished her drink and gasped. Gazing at the outline of the loch, as it was emerging under the draughtsman's paintbrush, the blue depths of the dye, in circles and ripples, darkening to an ominous watery slate in the centre, she said laconically, 'There is one way of dealing with it all, is there not? One way ...'

I said nothing. Though I'll own now what I knew then: the thought had crossed her mind to murder her husband.

9

THEY CANNOT PUNISH US for our thoughts, for our plans, for our knowledge, can they? Our own consciences have to do that job in the end. It didn't matter then, if that was what she intended, if that was what she was thinking.

But you also know that what your mother planned was not what occurred. Let me tell therefore, what happened on the opening night of her opera.

Mr Ogilvie and the board members who had been at the soirée did not forget their promise. Mr Ogilvie gave a generous subscription and sponsored the *ridotto* for Marie Eliza's opening night. The costume chests were stripped bare. Masks were fashioned from papier mâché, peacock feathers and scraps of hide. Ices were brought in, coloured sherbets, pastel blue, green and pink, crisp snowflakes melting in the heat of the theatre. Bowls of punch were ferried across from the Maut Ha.

My old orange seller friends were all there for the first opera of the season, all with their baskets piled high, their faces powdered, their paps crammed into corsets, freckled from the summer, fat from the food their lovers had gifted them, wearing masks of dyed linen and velvet with feathers and shells pasted to the temples.

It was late in the afternoon. The dress rehearsal was in its final stages, but we had stalled in the middle of the last act as Marie Eliza had been called to deal with the pony, which was shitting indiscriminately all over the wings.

I was loitering at the side of the orchestra pit when Jeanie approached me. She put her basket down and planted her elbows on the stage.

I embraced her. I felt conscious of my rags and shredded skirts, as if she might have taken my fortunes to have fallen. 'It's my costume,' I said. 'I am in the opera.'

'I know.'

'I am the Ballad Singer.'

'I know. It's perfect for you. I'm sure you will do a fine job.'

I didn't know how to take that. 'Thank you.'

'Izz,' she said. She drew me close, speaking so low that I had to press my ear to her lips to hear over the sound of the orchestra practising. 'Do you know Evelyn? She is sweethearts with one of the chairmen who stand at the fountain in Parliament Close.'

I shook my head.

'The big chairman. Muckle Paws. She's a flower seller. You might not know her. It doesn't matter. But her Muckle Paws told her that they are going to burn down the theatre tonight.'

I felt my body chill. 'That's ridiculous. Who is going to burn down the theatre?'

'Keep it to yourself Izz, I'll be skinned for soup if I'm wrong.'

'If you think you are wrong, then hold your tongue.' I could not help but feel this was Wenzeslaus's latest, last-ditch scheme, to put about rumours in the hope of cancelling the opera.

Jeanie's face was pinched. 'I am not mistaken. The chairmen know everything that passes in the city.'

'Then they should know who is starting this rumour.'

'It is not a rumour. There is a mob of men, kirk men, lay preachers, zealots, ministers and more. They say a woman should not have written an opera. That it is unnatural. That it is worse than devil worship.'

'Devil worship!'

She widened her eyes. 'I am only passing onto you what I heard. But Izz, be careful. Be sure and stay close to the doors tonight. I cannot afford not to come, but if you can, then perhaps you should not—'

'Of course I'll be here.' I had no intention of deserting my debut on the Canongate stage. 'Who has started this gossip?' I demanded.

'I don't know. But you would be best to make sure you are not caught up in it.'

I studied Jeanie's face, the harrowed lines, the wide, hazel, staring eyes. She was earnest. It did not make sense to me though. The kirk men had had all summer to torch the theatre, if they had wanted to stop it from opening again. It was common knowledge that the opera was to open the season. There had been playbills slapped all over the city. Why would they wait until her opening night?

Unless it was spectacle they wanted. Something to set an example, like the burning of witches.

Something in my gut sat ill.

I wanted to press Jeanie more, but Marie Eliza emerged at that moment, a little unsteady on her feet and with the sweet, faint scent of horse and hay on her. Jeanie, seeing her, dropped the faintest of curtseys — which riled me for some reason — then withdrew into the pit and began arranging the oranges in her basket.

I didn't trust my mouth not to blurt out what I had heard. 'Are you well, Marie?'

She dropped her voice. 'I have said to call me *Maestra* in the theatre, have I not?' she said briskly.

'I'm sorry, I forgot.'

'No, I'm sorry Izz, it's just — for the singers. To set an example. It is hard enough without feeling that they don't respect me. I cannot help but feel illness in the air.' Her gaze flickered around. 'Wenzeslaus has not arrived yet.'

'He will be here.'

'I have an ill feeling, Izz.'

I bit my tongue. 'What good would sabotage do him? He is leader of the Playhouse orchestra. His retainer, his contract depends on this too.' My head was dizzy and I did not know what to say.

'Then he will do something rotten, I just know it. He will appear in some humiliating costume. He will steal the show. He will do something. I know it.' She muttered darkly to herself and flicked at a strand of hay on her gown.

I dwelled on Jeanie's words but kept my mouth shut.

At that moment, as if conjured by her fear, a man in a black woollen habit with the hooked beak of a foul clenger mask obscuring his whole face, strode up to us. The nose of his mask was stuffed, and he carried a pungent odour of herbal poison. I started. Marie Eliza yelped as if death had crossed her path.

The man removed the mask. It was Wenzeslaus.

She stared at him, stricken. 'What do you mean to do, frightening me so?'

'It is my costume. For the *ridotto.*'

'For God's sake, Wenzeslaus.'

'You said the musicians were to be masked unless they were playing.' He feigned innocence.

'You could have chosen something less ghoulish,' she replied. 'A plague mask.'

'It's a Venetian classic. *Il Medico de la Peste.*'

'Looks like a foul clenger to me,' I said. He glared at me. I made to leave but Marie Eliza grasped my arm.

'We must rehearse the third act again. That pony, Wenzeslaus — where did you get him from? He has never been near a rider it seems, let alone a stage, in his life.'

Her husband shrugged. 'The riding school on the Pleasance.'

He replaced his grotesque mask and began taking out his violin, making a racket tuning it, digging his bow into the strings, scraping awful sounds from it.

She put her hand on her stomach and tried to conceal her wincing. She began to walk away.

'She will have that baby on the stage,' her husband muttered. 'If no one stops her.'

I do not know whether he intended for me to hear. Certainly when he caught me staring at him, he went back to sawing the strings of his violin.

I made my decision.

I caught up to her as she was instructing the singer who was to play Beggar Jeannie. 'Maestra, I must have a word.'

'Not now, Izz.'

'It is urgent.'

She looked aghast to have heard me spoken so, but let me pull her aside.

I kept my voice low and held her eye. 'There is a riot planned. One of the orange sellers told me. Some men — kirk men — are bent on burning down the theatre.'

'Tonight?' Her voice was a wisp.

I nodded.

'But why?'

I didn't answer. I think she didn't need me to. 'Who told you?' All of a sudden she could barely breathe. She reached out and clung hold of one of the scenery braces. I could see the thoughts travel through her, from her head through her body, draining the blood from her face with them.

'Jeanie,' I said. 'She's trustworthy. She heard it from one of the girls who had it from a chairman.'

Marie Eliza swayed and closed her eyes. She looked over at the orchestra pit. 'I know how this has come about.'

'You cannot halt the opera,' I said. 'You must not.'

At that her spine straightened. The burden of her baby became, like it had been that afternoon of the soirée, light as a cloud. She drifted away from me in something like a fever or a stupor. But even at that time I was thinking: *she looks like a bear about to strike.*

10

SHE EXCUSED HERSELF from the rehearsal, instructing Guadagni and the insipid Miss McGregor (the Younger Sister), to finish the third act themselves. She instructed Miss McGregor's mother (Mrs McGregor, the singing teacher) to step in and fill the part of the Older Sister, which was to be taken during the performance by Marie Eliza herself.

I hurried at her heels, following her across the stage as she snatched up her belongings; her score, her purse, her cloak.

'Where are you going?'

She didn't answer. I saw her look across at the orchestra pit again. Wenzeslaus had disappeared, leaving his violin lying on his chair. Her gaze roamed the theatre, searching for him. She climbed the barrier, one hand under her bump, the other rucking up her stiff skirts, took his violin and thrust it into my hands. Then she climbed back over, grabbed it from me and concealed it under her cloak.

'If he doesn't want there to be an opera, then he doesn't have to play in it,' she said.

'What about a first fiddler?'

'They will make do.'

'You cannot be certain it is he—'

She did not answer that. I scurried after her and followed her unsteady, lopsided, bump-heavy march, all the way out of the theatre, up the Netherbow, back to Fountain Close.

At the top of the turnpike she was short of breath and held onto the door jamb. I ran ahead into the tenement and fetched her the only liquid I could find, some dregs of creamy slime at the bottom of the porridge pot, which I decanted into a cup. She drank them gratefully. 'He will have to come for his violin. He will have to,' she said. 'And when he does, I will talk to him. That is all.'

In the parlour, Angelica was playing on the rug with Tommy. They had a pile of sticks they were arranging into a little house. Angelica would smile and blow it down while Tommy cried and then she would build it again, soothing him, and he would clap.

He came scurrying over to Marie Eliza and clutched her legs. She closed her eyes. With some effort she bent down and wrapped her arms around him, squashed her belly into him, put her shaking fingers into his curls and held on tight.

She held him close for a moment. 'Angelica,' she said quietly.

The girl rose and took him from his mother. With Tommy fussing in her arms, they left the room.

She fell back onto the divan, that I had seen her fall onto so many times. The violin slipped from under her cloak and her hand whipped forward to stop it from crashing to the floor. She gripped it with a shaking hand, her fingers circling the neck as if she would throttle it.

I stood at the window and watched the comings and goings past the mouth of Fountain Close. Her thoughts seemed so loud I could hear them ringing, chattering corbies in the eaves, with the one recurring refrain: *stop him stop him stop him.*

There was movement at the close's mouth. A cloak. Two dark legs. It could have been anyone at that distance.

I saw the leather beak of the mask come into view and I knew. 'He is coming,' I said.

She lurched forward, still gripping the violin neck. She heaved herself up off the couch and moved to the window.

'He is going past,' I said. 'He is heading to Parliament Close.'

'Or the castle,' she said. 'Where the soldiers are.'

As she rushed out of the door, the violin scraped the frame, leaving splinters spiking from its raw side.

11

I RAN AFTER HER. By the time I had traced her stride as far as Carrubber's Close it was too late.

He was lying against the wall. She had the violin held aloft. She had been beating him with it. The blood-streaked scroll was dripping and she was poised for another blow.

The body moaned. Her raised hand stopped in its tracks.

A chill crawled up my neck, and Marie Eliza froze, then began to shake.

He moaned again. The pitch of the moan.

She screamed. And all I could do was clutch her with one hand and smother her mouth with the other, for I did not want her cries to bring the Town Guard running. She had done it. She had done it, and it was done, and there was nothing more we could do, but screaming would not bring him back.

When she was quiet I crept forward and removed the beaten leather beak mask from the slumped man's face.

He had blood seeping from his eyes and smearing his cheeks. He was bruised and purple, but there was not enough blood to disguise the fact that instead of her husband, Marie Eliza had bludgeoned Guido Guadagni.

12

'Y ou need to come now,' I hissed. 'Drop the violin. Leave it here.'

It was still daylight, an early autumn evening, close of business time, and the Netherbow could not have been busier. Passing by the mouth of Carrubber's Close were wagons, crowds of apprentices, servants collecting groceries for suppers, people heading to the concert or to the ticket booth of the opera house, or to the taverns. We could have been seen at any moment.

She was gurgling and gasping.

'You need to get to the theatre before Wenzeslaus does,' I said. 'Tell them to close the doors, don't let anyone with him in.'

We looked at each other, and though neither of us spoke the words aloud, we both knew there was a simple solution to stop her from being hanged. *Blame Wenzeslaus.*

'You have to pretend you know nothing of what happened here. You must arrive at the theatre and the opera must go ahead.'

'Who is going to sing Guido's role?' She was shaking. 'I have no understudy.' That was what was on her broken mind.

'Sing it yourself. Feign confusion when he does not appear. Then take his part. I will take the part of Evelina.'

'Izz.' She tried to clutch me then, and I flinched from her bloodied hands. I did not want his blood on my shirt or my gown. She had some speckles on her palms that she had transferred to her hair and cheeks when she grasped them. I wiped her down with the dark fabric of her cloak. There would be water at the theatre.

The bells had rung for six thirty now. I prised the smashed violin from her hand and let it drop onto the cobbles. The bridge pinged from beneath the strings and went tumbling into the gutter.

Just as I thought I had her by the hand, she slipped from my grasp and plunged towards Guadagni's body. He was gurgling. A part of his soul was still in there. She tore the mask away from his face and kissed him again and again, and when she resurfaced, her own face was covered in his blood.

'For fuck's sake.' I could not help myself. Somehow I wrangled her back up the close, wiped the blood off her face with her cloak again, then got her into the swell of traffic at the Netherbow. Don't ask me how I did it. I do not know myself. Those moments were strange and felt like a dream even as I lived them. I don't even want to think of them now.

It was crowded on the Mile. I took her straight down Dickson's Close, from where we could cross into Cant's and into the labyrinth between the Canongate and the Cowgate. I didn't want anyone to see us approach from the direction of Carrubber's Close.

She was already a ghost by then. Her eyes were holes in her face and I could see her own soul evaporating from her open mouth, from her pinned eyes, as she darted her face in every direction. She was crumbling to nothing, disappearing.

'Why?' She howled. 'Why him? I could have sworn ... I could have sworn ... Why would he choose that mask?'

'Stop it.' I shook her.

We were at the rear of the Marquess of Tweedale's when we heard the cry ring out. 'Murder!'

It was a hollow scream; the sound of rage and terror. Marie Eliza sank against the wall.

She covered her ears while the sound rose over our heads, found its way through the narrow passages, seeped between the stone walls. 'Murder! Murder!'

I grabbed her. 'If you do not get to the theatre and clean yourself up now, you will hang.'

That last word jolted her out of her stupor.

Her feet slipped and scuffed on the straw as she tried to get purchase on the cobbles. She limped along, clutching the wall, scraping her bloodied cloak against it, inch by inch, as if she was fighting a ghoul trying to pull her backwards. By the time we reached the back end of Playhouse Close she was drenched in sweat.

'I cannot go further. I am punished. I am cursed.'

'Pull yourself together. You will get on that stage and any penance will be had afterwards. Think only of Guadagni. You owe it to him.'

Her eyes were pleading. 'He is ... He is ... He ...' she whispered. The shadows in her eyes sucked the life from mine. I remember grabbing her, shaking her, holding her upright. She let me support her up the steep close until we reached the theatre.

The clamour in the street was fierce. The Town Guard had been raised and men were traipsing down from the Luckenbooths, closes were being shut off, soldiers brought in marching pairs from the castle.

We passed through the wooden door that led to the box office, and let it slam behind us, cutting off the outside noise. The quiet was swaddling.

I let her rest against the panels for a few seconds. Most of the players and singers were already upstairs in the dressing rooms. Footsteps rumbled over our heads. The man who worked the ticket booth came around the corner whistling one of her arias, the one Beggar Jeannie sings when she finds the swan. He tipped his hat to us both.

'You are safe,' I said to Marie Eliza. 'Now, go put on Guadagni's costume. Take his role. I will take yours. Mrs Brown can be the hag. Sing as if nothing has passed. Let this be your last act, and after that you can suffer all the penance you wish.'

She stood up straight, lifted her head, took three or four breaths and walked towards the turnpike that led to the dressing rooms. I went into the theatre to find a rag and clean the hag paint from my face.

That is the last clear memory I have of Marie Eliza.

13

I WAS IN THE STAGE WINGS when they came.

The patrons were already being let in. The oranges were being sold. People were roaring gaily at each other behind masks. Screaming sweet nothings. Shouting pleasantries.

I went over and over the lines of Evelina in my head, to distract myself. Again and again I silently heard her murderous words. I lived out, through my balled fists, the moment she pushes her sister into the loch to drown. I thought if I lived only in the opera the rest could disappear, at least until it was over.

Costumes and excitement filled the theatre with heat. News of the murder was whipping from tongue to tongue. I heard someone backstage say that one of the actors had been killed. Someone else replied, 'Nonsense, they would have stopped the play.'

We waited for minutes that stretched longer and longer as the orchestra fidgeted and tuned up and retuned and played some hornpipes to sate the restless crowd. Wenzeslaus the first fiddler had not arrived. Perhaps it was he who was involved in the murder? But it could not be. For shame, a musician? Heavens, no. He was probably adjusting his costume. He was pissing. He was in the Maut Ha. Someone had better go and fetch him.

Again and again I said the lines of the murderous sister in my head.

I heard the fire before I saw it. A crackle in the ears, like stones dragged across glass. The cries of the patrons as they scrambled over chairs and barriers. Their costumes were cumbersome, huge skirts and petticoat cages, panniers and giant sleeves blocking their escapes. The musicians flung their instruments down and fled. The stage was stampeded. The pony in the wings reared and knocked out a stagehand.

It was chaos. One of the clarinettists was screaming his name and that is how I knew your father had come with the mob and the torches to destroy that thing his wife had created; that thing that tormented him so deeply with jealousy and envy, that thing he himself could not produce.

I want to say that I saw him. I have a memory that he was not wearing his plague mask and his face was dour and rageful; that he had in his hand not a violin, but a flaming torch, a tallow candle he had torn from the theatre wall. If I think hard on that night I tell you I saw him with a torch. The image is clear, burned on my brain. His face, an inferno of jealousy.

But the truth is there was too much wild panic in that theatre for me to ever truly say what I did see.

I waited until the last minute, rooted in panic. I waited until the fire crept over the orchestra pit and towards the stage, because I sensed that whatever hell was in the theatre, there could be worse awaiting us outside. I waited for her. I waited because I wanted to hear just one note of the overture to her opera, before I ran. Just one. But it never came. It never came.

So there Cecilia, there you have it. That ballad was for your mother. I spread those words to preserve her. I did not make the lie, but when it was made I latched onto it.

For though sometimes I hated her, for though she could be terrible at times, she was not the sole architect of all that came about. She was not innocent, but nor did she mean to do what she did, and I could not bear for others to hate her.

We are woven by the things we do not want to come to pass, as well as the things we do. We are counterpoint. Sometimes we find strange harmonies in uncomfortable discords.

I could not turn her in. I could not have borne it for her to go to the noose.

ACT V
SCAFFOLD

1

THERE IS A SCRATCHING in the hall outside the parlour.

Cecilia Abercorn's ears spring alert. She did not realise she was napping, and now a great rat with red eyes has entered her dreams and she pins her spine to the chair in defence; takes a gulp of air. There, on the side table beside her, are the filthy scraps of paper she has been collecting daily from the Tolbooth. They flutter gently. The twitching of the rat's whiskers fades.

The parlour door scrapes back, and Cecilia's mother is a murderer now, a woman who beat a man to death in his face, his *face* of all places, and nothing can take that knowledge from her.

It is Angelica, in the doorway.

What does she want? She never comes down from her box. *Did I not empty her bedpan?* Cecilia thinks.

Angelica stares at the papers. She says, 'I came down because I heard you sobbing.'

'I was not sobbing. You misheard.'

'You were sobbing in your sleep. I wanted to know what was troubling your dreams. But now I know.' She gestures towards the papers. 'What has she told you? Is it the truth? Let me see.'

Cecilia looks at the pages Isobel has written. Sometimes she goes to the Tolbooth to fetch them herself. Sometimes they arrive here, brought by a cadie. They are like an endless snowstorm, an ash cloud slowly dropping its dust on her doorstep, flake by flake, until she is covered in a dead white mass. How is she to know if the pages tell the truth? A story is a story is a story. When there is nothing else, what stones are there to build truth from?

'Let me read them,' Angelica says.

This woman she always knew as her sister, but who was more like the terrifying force of a deathly mother to her — she is powerless now, to stop her taking the pages and leaving the room. Or perhaps she doesn't want to stop her. There is loneliness in being the only person to know a story, there is a heaviness in carrying it alone.

She hears Angelica's footsteps retreating, up the stairs. Above, she hears the slow, grating grind of Angelica's confessional doors sliding shut again.

The house is silent.

2

ISOBEL HAS BEEN EXPECTING CECILIA to come again for days now. It has been almost a week since she sent the final pages to her. She has had no money come her way, and she has no more paper to write on anymore. For days now, she has been trying to bribe the guards with a flash of her tits, a feel of her undercarriage, to bring her soap and a cloth, some rouge, an old wig. Her dress is in shreds. She is certain that when she sleeps, the woman and her child who share her cell now are stealing pieces of it. They must tear away whole panels and secrete them to someone through the public hatch, or out of the window, to someone who must sell them on. Most of the skirt is gone now, and all of the copper embroidery.

They took her wig, her pattens.

Her silk shoes she sold for paper and ale.

Isobel has no more adornments left on her body than she had when she first set foot in Edinburgh. But the person underneath, who has emerged, is changed. She is no longer set on a path towards her life, but on a path away from it. She has the sense that she has passed an apex, that she should have kept her wits more firmly clasped to her, when she grasped hold of that thing she held in her palm for a while, that glorious thing she had when she sang at St Cecilia's Hall.

If she pleads not guilty there will be a trial.

If she pleads guilty, then at the very least she will be transported for aiding a murderess, or for lying. Perhaps she could start again, in Australia, emerge again, adorn herself again, and climb the treacherous mucky hill to greatness again. Isobel doubts somehow she would even survive the journey.

Besides she belongs in Edinburgh, and here she will die. She hears it is too hot in Australia. She will refuse transportation. She will plead guilty and she will take the gallows.

The Highland guard with the kilt and the religious fervour is back. Now he is slamming his fist against the door. He does it a few times before scraping it open.

The woman and her daughter scuttle forward on their hands and knees, like lizards, to see who is come. The Highlander kicks them. He actually kicks them back, like they are rats.

Standing behind him is a figure.

At a glance, Isobel sees it is Clessidro, sighs and looks away. But then she looks more closely.

As the light pours in from outside she sees the silhouette. The clothes do not belong to Clessidro. Nor is it Cecilia. It is someone else entirely, someone she knows only in her nightmares, but who has not made his presence felt for some time now.

Isobel screams.

It is Guido Guadagni. He has risen from the dead, and in his hands he is carrying a harp, with three gleaming swan feathers attached to the neck.

3

ISOBEL FALLS TO HER KNEES.

He has come back. He has been dragged from Carrubber's Close, dragged from the loch of the dead, with a bloodied wound in his face. He has come back with the harp in his mouth, the three feathers plucked from the swan. He has come back, ready to accuse, and he is speaking now.

'Get up, for God's sake,' he says. 'I'm not bloody Jesus. Did you know I still had his wig, his waistcoat? You didn't, did you? I couldn't let them go. His shift I've never washed. Still smells of him, I think anyway. Cinnamon.' The fingers play on the shift. The harp, under Guido Guadagni's arm is not a harp, but a foul clenger mask, a masquerade replica of an old Edinburgh plague mask with a hooked beak and a brow of feathers, a nose stuffed full of rosemary.

What made Isobel think it could be otherwise? Guilt?

'Oh come on, get up. Stop this penitential pageant. I thought you were an atheist anyway.'

Isobel's head lifts at the voice. She has not heard it for years. Not for twenty-two years, although she always knew it was alive, somewhere lurking among the covered over, bricked up, concealed spaces of the body it now resides in, built upon by another voice entirely.

4

CECILIA IS ON A PILGRIMAGE.

She does not know what to think anymore.

She is afraid to ask for Isobel at the Tolbooth gate, she is afraid to write and ask her what happened next: how did her mother die and how did Isobel survive? Where is her mother's body now if not in the graveyard?

She is afraid of that empty grave.

She traipses the streets of the Old Town, trying to see back through twenty-two years. It is hard to imagine spaces where there are now buildings and doorways. It is hard to see through the stone and down the blocked-up closes. Everything is sanded down, cemented in, made fresh. In Edinburgh, change is feverish.

She begins at the Netherbow.

Fountain Close. She had no idea, when she penned the address and wrote the name Isobel Duguid, that she was writing to the place where her mother and father had lived, the place they had lived while she was growing inside her mother, the last place they had lived before dying.

The ground slopes away, burbling its load towards the Cowgate. The darkness between the buildings smothers her vision.

It is a dingy, ugly place to Cecilia. She grew up between the short, pale stones of London. If the Marquess of Tweedale's gardens are still there, they are invisible to the public, green secrets hoarded in a grey landscape.

She continues up towards Carrubber's Close, crossing the thoroughfare of the High Street. The name of that close has struck fear into her since she first heard Isobel Duguid's ballad.

It had reached London on a broadside. A sheet of browning paper, fluttering, dropped by the pigeons of gossip, passed mouth to mouth, hand to hand, printer to printer, a story too juicy to ignore, a story of exotic savagery — foreigners! in Scotland! Murder! What could be better! — sung on a street corner by a woman with no teeth, whose daughter skited in and out of the crowds, picking the pockets of the people who stopped to listen.

Cecilia would have walked on. But Angelica — whom she was accompanying to a hanging at Tyburn — had stayed her, and gripped her arm so tightly she had left welts.

'I know that story,' Angelica had said.

Cecilia was baffled. She thought the devils had finally taken away her half-sister's dark wits, something she almost expected to pass every day. Angelica had led her frantically to a cool cathedral nave, close to the Mayfair, and had told her in quick whispers that the woman had been singing about their father; about Cecilia's mother.

'That woman?' Cecilia felt her face go cold. 'That woman with the filthy skirts? What could she know about us? About our family?'

Cecilia had never considered there might be any kind of scandal hiding behind the soft tragedy of her entrance into the world. As she understood it, she had been born to a mother who died in childbirth, to a father who passed away of a broken heart. They had been ferried, scurried, in haste to London by an aunt of Angelica's (Angelica's mother being confined to the cloister in Spain), and had been brought up tenderly in a fine, pleasant but dull household, where music was the only indulgence.

At first Cecilia had thought, 'Here goes. Her sense of reality has gone the same way her mother's did.' But Angelica had been lucid enough to explain that the ballad *singer* was not the ballad's *author*.

This was ten years ago. It took Cecilia ten years to find the author of the ballad, to track down Isobel Duguid.

First she found a husband who collected ballads.

Then she had to persuade him to collect in Scotland, and then in Edinburgh, which was the hardest part, for as we have seen, had he put his foot down for pastoral Perthshire or the islands, then who knows how long it would have taken her.

She has climbed mountains to stand where she does now, on the Netherbow, staring Carrubber's Close in the eye.

This was her ambition. It has governed her life, and she has climbed it the very same way Izz Duguid climbed her greasy cliff.

Does she believe Isobel?

How much does it matter? None of it would bring back her mother, her father.

She steps into the close. There is no blood on the wall. There are no markers of the violence the stones have seen. But there is a turnpike stair, and to reach it there is indeed a sharp step. Cecilia glides her foot along its edge. She thinks of the knocking of stone on scalp; she remembers what she has read, about her mother kissing Guadagni's bloodied face. Should she, Cecilia, have some memory of this? Did the image of the blood transfer itself down the tubes and organs of her mother's body, to her, like Christ onto his shroud? Does she carry around traces of the castrato's blood?

Cecilia tries to feel something, some horror or sadness, but just as when she was reading her mother's opera, she feels nothing. She is numb. Anesthetised to the devilish tale by her desperate thirst for it.

She walks back out of Carrubber's Close, passing a cadie, who gives her a good hard stare, the stare of a local at a foreigner.

What if Guadagni had brought her up instead? Since she never knew either parent, does it matter who they were? Does it have any imprint on her?

She is not a murderess. She has not killed anyone, and nor will she. The chain is broken. She has not inherited her mother's fateful urges to kill.

Her hand flies to her mouth as the clock strikes five, and she realises that somewhere at the top of the hill she is sending a woman to her death.

5

INSIDE HER WOODEN BOX, Angelica reads Isobel's tale by the light of a smoking candle. She is pleased with the way Isobel has characterised her, that she has not neglected to mention her taste for the Inquisition, her penchant for lace, for hangings.

Angelica no longer attends hangings. She has collected enough sin, enough pain in her mind for her to spend forever in contemplation, in her world of darkness. In her confessional box. Now she lives almost entirely in the dark. She has succeeded in negating the body, in cheating God of cheapening her into flesh. She has become a mind floating in darkness, an idea, a soul, a vessel of thought, venturing outside her own thoughts only briefly, to attend to her hunger or her need to produce waste.

She reads on and recognises herself in Isobel's pages, clambering up closes, down cobbles, bearing Tommy, negotiating her stepmother's whims and moods. Isobel has been too generous about Marie Eliza. To Angelica, her stepmother was a woman with a rapacious appetite and no self-control, a woman who wanted the world, who let herself cave to temptation in the expectation that she could always repent afterwards. She was, to Angelica's mind, a Catholic woman in a Calvinist city, who wanted to be mother, lover, wife, composer, singer, lady and, when the fancy took her, simple maid. This is too much.

She remembers the day Marie Eliza seized Tommy from her at the hanging. She remembers the days when Marie Eliza covered her eyes when the child clutched her legs, and asked her, Angelica, to take him away. She remembers Marie Eliza's pregnant belly and how it seemed to fill the small apartment. She remembers the sound of her weeping, she remembers the hulking sound of her father, going at Marie Eliza behind the closed bedcurtains.

She remembers the day, years later, in London, when Tommy was press-ganged and taken to sea. He never returned. Where is he now? Is he a pirate, stabbing other privateers in the eyes and stealing the gold from their ears? Or is he a pile of teeth on the seabed, a cautionary shanty some old coxswain who knew him once sings as the men on the deck chew their dried beef at sundown? When Tommy was taken, the last light in Angelica's heart, the last flickering flame of goodness and hope, went out.

Now she wants nothing, none of the world. The only thing she wishes for is to eliminate desire itself, base, corrupting desire, desire for anything, desire for power, desire to create something, desire for glamour, desire for another person's body, desire for desire's sake. Desire which corrupts thought, because it is the boatman steering between the mind and the flesh. Marie Eliza had put Angelica off desire for life.

First, she corseted herself in widow's lace.

Then she shut herself in a box.

Every day she thinks on the sins that stem from the body. Angelica is the keeper of sin. She keeps it locked away, in her heart. The key is lost, and besides the mechanism is too rusty these days to ever open.

6

ISOBEL RISES.

She looks into Marie Eliza's eyes. Marie Eliza is carrying the mask Guadagni was wearing when he died. She is wearing the very breeches; the bloodstained shirt. How did she get hold of them? Has she kept them for all these years in her trunk, in the corner of their shared room? She notices Marie Eliza still has on her Clessidro shoes and stockings.

'That woman,' Isobel says. 'Mrs Abercorn. She's your daughter. She found us.'

'She is not my daughter. How can she be my daughter? I have not had a daughter since the day she was taken away. How could I be a mother to her?' Her voice is cold, but Isobel sees her hands are trembling. Her fingers squeak up and down the leather beak of the mask. The sound is unbearable. They hear a mouse skitter somewhere, under the straw.

'I would have stayed hidden forever,' Marie Eliza says. 'But you couldn't keep your mouth shut or your conceit from the stage. Was it worth it? All the paste emeralds, all the candelabra concerts? They didn't even like you. Even when you stole *my* melody, the patrons hated you. They only clapped along to that ballad because they knew if they didn't, they would lose me. Now look at you.'

341

Isobel pouts at Marie Eliza. 'Hold your tongue. I did not steal your melody. You stole that melody from a country ballad. There's no worse theft than taking something that can never belong to you.'

'It was a *motif* Isobel. That is what motifs are! You take them. It's not theft.'

'Then it's not theft then for me to take it back for my own ballad.'

'It's different. I changed the tune. Those extra notes were made by me, they were not in the original.'

Isobel is to be hanged in a few days and why are they arguing about the morals of composition? But it bristles in Isobel's breast to think she might not be able to win this one. Now she understands a little of Jas le Corbie's belligerence.

'There's not such a difference between you and Clessidro after all, is there?' She bleats. 'Are you listening anyway? Your daughter is living on Young's Street, with a man named Percy Abercorn. You should see them.'

'She died when I died,' Marie Eliza says. 'That's what your ballad says, doesn't it? So, it must be true.' She looks down at her clothes. The stockings, the threadbare weeds that she has come to know signify her strangeness to Edinburgh society. As Clessidro she had nevermore enjoyed the uncomplicated attentions of men, or the confidences of women. She had nevermore been allowed inside the houses of the New Town without being made aware that she was being looked at as a curio, admired as an artist, yes, but held distant as something reverent, and precious, always one who didn't quite belong. When she made conversation with patrons after the Edinburgh Musical Society concerts, she knew the patrons were thinking of her private parts, even as they asked her probing questions about Handel.

Worst of all, she has had to live beholden to Isobel Duguid; she has had to watch her crawl out of the ashes of *her* — Marie Eliza's — life and ascend like a phoenix daubed in greasepaint. She has had to cajole and weasel the committee of the Edinburgh Musical Society on Isobel's behalf; the patrons she used to serve, until Isobel ascended to the very position *she* — as Marie Eliza — used to enjoy, the *prima donna* of the stage. Could God or his minions have devised a baser torture than that?

How she kept up her deception as Clessidro is only down to her own notion of penance. She has forced herself to live the way her lover lived. She has forced herself inside the body of a castrato. To be in his body, his life, to live as him is the only thing she has left of him. Seeing through his eyes helps quell some of her guilt and the shameful loneliness that tears her apart. 'It is a comfort,' she had said once, when Isobel asked why she kept his handkerchief, his shoe buckles. Guido Guadagni's body went into a pauper's pit in Greyfriars, but Marie Eliza kept his trinkets — and apparently his clothes — like they were his coffin, something she could step into when the urge grew strong. 'Look, I keep his locket by my breast too.' She had once showed Isobel a bloodied lock of his hair she wore beside her heart. She is an incomprehensible woman sometimes, Isobel thinks.

Marie Eliza's hands are still trembling. She stinks of the drink. There is a humming all around her, as if her very skin cannot keep still. Traits she had when she was younger have distilled stronger as she has aged.

'As soon as Cecilia was born, she was no longer mine. When the midwife took her away. When the wet nurse was summoned to suckle her. When she was bundled off to Angelica's aunt's in that wagon. I heard, I did not see her leave. I heard her cry, and she died then, when I died.'

Marie Eliza shifts her weight very subtly; Guido Guadagni stands there once again. The sight makes Isobel uneasy. She doesn't like them shifting between one another. It makes her think of *The Twa Sisters*. What other reason could he have for surfacing, than to claim the necks of them both?

'Where did you go these past weeks, after you left Fountain Close?' Isobel asks.

'Where do you think? I took sanctuary, first at Holyrood and later in the Magdalen Chapel.'

'And why are you back now?'

Marie Eliza looks at her scuffed shoes. 'I heard word that you wrote it down. Everything that happened. Everything.'

She has not changed, Isobel thinks. Her curiosity will kill her one of these days. *I will die if you do not come.* Yes, of course you will.

She remembers the day Marie Eliza gave birth to Cecilia. Cecilia slipped out in her caul, lucky as a mermaid, but even as her mother fed her for the first and last time, and her father languished in the Tolbooth up the hill, Isobel was in the next room, smoothing out the breeches she'd filched from the theatre wardrobe, laying out the ruffled shirt, spreading open the embroidered jacket, preparing the name Clessidro: water thief, hourglass, time turned about, given a second chance to pass like sand through the centre of the earth.

When the midwife left, she had her bag in one hand, and in the other the coin Isobel had given her, to put about the rumour that Marie Eliza Herz, shocked by her husband's brutality and her lover's death, had not survived the birth of her child. Marie Eliza was already dead.

The child was taken with a leather purse of goat's milk, by Angelica along with Tommy, and bundled on the first stagecoach to London. It was imperative Angelica be got rid of as soon as possible. She was not allowed to see her dead stepmother. Isobel knew she suspected though: she had always suspected something. Isobel understood now that Angelica had suspected Isobel was at the centre of it all, and she had told Cecilia Abercorn as much.

In Greyfriars Kirkyard a casket was lowered into the ground with nothing in it but the libretto and a single page of score of an opera that was never sung.

Marie Eliza went into a cocoon, a death bride, spun herself a new body, then emerged as Clessidro. Clessidro lived happy and free for a while. But his past kept burbling up his throat, and he took to drink. Isobel, who had burnt her conscience long ago on the nights when she sang for her supper beside barrels of fire, beside gallows poles, became the toast of the Edinburgh Musical Society. Sort of.

Isobel had procured then, with her wits — at a price — the woman's freedom, with a plan that would yoke them both together, and keep Marie Eliza in her debt forever.

What is this age, if not of bright ideas?

Isobel was a *Lumière* and she was proud of herself.

'Give me this manuscript,' Marie Eliza says. 'I want to know what you wrote.'

'What do you think I am, a printer's shop? There's only one copy of it. And you know where to find it.'

'I can't. I can't go there. I can't look at her. Won't you tell me what it says?'

'I think if you credit me with honesty, you know exactly what it says.'

Marie Eliza's face is bloodless. 'I gave you your fame. I let you steal my opera melody.'

Isobel gives her a warning look. She does not want to hear about that fucking opera motif – that *wasn't* Marie Eliza's to take – ever again, and she is not above losing her temper if she has to. But she doesn't want the guard to bar her from having visitors. 'I gave you your life, *Madam*, so don't let's compare bargains.'

'Away from my children. It was a devil's bargain.'

Isobel heaves a sigh. This is, she knows, her sin, her shame. When she stares down out of the grated window at Cecilia, who wanders the High Street like a soul in purgatory; when she thinks about putto Tommy or Widow's Weeds Angelica with her flamboyance for pain — surely the most lost of the lost that buffet around the earth — she feels the corner of her left eyelid twitch, and she knows that somewhere in her own crusted soul there is remorse. The twitch that keeps no beat but comes and goes, driving her mad for she cannot predict it nor tune her heart to its drumming — that is her conscience.

'Go to your daughter,' Isobel says. 'Go to her now. I am done here. I am for the noose. And I'm tired, anyway. My throat hurts.'

Marie Eliza goes to put on the plague mask. She holds it inches from her face, hesitates, changes her mind, takes it off again and strides from the cell.

7

CECILIA IS SILENT OVER LUNCH. Percy doesn't seem to notice. If he does, he doesn't say anything. He is preoccupied with the bones of his eel.

Once he is finished filleting the eel he says, 'The book is selling well, is it not? I had a note from Jamesons to place an order for a further twenty. It's said they have sent at least one copy to Pennsylvania.'

Cecilia eyes him coldly. She eyes the lattice work of fine grey bones on his plate. 'Percy, we have sent a woman to her death,' she says.

He fiddles with the bone pile. He looks to her then like a very pernickety, very scrappy little Sawney Bean, the Scots cannibal from the old ballads. Only Percy's Sawney Bean is picking on bones a hundredth the size of him.

'Did cook say that there would be pudding today? Dundee cake? Is it clootie, or clow-tee dumpling?' he muses.

She wonders if he wilfully does not care what they have done, or if he is careless — and which is worse?

'She's not a cook, Percy,' Mrs Abercorn says softly.

8

THE KNOCK IS SUBTLE AND SOFT.

Cecilia would have missed it, were she not sitting in silence, in the darkened parlour. Percy has fallen asleep at his writing desk.

She waits to see if Elspeth has heard. The clanging of pots and pans in the kitchen continues.

Cecilia's chest trembling, she rises. The cold whispering of a ghost surrounds her as she opens the door and stands face to face with her mother.

She recognises: her wayward, uneven mouth. The bulbous tip of her nose that she has never liked in herself. She recognises a slight lilt in her breathing, that had always irritated her when she found herself doing it. Cecilia is coming to understand that there are many things about herself that she has never liked. It is as if she already knew they belonged to her mother, and it is not dislike, it is anger, it is hurt, pure and simple.

Why is her mother wearing a man's breeches and a blood-stained shirt?

Why is she carrying a plague doctor mask?

Why won't she say something? Her face is cold as a marble bust.

Then Cecilia realises; she is frozen in shock. She is seeing the very same ghost in Cecilia's face that Cecilia is seeing in hers.

'Come in.' Cecilia stands aside.

Marie Eliza hesitates before stepping across the threshold.

'My husband is asleep in the parlour. We shall go upstairs.'

Cecilia is painfully aware of her mother's terror of her, as she treads the staircase ahead of her. The fear is pulsing from Marie Eliza. Cecilia knows that she could turn around and with one spiteful push dispatch her; shove her, have her slip and break her neck. She knows her mother knows it too. And why wouldn't she? Murderous vengeance could easily be a family trait.

But she doesn't. She holds the door to her bedroom open at the top of the stairs.

'Thank you,' Marie Eliza murmurs.

Cecilia gestures to the bed. She sees Marie Eliza looking around. 'Is Angelica . . .?'

'In the next room. Don't worry. She doesn't come out of her box.'

Marie Eliza's eyes widen. She nods uncertainly. 'Where is Tommy?'

Cecilia looks down. 'He went to sea when he was fourteen. I barely knew him.'

'He went to sea?' She chokes on her words. 'Fourteen? He was too young to go to sea.'

'He was press-ganged. He had no choice. They took him. I wrote to him for a while, but the Navy returned the letters.' Cecilia stares at her mother and shakes her head.

Marie Eliza looks at her hands. She steadies herself. She starts to speak. 'It's not as if I could have — I just — I will begin at the beginning, so that you know all that I—'

Cecilia cuts her off. 'I have sat through so many versions of this fucking tale that I don't know if I can bear to sit through another one.'

Marie Eliza is weeping now, but Cecilia will have none of it. She should have taken those tears and used them to quench her children's thirst. She should have pawned them for bread, and milk, and love. She should have screamed and fought and scratched that hell cat Isobel and her schemes.

Then the thought creeps in: if she had, she would have been hanged.

Would Cecilia have preferred her mother dead and infamous or alive and hidden? Such choice.

'Did she tell you everything? Isobel? In the papers she wrote you. Did she tell you the truth?'

'How am I supposed to know?' Cecilia wants her mother to say it, to ask her outright whether Isobel's papers have accused her of the murder. Whether Isobel confessed that Marie Eliza was still alive.

'Once it was done, there was nothing more—'

'You would have killed him,' Cecilia says bluntly. 'Wenzeslaus. My father. You would have killed him, and you would have gone to Italy.'

'I would have taken you with me,' Marie Eliza whispers. Her tears have sliced two clean paths through her paint.

Cecilia is thinking of the tansy.

She gets up, rummages under the bed. She is keeping the papers out of sight of Percy. She doesn't quite know what he would make of them, but she has a bad feeling that it wouldn't be nice.

'You can read them yourself,' Cecilia says.

Marie Eliza's hand stretches out. On top of the papers is the sheaf of her half-rotted opera. She lets out a gasp as she sees it; as she makes sense of how her daughter must have come to have it. There is really only one way. How can one person have inflicted this much cruelty on her own child?

Cecilia clambers quietly down to her knees. She shuffles close to her mother. Yet again, she is struggling to feel. But she knows what she must do.

She grasps Marie Eliza's hands, and calmly says, 'I will tell no one what is contained in here. I will take it to my grave. I cannot say I will forgive you, but nor will I ever accuse you. Perhaps there is a way for us to live with ... It is only up to you what you do next.'

9

I**SOBEL WAITS** in the soil and the filth.

Outside, across the chasm where the Nor Loch used to lie, where her mother's body was thrown, she can hear construction workers.

She tries to make music out of their sounds, but her foul mood means she hears only ugly chimes and strikes. They are killing off the last of the old city, trampling it under stone feet. Money is pouring into the New Town like blood from a sacrifice.

Twenty-two years of penance she inflicted on Marie Eliza in return for her silence. She has suffered enough.

Isobel is on her way to dust. Already the diggers at Greyfriars will be filling the pit with lime for the day's criminals. No lead-lined, resurrection-proof tomb for Isobel. Her body will not be preserved. She will not be able to creep back up through the soil and look her killers in the eye.

She might not even get as far as the graveyard anyway. She could end up reconstituted, her skeleton an idea in a university man's thoughts. She will be broken and rebuilt in a new image. She will become a tale, a cautionary tale, with a moral.

Isobel has had her moment.

Her emerald earrings already belong to someone else; sold to pay a lawyer who drinks daily in the Fortune Tavern and comes to visit her at five o'clock only to see if she has anything to complain about; to see if she has fucked the guard yet and can plead her belly.

Isobel has no desire to plead her belly. Her belly is a coven and she will not birth a child, who will shape shift into something else, like Marie Eliza's child, who turned into Mrs Abercorn.

There is a knock. 'It's ti-ime,' the turnkey sings. He needn't sound so smug.

He has a priest with him. No, it isn't a priest, it's Angelica in her devil robes.

No, it isn't Angelica. It is a minister. No priest for Isobel, no Angelica. Isobel warrants only the stern words of the kirk. She is absolutely certain that under this minister's rules she counts as one of the unelect. There is no place for her at heaven's table.

She is relieved. Heaven sounds exhausting. Having to be good, all the time.

She has no desire to absolve her sins. She doesn't have the money, and if she did, she'd have spent it on jewellery and fine foods instead of redemption. Perhaps in hell she can be herself.

And now, the procession.

Now she is walking with her head held high, walking past crowds of a size she never could have dreamed of performing to, all turned out for her. She has never beheld such a ripe, voluble crowd; such appreciation.

She blows kisses.

She curtseys. She is going to die not only for her own sins, but for another woman's, and if she has learned anything in her unphilosophical life it is—

But wait.

There is Guido Guadagni, standing once again in the Lawnmarket.

10

I SOBEL BLINKS and sees back through time.

Guadagni, bleeding.

Isobel can see in Marie Eliza's face that she hears now the voice of her lover in those sickening breaths. She is a hair away from snatching at his mask. Isobel holds back her arms.

If she has a shock, labour might begin, and the last thing Isobel needs is a woman giving birth into the blood of the murdered. How in holy fuck are they going to get out of this one?

Instead, she herself reaches forward and removes Guadagni's mask.

Marie Eliza groans.

That groan is unlike anything Isobel has heard. It becomes the dirge to her ballad, the drone of the pipes.

Isobel blinks.

Guido Guadagni takes off his mask.

He takes off his wig. He takes off his waistcoat, and his breast bindings, and his trousers, and now there is a woman standing on Edinburgh's Royal Mile in her sark, her thready wild hair around her, paint smeared on her aged face.

She is bare. Her insides are exposed. She is a relic of the past. She no longer exists, though she will always exist.

The crowd stops jeering, to see this strange spectacle.

What will happen?

Will she be carted away? Will the guards remove her, for she is blocking the procession?

Isobel has stopped walking now. She sighs. This is just like fucking Marie Eliza. Classic, typical Marie Eliza. She waits until the last minute, and then she cannot control her impulses. She has to just do the thing that has come into her head. She can't stop herself. This will not have been planned. It will be a whim. And now she has stolen the scene at Isobel's final performance, *again,* she has held her from the stage. Isobel has prepared herself to die on the scaffold, and die she will, today, come hell or high water.

'Stop!' Marie Eliza screams.

There is such silence on the Royal Mile. Even the construction workers stop banging.

The guards look to the wardens. The wardens look to the minister. The minister looks to Isobel — accusingly — as if he is suggesting this might be part of her devilish design.

'It was me who killed him,' Marie Eliza cries. Paint is streaked down her face, hideous, ghostly, broken. She drops to her knees on the straw-strewn setts. 'I beat Guido Guadagni to death because I thought he was my husband. I thought he was Wenzeslaus. I meant to kill my own husband. And so I did, by having him blamed for the crime.' Her cries echo round the high buildings.

Very quickly a hullabaloo strikes up. The price of a window view has just risen by sixpence, now two shillings, now three. Some voyeurs are hanging out of the frames so far they risk their own deaths in the muck.

An officer finally pushes through the crowds to Marie Eliza.

Isobel breathes a sigh of relief. Perhaps she will be carted away to the Bedlam and they can get on with the hanging. She doesn't like this kind of pause. It is the wrong kind of attention.

But now a magistrate has been hustled from the coffee house and that tall dragoon guard from the palace is talking with him. Two lawyers appear from a room above the Luckenbooths, black gowns spread behind them, and soon no one is even remembering to look at Isobel, as the confusion, the consultation, continues.

At last the magistrate returns to the coffee house. The kilted man bellows: 'Back to the Tolbooth with her.'

Isobel grits her teeth.

11

THEY SIT SIDE BY SIDE on the straw, backs against the Tolbooth's shit-caked cell wall.

It is a bright, sunny, crisp day in Edinburgh.

Light pours like honey through the cross-barred window of the gaol. The view extends over the rooftops to Fife. The sea is sparkling. It is a day when ships will have no trouble landing their cargoes, of oranges, cinnamon and lace.

On a day this ripe with promise, a young girl could skip along the hedgerows to the large, smoky, reekie city, with nothing but song and hope in her. In the heart of the city, a girl could fall in love and believe she could grow up to write an opera.

Light makes everything plain and clear. It is the maze in the heart of the Old Town that seizes it, distorts it, disguises it. Turn a corner and you are confronted with the tall dead end of your own darkness.

But isn't that a truer way to live?

Isobel's foot beats an idle tattoo against the stone floor. It sounds like a death knell.

Marie Eliza is too weak and overwhelmed to ask her to stop. Her past is rushing at her like an angry cavalcade, and hold up her arms she might, but there is nothing she can do to stop the horses from trampling her to death.

She should have died a long time ago. She should never have let Guadagni return to tell the truth. She should never have let Isobel anywhere near the Abercorns.

Facing Cecilia, staring into her eyes — eyes she had not seen since they were barely opened — was worse than death. Truth be told, she would rather look into the eyes of St Peter and feel his scorn as he turns her away; she would rather stare into the eyes of Satan and behold her eternal fate, than look into her daughter's eyes again.

Tomorrow Marie Eliza and Isobel will face the magistrate. They will not plead their case. They will tell the truth. They will excavate the bones. They will drain the loch. They will pull up the paving slabs. Together, they will write a new ballad.

'Do you remember arriving in town as Clessidro?' Isobel says. How rasping her voice has become.

She would like to still be that person who stood at the mouth of the fleshmarket, watching the new Maestro Clessidro's carriage trundle up and over the setts, rattle across the new bridge, the carriage she and Marie Eliza had paid for with their last pennies.

They had sent a letter to the Musical Society, announcing Clessidro's arrival.

'I remember being certain someone would recognise me,' she said.

'They did not want to.' Isobel looks sidelong at her. Marie Eliza has the clenger's mask on again. She is twiddling it around her nose. It is the same colour as the blood on her shirt. 'I painted you well enough, but if anyone had wanted to see they could have. Your eyes are the same. Your expression. Your voice. Your Italian accent was murderously bad.'

'Anything can change into anything here.'

'You took a ballad and turned it into an opera.'

'You took my life and turned it into a ballad.' Marie Eliza looks sidelong back at Isobel. She begins to laugh. It's a hideous, unbridled laugh; the laugh of the mad, the laugh of the damned; the laugh of a woman who understands that she has lived, and now the jig is up.

The Highland turnkey pokes his head around the corner. 'Stop having fun.'

The two women look demurely at their feet.

There is nothing left to say for the moment. The secret is out now; it is running amok through the Old Town, screeching with glee, whipping up and down the drainpipes in its nightgown.

Isobel feels as if a haar has been peeled from her, leaving her naked, and it is a cool, fresh relief as well as a terror.

Isobel puts her arm around Marie Eliza. 'Let your conscience be clean. Justice will be done.'

'How can it ever be clean?'

Isobel thinks on this. She realises then that Marie Eliza has carried this restlessness around with her. She may have appeared to transform, but unlike Isobel, she never changed in her heart. She never rewrote the story and forced herself to believe it. She never forgot. She simply never spoke of it.

Marie Eliza brushes Isobel's hair with her fingers, combing the black locks. Pewter threads are beginning to emerge, burnished strands. She hums a tune.

Isobel pinches Marie Eliza's cheeks to bring the blood.

They breakfast on porridge and water. They dress themselves in the clean white smocks Angelica has supplied for them, no expense spared, the finest linen.

A man arrives with a basket full of plaster of Paris, and a flacon of dirty fountain water, to take an impression of their faces — death masks. 'I thought I could get aheadae the game,' he says optimistically.

They exchange a glance. 'Why not?' they say at the same time.

Side by side, they sit as the lead white slop hardens into a chalky cast on their faces. It pinches, smarts. It is stealing the last of their expressions, the lines and wrinkles that are the closes and alleyways of their lives, the etchings wrought on their lips and cheeks.

They sit in companionable silence for a short while, as the death mask man converses with the guard, asks him if there are any more in the condemned cells to be hanged soon. A few stragglers and gawpers file past the cell door, eager to see the 'twa murderesses' on the morning of their fate. What they make of the two women, sitting with their backs against the wall, their faces caked in oozing, cracking white paste, is anyone's guess.

'Isobel,' says Marie Eliza, without moving her lips.

'Aye.'

'Will you sing *Stabat Mater*? It would bring me great peace.'

Isobel tries a few bars, but she can't move her lips enough to get past the first two notes. 'I don't think I can,' she says. 'Will you sing *Erbame Dich*?'

Marie Eliza tries. It's no good. The plaster is too thick. 'No. Can't.'

The sounds of the Old Town bleed through the open window, echo round the Tolbooth cell. 'Will you sing me *The Twa Sisters?*' Marie Eliza whispers.

Isobel remembers the day at Duddingston. Her voice, cast to the wind. Like ashes. Somewhere out there, in the wild city it still resides. It will be caught, heard, sung again. The music never dies, only the people. She hums the melody, and then she can't help herself. She is back in Parliament Close. She is in the Cowgate at dusk. She is on the St Cecilia's stage. She is not singing *The Fiddler's Wrath* but *The Twa Sisters*, the song that twined her life to the woman who sits next to her. And she can't help it. She sings, and her mouth, her soul opens. She sings and the death mask cracks. White powder crumbles into her lap.

'Fuck's sake,' the death mask man mutters.

Marie Eliza laughs. She cackles. She joins in, sings a roaring, rambling descant. They sing together and their voices carry out of the tiny window into the cacophony of the High Street.

As the procession comes to lead them from the Tolbooth, Isobel sees Marie Eliza take one last look over her shoulder, down towards the Canongate at the Playhouse that has not been there for some twenty-two years.

12

I T IS A GOOD, STURDY GALLOWS. Thrown up that morning, the wood sanded and pale, the light hitting it just so. The double nooses trap clouds in their 'O's. They can see them from halfway up the West Bow.

If Isobel's hands were not bound in irons she would reach across and squeeze Marie Eliza's.

Such a crowd on this jubilant, sunny day. It is still early, the warmth in the air full of promise, the animal smells mingled with the dew.

Isobel has too much pride to feel melancholy. She has been stifled by the gaol these past months. This is her emergence. She feels like a swan, in her white gown. They are like two swans. Sisters.

Cecilia could not persuade Percy to attend.

Percy has his mind on his desk. Percy has his mind in his books. Percy has important things to do, people to meet. Percy is thinking of his next book. Percy is arranging travel, perhaps to the Orient, certainly to Germany, for Percy hears there are folk tales there that have not yet been collected, and now Percy has in his mind that, owing to the success of his book, he is the man for the job.

Percy is heading for the heavens, on the clouds of his own thoughts and brio, and the hanging of two women does not interest him.

So Cecilia stands there alone. She has paid handsomely to see her mother hang; a good window at the bottom of the West Bow. Second floor. Eye to eye with the noose. Nose to nose with her own sins.

Angelica will stand in the crowds, looking up. She will pray fervently, noisily, the second the traps drop.

The minister is raving, the usual passages about death and damnation. Isobel can't be bothered with his bluster. He is trying to steal the show.

She looks at Marie Eliza. Marie Eliza looks back at her, and her face is the prettiest, the purest Isobel has seen it, since the night in the rainy pleasure garden.

They walk up the steps in perfect unity. They are barefoot, though the ground is cool. Both women have learned that discomfort is part of the illusion, the performance.

Isobel doesn't even flinch when a splinter lodges in her sole. The naked wooden boards feel beautiful against her skin.

Though the hood placed on her head muffles her ears, she still hears the sound of the crowd. It's a bare-toothed lowing, a spreading of fire, a tidal wave that swells as the voice of the minister rises. She hears Marie Eliza whimper. She is about to meet the man she murdered. What can she be thinking? Of the state of her dress, of how she has aged and he has not? Or is she thinking of forgiveness? Of grace?

The wood creaks. Isobel shifts her weight. The earth disappears from under her. And as her body drops, the baying of the crowd turns into a gasp, then a whoop. The crowd whoops and cheers and claps. Claps. People are actually applauding her death. The fuckers.

They are clapping with such gusto, and the thought that goes through her mind, as she reaches out her toe for one last touch of Marie Eliza's cold, sweating foot is this: if only she had known earlier it was this easy to please a crowd of enlightened people.

Beside the gallows, a girl in a pinafore begins to sing.

'Come false-hearted women,
Come friends who betrayed,
Hear the tale of two lassies
And the price they paid,

The one was fair
The other poor
The man they killed
Was a capon Moor

The fair one planned to murder-o
To stab and kill her husband
The poor one thought she spied him,
But lo, it was her lover-o'

Isobel takes her last, strangled breath. Marie Eliza gasps. Even her final sigh is melancholy, sensual.

The ballad is sung. The words are out there, mingling with the sounds of the cattle and the pigs.

Cecilia closes her eyes.

CURTAIN

Acknowledgements

Thank you Daisy Parente, for your tireless efforts in championing all of my work but this book in particular. You could not have found me a better editor for it than Rachel Morrell. Rachel, thank you for understanding my strange and warped world and for stepping into it wholeheartedly. Your edits and ideas have made the book so much better, while allowing it to be itself, and for that I cannot thank you enough.

Thank you to everyone at Black & White, the designers, PR, Rights and Production teams, Fiona Atherton, Hannah Walker, Thomas Ross, Tonje Hefte and Emma Hargrave, who have taken such great care of the book.

I am extremely grateful to Scottish Book Trust for the Robert Louis Stevenson Fellowship, which allowed me time to begin researching the book, and to Creative Scotland's Open Fund for putting their faith into me and enabling me to have time and space to develop my writing.

Huge thank you to Joan Baez for allowing me to quote from the lyrics of her beautiful song 'Diamonds and Rust'.

Thank you to the book's early readers: Ruth Boreham, Claire Heuchan, Lynsey May. Your insights and encouragement kept me buoyant in those doubting moments all writers have.

Thank you to Dona Easton at St Cecilia's Hall. I must have been standing under a lucky star the morning I first bumped into you. Your knowledge, research tips and feedback have been invaluable and the book would not be the same without you.

There were a variety of research books that helped me understand the eighteenth century music world, but I want to particularly acknowledge the PhD thesis of Sonia Tinagli Baxter, *Italian Music and Musicians in Edinburgh c. 1720–1800*.

Thank you Eli Wieland and Tim Ribchester, for your patience in explaining operatic singing terms to me, and for recording some of the lost works of Maria Barthelemon that I came across in the British Library.

Thank you Caraigh McGregor, for always being my grammar guru and most wonderful friend. (And for taking time to approve your own acknowledgement).

Thank you Gabriel and Harry, for understanding that Mummy needs to work sometimes, and Alex for reminding me when I need to hear it that making up stories is not a frivolous pursuit. This book would not be here without you.

Thank you to my mum and dad, for making me do my violin practice, and for the singing lessons (even though we all knew I was terrible). Particular thanks to my mum, Liz Ribchester, not only for being the Nanna every creative parent needs in their life, but for your patience in teaching me how to read.